What To Do About
Wednesday

USA TODAY BESTSELLING AUTHOR

Jennie Marts

Thanks for choosing to read the Page Turners Mysteries! These books are a mix of romantic comedy and cozy mysteries and I hope you love them! If you do enjoy them, please consider leaving a review.

And be sure to check out all the adventures in the *Page Turners* series:

Another Saturday Night and I Ain't Got No Body: Book 1
Easy Like Sunday Mourning: Book 2
Just Another Maniac Monday: Book 3
Tangled Up In Tuesday: Book 4
What To Do About Wednesday: Book 5
A Halloween Hookup: Book 6 – A Holiday Novella
A Cowboy for Christmas: Book 7 – A Holiday Novella

Be the first to find out when the newest *Page Turners Novel* is releasing and hear all the latest news and updates happening with the Page Turners book club by signing up for the Jennie Marts newsletter at: Jenniemarts.com

My biggest thanks goes out to my readers! Thanks for loving my stories and my characters. I would love to invite you to join my street team, *Jennie's Page Turners* where you can become an honorary member of the *Page Turners Book Club!*

This book is dedicated to
Lee Cumba
My mom and mystery mastermind plotting partner
Thank you for your never-ending support
And for always believing in me and my dreams

Brittle leaves crunched under Piper Denton's feet as she practically danced up the stairs to her new apartment. Which went to show the importance of the moment, because Piper didn't do much dancing. She was more of a side-to-side swayer with an occasional awkward clap thrown in, usually right after the beat that called for onc.

But today was different. Today was the start of everything.

And nothing was going to get her down. Even the weight of her backpack, also new, purchased the day before with a week's worth of tips, didn't bother her. The heaviness of the textbooks served as a symbol of her first day of college—and her newfound sense of freedom. Freedom to finally live her own life, just the way she wanted it.

She realized she was smiling, her face unaccustomed to the expression but trying it out like a woman would test a new hairstyle or fashion choice. Thinking of fashion, she wished again she would've grabbed her favorite blue sweater before leaving the apartment as a brisk breeze sent a shiver over her bare arms.

The sweater had been Drew's favorite too. He'd always said it brought out the blue in her eyes. Her uncommon smile fell, and a different kind of shiver ran through her at the thought of Drew, followed by a stab of pain and the sensation of a giant fist tightly squeezing her heart.

Stupid boys.

The scent of garlic wafted through the air as she pushed through the door and pushed down the heartache caused by the boy who had recently left her behind as he'd headed to a university halfway across the state.

They'd planned to attend the same school, but Piper hadn't quite made the cut, so she was stuck in town going to the local community college. But it was still college. And she was still out on her own for the first time. And that's what really mattered.

Who cared about Drew? *Stuff. Stuff.* So what if he was the first boy she'd fallen in love with? *Stuff. Stuff.* So what if he'd broken her heart?

She pushed the feelings down, driving them deeper like a camper crams a sleeping bag into a stuff sack. She was great at burying her feelings—had been doing it for years.

Letting out her breath, she put her high school boyfriend behind her and focused on the future ahead of her. Focused on the thing she'd always wanted—to live a normal life, one she was in control of. One that didn't depend on anyone else or have anything to do with her crazy mother.

She'd taken the first step to that control weeks before when she'd enrolled in college, then moved out of her aunt's house and into an apartment with another student.

She didn't have much to take with her, but that didn't matter either. She was finally making her own choices, her own decisions, and doing things her own way.

Her new home was only a few blocks from campus, on the ground floor of an old Victorian that had been converted into two furnished apartments. Although calling them furnished was a bit of stretch, but each bedroom did have a bed, a dresser, and a wobbly nightstand. And the main room had a lumpy broken-in sofa as well as a scarred kitchen table and four mismatched chairs. All the furniture appeared to be garage sale stock, but it worked. And it was better than what she'd had—which was nothing.

A furrow creased her brow as she squinted at the apartment door. It stood slightly ajar, as if someone had walked out and not gotten it pulled tightly behind them. She'd have to talk to her roommate about that.

That and leaving her makeup all over the bathroom counter. Piper didn't even know what half of that stuff was for. She could handle the seventeen bottles of hair product in the shower and all the garlic she used in her cooking—she could stock up on vanilla-scented candles, but Piper was nuts about closing and locking the door.

She'd watched way too many movies and read too many stories about college co-eds who had been assaulted simply due to the ease of a circumstance. That's why she'd never taken up jogging—too easy for a would-be rapist to snatch her from a wooded path. Well, and the fact that she hated running.

Maybe she and Brittany needed to set some ground rules—come up with some roommate guidelines.

Wow—that certainly sounded like a responsible, mature plan of action—maybe she was getting the hang of this adulting thing after all.

Piper pushed through the door, and her breath caught in her throat.

Oh no!

Her heart stopped as her eyes flicked across the room, taking in all the details at once.

The stark white of the filmy gauze curtain fluttering at the window, the shattered bits of the blue plate—one of the set her Aunt Cassie had given her—and the scattered strands of spaghetti sprayed across the floor. A crust of garlic bread leaned against the kitchen chair next to a lone meatball that must have rolled across the hardwood.

And the sight of her new roommate sprawled across the floor, a tan plastic bag wrapped around her head.

Her mouth went dry as she stared at Brittany, not

quite able to comprehend what she was seeing.

The girl's body was splayed across the floor, her arms loose at her side. Piper noted several red scratches down her throat and the awkward way her leg jutted out to the side, her skirt flipped up, exposing the top of her thigh. She wore an odd-colored pair of green tights that didn't quite match the green in her shirt. A small tear ran up the leg of her tights. She would hate that.

Piper hadn't known her long, but she knew Brittany well enough to know she wouldn't leave the apartment without changing those tights. Plus, they didn't really match that outfit.

Her cardigan fell open at her throat, a jagged piece of the collar torn and missing, and the odd shade of the tights clashed with the teal blue of the sweater. *Piper's* sweater. No wonder she couldn't find it this morning. Brittany must have worn it to class.

What the hell was wrong with her?

Why was she even thinking about this girl's outfit? Why was she thinking about her sweater and her odd, ugly tights? Nobody was going to care—least of all Brittany.

But it bugged Piper. That small tear, the tiniest of pale leg showing through the jagged lines of ripped nylon.

A large red stain covered the girl's chest, and crimson splotches dotted the floor around her body.

Piper shook her head, the slightest movement, just enough to try to shake the image and convince herself she was imagining the gruesome scene.

One of Brittany's shoes was missing and a dark smudge marred her ankle.

Piper blinked. She didn't understand. But she knew she should be doing something—reacting in some fashion. She couldn't just stand there.

Do something! Help her!

Her paralysis broke, and she dropped her backpack. It

hit the floor with a resounding thud as she ran toward Brittany, dropping to her knees at her side.

Her hands were shaking as she pushed up the plastic bag and held her fingers to Brittany's throat, desperately trying to feel a pulse.

There was nothing.

Her skin was cold, and she didn't appear to be breathing.

Tearing the bag from her head, Piper let out a strangled scream as her roommate's eyes, red and bloodshot, stared vacantly into hers.

Rearing back, she pushed herself away from the girl, crying out again as her fingers touched the red sticky substance.

Bile rose in her throat, and she turned her head and vomited across the hardwood floor.

Get help! her brain screamed at her.

She tried to pull her phone from her pocket, but her fingers couldn't seem to work, and it hit the floor with a clatter. She grabbed for it before it slid into the mess.

Her hands were shaking so badly she could barely operate the phone, but she finally got the three numbers pressed and held the phone to her ear.

"911 Operator. What is your emergency?"

"M-my roommate. I think she's dead." She wiped the back of her hand against her mouth, her stomach threatening to roil again.

"Can you tell me where you are?"

"I'm at home. In our apartment." She gave the operator her address. "Can you send someone, please?"

The operator repeated the information and verified Piper's name and phone number. "I've already sent paramedics to your address. Can you tell me your roommate's name and how old she is?"

"Um. I don't know exactly. I think eighteen, like me.

And her name is Brittany. Brittany Burke."

"Is Brittany conscious, or does she appear to be breathing?"

"No, she's not conscious. I tried to find a pulse, but I couldn't. She's not breathing either. She's just staring me, and her eyes are all bloodshot, and her mouth is kind of purple like there's a bruise around it. I just came home and found her lying on the floor, and she had a plastic bag wrapped around her head."

"Is she bleeding?"

Piper glanced down at the red substance on her hand. It had started to dry, and she could see now that it wasn't blood. It was spaghetti sauce. "No. I don't think so." Her shoulders slumped forward, and she tried not to cry. "Who would do this? Why would anyone want to hurt Brittany?"

"Okay, hold on, Piper. The paramedics are almost there. Is anyone in the apartment with you?" the operator asked. "If someone did this to her, do you think the assailant is still there?"

Oh gosh. She hadn't even thought of that.

Her eyes darted around the room, her heart slamming against her chest.

What if the killer were still in the apartment with her?

She backpedaled across the room, crying out as her hand slipped in the spilled spaghetti sauce. How could she have mistaken the tomato sauce for blood?

Wiping her hand on her jeans, she left a smear of sauce streaked across the side of her thigh as she scrambled to her feet and ran from the apartment.

She felt terrible for leaving Brittany in there by herself. But not much worse could happen to her now.

Pushing through the front door, she saw the fire truck pull up to the front of the house, and she waved them through the door, pointing to her apartment. "She's in there."

She told the operator the fireman had arrived and disconnected the call, then shoved the phone in her pocket and hugged her arms around her middle.

A police car pulled up, its tires screeching as it braked to a halt, and a tall familiar policeman stepped from the car.

"Mac!" Piper yelled, launching herself off the steps and into the arms of the policeman.

The man hugged her to him then pulled back and studied her face. "You okay?"

She nodded, not yet trusting her voice.

She'd met the policeman, Officer Mac McCarthy, earlier that summer when her book club had gotten involved in the mysterious disappearance of a neighbor. Since then, Mac had become a friend to all of them, and more than a friend to Zoey, the newest member of the book club.

"I heard your name on the scanner, and I was only a few blocks away," he explained. "I already called Cassie. She's on her way."

"Thank you," she whispered. The thought of her aunt arriving and taking charge had her knees buckling with relief.

Mac grabbed her before she fell. He guided her to the porch and eased her down on the front step. "Can you tell me what happened?"

She relayed the events of the last ten minutes.

"Do you have any idea who might want to hurt this girl?"

"No. Everyone liked her."

Even Piper. And she didn't often warm up to people quickly. Especially people like Brittany.

She was one of the popular girls—the kind who always knew what fashions were in and whose hair always looked great. One of those girls who was pretty without even trying.

Brittany. Even her name was cool.

Piper had been so excited to find a roommate, she wouldn't have cared if she were a neat-freak, a hoarder, a cheerleader, or an introverted computer geek. But Brittany had been none of those.

She'd been nice and sweet, beautiful and popular. She'd had tons of friends—the opposite of Piper, who considered herself one cozy Snuggie shy of being a hermit. But the two girls had got along well—so far.

Everyone had loved Brittany.

Well, apparently not everyone.

Someone hadn't liked her at all.

But Piper had. They'd really started to get to know each other, had even shared a few stories over a cheap pepperoni pizza the night before.

Piper had even started to imagine they could become friends.

Even though the only things they'd seemed to have in common were that they both had blond hair, an affinity for pizza, and were evidently about the same build. Or so Brittany had seemed to think when she'd excitedly told Piper they could share clothes. Which was how her favorite sweater must have ended up on the dead girl's shoulders.

A shudder ran through her.

Mac took off his jacket and draped it around her petite shoulders.

She clutched the lapels and pulled it around her, pulling her knees up and resting her forehead on them.

How could this have happened?

Her day had been going so well. Her life had been going so well.

Other than that whole thing with her boyfriend breaking up with her.

But she'd moved out and had a place of her own.

What would happen to her now?

Ugh. She was a terrible person.

She should be thinking about what was going to happen to this girl, how her friends were going to feel, how devastated her parents were going to be. But all she could think about was how the hell she was going to find another roommate to help her pay the rent.

A moment ago, she'd been so happy, so excited, she was adulting.

Now all she could think was 'mommy.'

Well, not really 'mommy', because she couldn't count on *her* mom for anything—except to not be there when she needed her.

Why did Brittany have to die?

Why did she have to ruin Piper's first day of college?

Clasping her hand over her mouth, she silently took back her words. Even though she hadn't spoken them out loud, she'd still thought them. They were still out there, hanging in the air, like a load of damp laundry on a cloudy day.

Pushing back her anger at this stupid girl for dying on her and wrecking her first days of college, she slumped against the steps, waiting for her aunt, and made a mental note to talk to her therapist about these horrible feelings.

Then made another mental note to actually get a therapist.

A sensible blue minivan pulled up, and she lifted her head. Relief flooded through her as she saw her aunt leap from the car and race toward her.

The van doors slammed as two other women climbed out and hurried up the sidewalk.

The cavalry had arrived.

The cavalry—otherwise known as the Pleasant Valley Page Turners—was her aunt's book club who had adopted Piper as a new member earlier that spring.

'Book club' was a loose term for a tight-knit group of women who cared more about each other and spending time together than they did about their monthly book choice. They met every Wednesday, and the women had taken Piper under their collective wing and become the closest thing to a family she had.

Sunny and Maggie had known her aunt since college, and Edna was Sunny's neighbor.

Even though Edna Allen was in her early eighties, she had the spunk and spirit, not to mention the dirty mind, of someone much younger. She kept the women on their toes, frequently in stitches, and was more often than not the one who came up with the crazy hare-brained schemes which usually landed the group in hot water.

Each woman brought something different to the table, and Piper loved them all.

Especially Cassie, the woman who'd taken her in and treated her like a daughter when her own mother had left her on her doorstep and rode off on the back of a motorcycle with a tattooed biker named Spider.

Piper wasn't much of a crier, and she'd been holding it pretty much together until she saw Cassie, and her aunt folded her into her arms. Then the floodgates opened, and Piper sobbed into her shoulder, clutching Cassie's mom-sweater in her fists.

Her plus-sized aunt often complained about the few extra pounds she carried, but Piper thought the extra weight just made her aunt a better hugger, and she loved the way she could sink into the comfort of Cassie's arms.

"Are you okay, honey?" Cassie asked.

Piper nodded into her chest. "I'm fine. But Brittany isn't. She's dead."

"I know. Mac told me when he called."

"You must have been so scared," Sunny said, throwing her arms around both of them.

"How did she die?" Edna asked, huffing up behind Sunny and joining in the group hug. "I've heard the suicide rate is higher for college kids these days."

"She didn't kill herself," Piper explained. Not unless she suffocated herself. "She was murdered."

"Oh no," Cassie cried, squeezing her tighter. "Mac didn't tell us that."

Edna peered over Piper's shoulder. "What happened?"

"I don't know. I just came home and find her lying on the floor. She had a plastic bag wrapped around her head and scratch marks on her throat. L-l-like she'd been trying to claw the bag away."

The memory of her face and her red-rimmed bloodshot eyes flashed through Piper's mind, and bile threatened to rise to her throat again. She swallowed. "I called 911, but she was already dead when I found her."

"Oh honey," Sunny said, rubbing her back.

Edna had already inched toward the door. "I'll just see if I can find out anything more." After watching copious amounts of crime television and reading numerous murder mysteries, the elderly woman considered herself a bit of an amateur sleuth. And the scent of a murder had her craning her neck and bouncing on her orthopedic shoe-covered toes to get inside.

"Edna, no. Let the police—" Cassie said, but her words fell on deaf ears because Edna had already snuck through the front door.

A few minutes later, she was hustled back out again by the familiar detective.

Mac had a scowl on his face and a firm grip on the geriatric Nancy Drew's arm. "No, Edna, you *cannot* spend a few minutes studying the crime scene," he was saying. "Although I appreciate your enthusiasm, I don't want you compromising anything the *real* police actually need to see."

Edna huffed and pulled her arm from his grip. She smoothed her cap of silvery-white curls. "Well, excuse me. I was just trying to help."

"I'm sure."

She ignored Mac and put an arm around Piper. "I'm so sorry, honey. You must have been so scared to find her like that."

Piper nodded, swallowing at the tightness in her throat.

"And I'm pretty sure she's wearing your sweater."

"She is."

"I wouldn't plan on getting that back." Edna leaned closer. "And it didn't really do anything for the outfit. It matched her shirt, but those green tights were hideous."

"All right," Mac said, pulling a notebook from his pocket. "Besides her unattractive hosiery," he paused to narrow his eyes at Edna, "can you tell me anything else about what happened? I need to know who her friends were, what her day looked like today, was she expecting any visitors, that sort of thing."

Another police car pulled up, and Mac waved two officers inside, letting them know he was getting the statement from the witness.

Piper sank down on the front steps again. "I don't know. We've only been roommates a few weeks. It seemed like she was friends with everyone. We go to the same college, and we both started classes today."

"On a Wednesday?"

Piper nodded. The day had seemed so special—so many firsts—too special for an average Wednesday in the middle of the week. "We start on the date rather than the day," she explained. "College isn't like high school." Although she wished for a moment she could be back in high school, back in Cassie's guest room, with her cousins down the hall and the delicious scent of whatever Cassie was baking wafting through the house.

But that wasn't the case. Because now not only was she in college, but she was also involved in an actual case, a murder case.

"I can check on her class schedule," Mac said, making another note in his book.

Edna inched closer, stretching her neck to peer at his notepad.

He gave her a look, then shielded the pad. "What about close friends or a boyfriend?"

"Yeah, she had a boyfriend. Kyle. I'm not sure of his last name. But I could find out. She told me they'd been dating since high school. I've only met him a few times. But she said they'd been having some trouble lately, and she told him she needed some space to get settled and start classes."

Tears clouded her vision, and she dropped her head into her hands. "This is so unfair. She had everything going for her. Her life was just starting."

Cassie sat on the steps next to her and rubbed a hand across her back. "I know, sweetie. It is unfair."

"How about the grocery sack? Does it have any significance to you?" Mac continued with his inquiry. "We're trying to determine if it was already in the apartment or if the assailant brought it with him. It was from the Spend Thrift. Is that a store where you normally shop?"

Piper shook her head. "No. Never. I don't have a car, and it's all the way across town. And Cassie doesn't shop there either, so I'm sure it wasn't mine. It could have been Brittany's, but I doubt it. We only had a few plastic sacks, and we kept them in a bin in the pantry. But as far as I remember, they were all the white ones from the Price Right down the street."

Mac asked her about a million more questions, but she didn't have a whole lot to tell him. She promised to write down anything else she could think of and let him know if something new came to her.

Mac snapped his notebook closed. "I'm sorry, kid, but you're not going to be able to stay here until we've cleared the scene."

"It's fine," Cassie said. "You can stay with me."

"But what about my books and my clothes? And how am I supposed to get to campus? I still have to go to class. And to work." Piper had started a job at a local coffee shop a few blocks from her apartment. She'd only been there a few weeks, but it had worked perfectly for her since she didn't have a car.

"I can go in with you, and we'll see if we can let you grab a few clothes and your textbooks, but otherwise, we'll need the apartment until we can make sure we've collected all the evidence. I'll let you know when it's okay for you to move back in."

Piper sighed. Her day had started out with such promise. Her future was bright and unfolding in front of her. Now it felt like she was taking a step backwards—letting go of her new home and moving back in with Cassie.

It's only temporary, she reminded herself. And if she were being honest, she wasn't too excited to go back into the apartment just yet anyway. It wouldn't hurt to stay at Cassie's a bit and let the image of her murdered roommate sprawled out on the floor fade a little.

Although she wasn't sure that image would ever fade from her memory.

She glanced around at the Page Turners. "Thanks so much for showing up. I really needed you guys." Who needed a therapist when she had the Page Turners?

Edna reached for her hand and gave it a squeeze. "We're always here for you, honey. I'm just sorry this happened to you. You have so many exciting things to look forward to and your week should have been wonderful. You should be focused on classes and making new friends. Instead, your hump day just turned homicidal."

Three weeks later, Piper finally returned to her apartment.

The police had cleared it the week before, but it took a few days for Piper to feel comfortable spending the night there alone. Cassie had gone over with her a few days before and packed up Brittany's things, then her parents had picked them up the day after the funeral.

The service itself had been packed, and Cassie and Edna had attended with Piper. Cassie had gone as support, and Edna had claimed that's why she was attending as well, but she also kept a sharp eye on the other attendees, declaring the killer often showed up at the funeral.

It gave Piper the willies to think she could be in the same room as Brittany's killer.

It also gave her chills each time she walked into the apartment and couldn't keep from staring at the spot where Brittany's body had lain.

She was grateful Edna had given her a ride over today and offered to come in with her. She would eventually have to get over it, but for now, she was thankful for the company.

"I've got your purse and the cookies if you can grab your backpack and that duffel bag," Edna told her, balancing Piper's purse on the tub of treats as she pushed the car door closed with her hip.

"Got it," Piper said, hefting the backpack and duffel, then plucked her purse off the tub and dropped the cross-body bag over her shoulder. She led the way up the sidewalk and into the house, digging in her pocket for the keys.

But for the second time in as many weeks, her heart jumped to her throat as she noticed the door to her apartment stood slightly ajar.

She stopped in her tracks and reached for Edna's arm, motioning to the older woman to stay quiet.

They took a few steps closer. Edna's eyes widened as a thump sounded from the other side of the door. "There's someone in there," she whispered.

"Should we call the police?"

Edna shook her head then reached into the front of her shirt and pulled a portable can of Mace from her bra. Edna was famous for the items she produced from her brassiere, often using the wardrobe piece as more of a purse than an article of clothing. "You push open the door, and I'll be ready to squirt the spray."

It didn't sound like the best plan in the world, but it was the only plan they had, and Piper set down the duffel bag and backpack and tip-toed to the door. She turned to Edna and mouthed, "Ready?"

The other woman had set the cookies on the duffel bag and held the Mace at arm's length in front of her. "Ready."

Piper burst through the door, and it slammed open, banging against the wall and startling the man kneeling on the floor and running his hand over the floor where Brittany's body had been.

"Hold it right there, Mister," Edna hissed. "I've got this Mace trained right on you, and I know how to use it."

The man raised his arms above his head. "Now hold on. There's no reason to use it at all."

"Who are you? What are you doing in here?" Piper fired questions at him.

Edna kept the can pointed his direction. "Did you kill that young girl?"

"What? No, of course not. My name is Lester

Grimley. I'm the handyman for the apartment complex. The landlord asked me to come in and make sure the apartment and the floor was okay. You know, after the…incident."

Edna narrowed her eyes. "Do you have any ID? Some kind of work badge?"

The handyman was probably in his late fifties or early sixties, shots of gray peppering his otherwise brown hair. Even crouched on the floor, it was evident he was a tall man. He wore a faded red T-shirt and tan Dickies work pants, the hems scuffed and torn from wear. His body was lean and his arms were corded with muscles.

He looked strong enough to easily strangle a petite college co-ed.

Or overpower her similarly built roommate and her elderly companion.

Piper scanned the room for any evidence of foul play. Nothing seemed amiss. Besides the strange man in the middle of the room, and a small red and black tool bag on the counter. Piper kept one hand on the front door as she tried to peer into the bag looking for…what? A collection of plastic grocery sacks?

Why did her roomie have to get murdered by something as ordinary and common as a grocery bag? Couldn't the murderer have chosen something more original—and easier to implicate him with—than an item found in almost every home in America?

Ugh. What was wrong with her? She'd been hanging out with Edna too long. And they'd spent the last few weeks speculating on the murder. No wonder she was seeing danger in every corner, and handyman, and criticizing the uninspired methods of a murderer.

"I'm watching you," Edna told the man. "Don't make any sudden moves."

He rolled his eyes as he slowly reached in his back

pocket and produced a flattened leather wallet that he tossed toward them.

Piper grabbed it and flipped it open to reveal his ID. She scanned it quickly then held it out to Edna. "It says his name is Lester Grimley, and he lives on Fourth Street, which is just a few blocks from here."

"It also says I have brown eyes and brown hair. And I think I've got about fourteen bucks and a sandwich coupon in there. Satisfied?" His right eye had the slightest twitch.

It unnerved Piper. Like it was a 'tell' that he was lying. But what in that sentence was there to lie about? That his hair color was different or that the coupon was really for pizza instead of a sandwich.

What if he had something to hide in his wallet? Like a fake ID. Or what if he had a condom tucked into his wallet? *Ew.* She dropped the wallet on the kitchen counter as if it were hot and had just burned her fingers. She didn't want to know.

Edna shrugged and lowered the Mace. "Are you about finished here?"

He dropped his hands and pushed himself up, rubbing his knee as he stood. "Yeah. This was my last task of the day." He eyed Piper with a raised eyebrow. "Unless you have something else I can do for you."

Piper bristled, an eerie chill racing up her back. What an odd way to phrase the question. She took a step back. "No, I'm good. Except I guess for the window." She gestured to the side wall of the apartment. "Did you fix the loose latch?"

Mac had mentioned they needed to get that taken care of. They still weren't sure how the killer had gotten into the apartment.

Lester shook his head. "Not yet. I need to pick up a new latch at the hardware store. I'll come back later this week to install it."

"Just make sure you call ahead this time," Edna instructed.

"Yes, ma'am." He stuffed his wallet back into his pocket, picked up his tool bag and ambled out the front door.

Piper closed the door behind him, noticing the way he walked with the slightest limp. She turned to Edna. "Was it just me or was that guy a little creepy?"

"A little? I feel like I need to wash my hands." Edna pushed the Mace back into her blouse and came out with a small container of hand sanitizer. She squirted a smidge into her hands, then held the bottle out to Piper.

She shook her head. "I'm good." Not that she didn't appreciate the offer of a sanitary cleanser which had just come out of her friend's bra, but she was going to pass this time around.

"Suit yourself." Edna looked around the apartment, taking time to study the spot on the floor where Lester had just been kneeling, while Piper brought in the rest of her things from the hall. "Are you sure you're going to be all right by yourself here, honey? I could stay a bit if you'd like. Or even sleep over. It could be fun, like a slumber party."

"No. I'll be fine. I have to stay by myself eventually. Might as well start tonight." In truth, she would be happy to have the other woman's company, but she needed to put her big girl panties on and suck it up and every other stupid cliché she could think of that would offer her the bravery she needed to spend the night in the apartment alone.

"Any luck on finding a new roommate?"

"Not yet. I think most people already moved into their housing before classes started or they're freaked out about moving into an apartment where the last renter was murdered. Although I didn't put that particular piece of information in the ad."

"Smart."

"Whatever it is, I haven't had even a single call to ask about the place."

"Don't worry. It'll happen. The right roommate is out there."

❧ ❧ ❧

The next morning, Piper stuffed a granola bar in her mouth then grabbed her backpack and pulled the door closed behind her. She rattled the doorknob, confirming it was firmly shut before heading down the hall and out the front door.

A soft whining sound stopped her as she tramped down the stairs, and her pulse raced at the thought of the killer hiding under the stairs.

She swallowed, then took a deep breath and cautiously peered over the railing.

A wide front porch wrapped around the Victorian, and Piper braced herself to run or scream if a crazed murderer came into view.

She let out her breath as she spied a small scruffy dog cowering under the floor of the porch. Its brown and beige fur was matted and dirty, and by the visible outline of its ribs, it looked like it couldn't weigh more than ten pounds.

Poor little thing. He must be starving.

Already forgetting the threat of the crazed killer, she pulled the granola bar from her mouth and held it out to it. "Hey there, little pup. You look like you could use this more than me."

The dog tentatively leaned forward and took a small sniff, then shrank back against the wooden post supporting the porch.

"It's okay. I won't hurt you." She broke off a piece of

the granola bar and tossed it gently toward it.

She didn't have time for this. She had to get to work. Her shift started in ten minutes, but she couldn't just leave it there.

The dog looked from her to the granola bar, then ran forward, grabbed the offered bite and raced back under the safety of the porch.

At least that was something. And about all she could do now. If it was still there when she got home, she'd bring it something more. She tossed it the rest of the snack bar and hurried up the sidewalk toward the coffee shop.

Holding back a yawn, she tried to focus on the day ahead of her. She worked the morning shift and had classes this afternoon. Maybe she'd take the long way home this afternoon and hopefully wear herself out.

The night before had been spent in restless fits of sleep, and she'd woken from a nightmare around three. Too anxious to go back to sleep, she'd wandered into the kitchen and made a cup of hot chocolate. Taking the warm mug and the cookie tin into the living room, she'd spent an hour watching television before finally falling back asleep on the sofa.

She'd woken up that morning with a sore back, her eyes scratchy from lack of sleep and cookie crumbs sprinkling her chest, but she'd made it through her first night in the apartment alone.

🐾 🐾 🐾

Eight and half minutes later, Piper pushed through the door of The Pleasant Valley Perk coffee shop. The business name was a mouthful so most of the locals just referred to it as The Perk.

Her coworkers, Sarah and Fitz, stood behind the counter.

A few customers dotted the tables, but no one was in line. Fitz looked up as she walked in and offered her one of his gorgeous grins.

Piper's heart skipped a beat. Just like it did every time she saw the cute coffee maker.

Feeling her cheeks warm, she gave a little wave then headed into the back room to drop off her coat and purse.

Fitz was fun to look at, but there was no way anything was happening there. Besides the fact the hot computer engineer was totally out of her league, there was also the small details. One, he was her boss—well, he was the shift leader, so he was *like* her boss, and two, he was a friend of Drew's, which automatically made him off-limits.

The guys had been friends and teammates. They'd played soccer together, and Piper had met him a few times while they were in high school. She didn't know what his actual first name was, but his last name was Fitzgerald and everyone called him Fitz.

She called him the Brilliant Barista. Well, not actually to his face. But in her head.

Seriously, the guy was crazy smart. And totally hot. And literally oozed charm. But not in a smarmy way, more like an 'everyone was his friend' kind of way. He had the cutest smile. It lit up his whole face. And made his blue eyes do this sparkly kind of thing. His body was lean and muscled, the body of an athlete. And his skin still held the warm shade of a summer tan.

He wore faded jeans and scuffed low-top Converse sneakers and looked totally at ease in his clothes, whether he had on a nice button down shirt or a worn T-shirt that humorously declared his love for physics.

Fitz was smart and sweet and...*totally off-limits*, she reminded herself.

There was no way she wanted to get involved with one of Drew's best buddies.

Not that it mattered. There was still the little matter of him being completely out of her league and the small fact that with such a cute guy, she would be routed directly into the friend zone.

The Brilliant Barista poked his head into the backroom, another killer grin on his face. His blond hair was just a little too long, and his shaggy bangs fell across his forehead. "Hey, Piper."

"Hey, Fitz."

"You doing okay?"

"Yeah, sure."

He stepped into the back and leaned his hip against the counter. "You back in your apartment yet?"

She nodded. "Yep. Spent my first night alone there last night."

"How was it?"

"Creepy. And a little weird. But also okay. I didn't sleep very well, but I'm sure that will get better."

He had this way of really looking at her while she talked, like he was totally interested in what she had to say. Which made her blab out every inconsequential boring detail of her life.

The coffee shop was either slamming busy or deathly slow, and the baristas often had time to chat. Piper was usually the one blending into the wall, listening while she let others talk.

But she wasn't like that with Fitz. Whether it was the way he asked her questions or the way he appeared to actually care about her answers, he seemed to always get her talking. Over the last few weeks, they had worked almost every shift together, and she had spilled the specifics of the murder and the humiliating aspects of Drew dumping her.

"That's gotta be strange," he said. "But I'm sure it will get easier."

"I hope so. It took me forever to fall asleep last night."

Sarah, the other employee, called into the back. "We've got a line. Can you guys help?"

"Be right there," Fitz answered. He caught Piper's arm as she walked past him toward the front of the shop. "You know you can always call or text me. I mean, just in case you have trouble again. I'm a night owl, and I'm usually up late studying anyway, so it wouldn't bother me. Just remember you've got my number if you ever want to talk."

The employees were given a call tree when they started and encouraged to enter their co-workers' phone numbers into their phones in case they needed to call in or wanted to request a shift exchange.

She ducked her head and muttered a soft, "Thanks."

There was no way she would ever call him. And she was sure he didn't really expect her to. The guy was just being nice. Like he was to everyone. He was probably just worried she would be too tired to show up for her shift.

She didn't have time to think too much more about it as the shop was filling with their usual mid-morning rush. Fitz grabbed a stack of cups and started filling orders while she and Sarah rotated between the registers and preparing drinks.

🐾 🐾 🐾

Later that night, Piper tossed and turned, trying to sleep.

Her day had flown by. Fortunately, she enjoyed her classes, and it had been a warm day so she'd been able to walk home from campus the long way.

She'd passed a grocery store on her way back and had grabbed a few things, including a small bag of dry dog food. The scruffy dog had been gone when she got back to the apartment, but she put a plastic bowl of water and a little dish of the food under her porch, just in case. She knew what it was like to be hungry.

It had taken her a couple of hours to finish all her homework then she'd had a warm cup of tea and tried reading a book, in an effort to tire herself out.

But it hadn't worked. She'd been lying in bed for close to an hour and still felt wide awake.

Her body seemed to be on hyper-alert to every sound and creak in the apartment. Between the neighbors moving around upstairs and the wind that was blowing that night, the old Victorian was full of creepy thuds and groans.

She checked her phone. Again.

Eleven-forty.

Ten minutes past the last time she'd looked.

Her phone buzzed in her hand, startling her, and it flew from her hand as she jumped. It hit the floor with a thud.

Who was calling her this late?

Maybe it was the killer.

Maybe he was calling to tell her she was next.

Or that he was in the house with her. She'd seen that movie.

Leaning over the bed, she reached for the phone, then snatched her hand back as her mind reeled with visions of the murderer hiding under her bed waiting for the perfect moment to strike.

Her breath seemed to be stuck in her throat, and her heart pounded against her chest.

This is ridiculous. There is no monster under the bed.

She swallowed and leaned slowly forward. Gathering her courage, she shot her hand out, snatched the phone from the floor, and scrambled back in the bed, pressing her back against the wall and clutching the phone to her chest.

The stupid text better be worth it.

She peered down at the phone, and this time her heart

raced for a different reason.

The text was from the Brilliant Barista. "You asleep?"

Her hands shook as she fumbled with the phone, trying to touch the right spots to respond. "Not yet. Why aren't you?"

"I'm studying for a test. Thought I'd check in on you." Smiley-face emoji.

Hmm. Was that a 'isn't that funny' kind of smiley face, or a 'remember, we're just friends' kind of smiley face?

Did it matter?

"Thanks." Smiley-face emoji.

Two could play at this game.

"Wanna talk?"

Wasn't that what they were doing? Or did he mean *actually* talk? Like on the phone? Or did he mean he wanted to come over? She tried to imagine Fitz in her apartment, sitting on the faded blue sofa. A warm tingle slid down her spine.

What was wrong with her? He was just being nice. Being Fitz. He hadn't asked her if he could come over or take her out. He's simply asked if she wanted to talk, which could just as easily mean to continue texting. She typed a quick response before she could change her mind. "Sure."

She held her breath, then almost dropped the phone again when it buzzed in her hand. Her hand trembled as she touched the screen and held the phone to her ear. "Hello."

"Hey."

"Hey."

Wow. This conversation was going great so far.

"So, um, what test are you studying for?"

"Calculus."

"Yeah? Tell me about it."

"Oh man. You really do want me to put you to sleep."

She let out a funny giggly sound she wasn't used to hearing come out of her mouth. "What I want is for you to talk to me about something that will take my mind off the fact my roommate has just been murdered. And that it happened in the next room over from where I'm currently sleeping."

"Okay. I see your point. Well, I'm currently trying to solve a differential equation."

"Hmmm. Is that anything like making coffee?" she teased. "Because I kind of understand that."

"No. Not at all."

"Tell me about it anyway." Snuggling into her pillow, she pulled the covers up to her chin and closed her eyes, letting the sound of his voice relax and settle her troubled mind.

"I'd rather talk about you."

"Why? I'm far more boring than Calculus."

He laughed. "I don't believe that. I'm just worried about you, I guess. How's the search going for a new roommate?"

Her eyes popped open. That topic wasn't settling at all.

She let out a sigh. "Not well. I thought I would have at least a few inquiries by now. But I haven't had a single reply to my ad."

"What does your ad say? Maybe you're not making the apartment seem attractive enough."

"I didn't want to make it too complicated. So I put in, you know, just the normal stuff. Single female seeking roommate to split rent for furnished two-bedroom apartment in a renovated Victorian home. Close to campus, utilities included, blah blah blah. I said I was looking for a non-smoker who was semi-tidy. Then, in an effort to show I have a fun side, and believe me, it *was* an effort, because I've been told I'm not much fun at all, I listed three requirements. Must have: 1) a sense of humor, 2) an easy-going personality, and 3) a Netflix subscription."

"That is funny." He chuckled, and the sound of his laughter sent butterflies swirling through her stomach.

"I figured you'd have to be easy-going to live in a place which has just been swept for clues by the cops. And I wasn't serious about the Netflix thing. It was just a lame attempt to be witty. But it isn't working. I still haven't had a single call or email about it. I think people are creeped out by the murder. I know I would be."

Oh wait. I am actually freaked out—hence the midnight phone conversation with the Brilliant Barista.

"Yeah. That's a tough one. But I'm sure the right person will come along."

"So I've been told."

"Are you getting tired yet?"

"Not at all. Maybe you should tell me more about your equation, and I'll nod off."

"Good plan. I'll work through this last problem out loud, and if I hear you snoring, I'll hang up."

"Hey. I don't snore." Why did he say that? Had he heard she snored? Had Drew told him that?

The reminder of Drew and his relationship to Fitz was like a splash of cold water to the face.

"Listen, you've been really great, but you don't have to calculus me to sleep. I know you have more work to do, and really, I'm a big girl. I can fall asleep on my own."

"Oh yeah. Of course. Sure you can. I was just trying to help." His tone changed to sound more brusque and businesslike.

Crud. She didn't want to hurt the guy's feelings. *Or get hurt myself.* She kept her voice low, sincere. "You have helped."

"You can call me anytime."

"Thanks, Fitz."

"You are very welcome."

"Good night."

"Hey, Piper?"

"Yeah."

"For the record, I *do* think you're funny."

She let out a soft chuckle. "Thanks."

"Good night, Piper," he whispered.

"Good night, Fitz," she whispered back, then tapped the screen to disconnect the call and set the phone on the wobbly nightstand.

Flopping back onto the bed, she nestled into her pillow and closed her eyes again, but could not stop smiling.

❁ ❁ ❁

The next night, Piper sat curled on the sofa trying to study while she nervously glanced at the clock.

She'd received an email reply to her ad that afternoon, and her new roommate was scheduled to arrive any minute.

The email had been cordial and well-written. It had been signed only as L. Penny, which Piper found a little odd, but had decided beggars can't be choosers. With the rent due in two days, she was bordering on desperate.

According to her message, "L" had just moved to town and was planning to enroll in some classes and was 'super-excited' to find a place so close to campus and downtown.

Nothing in her email set off any 'crazy' flags for Piper, and she had her fingers crossed this L. Penny would be someone she could like. Heck, she'd take someone she could barely tolerate as long as they could overlook the small matter of the last tenant's untimely demise and could cover their share of the rent.

A knock sounded at the door, and she jumped, her nerves getting the best of her.

She pushed off the sofa and crossed the room, but paused, apprehension filling her as she reached for the door knob.

How bad could this person be? She claimed to have met the requirements Piper had listed and she met the main one that Brittany wasn't—she was breathing.

And she said she had the first month's rent with her, which was the most important qualification at the moment.

She needed someone to help with the rent and someone who wasn't squeamish about living in an apartment where the last tenant had been murdered. Period.

That was enough for right now.

If they could manage those two things—and had Netflix—she could pretty much deal with anyone.

She took a deep breath and opened the door.

That same breath caught in her throat as she stared at the blond woman standing there.

Her voice cracked as she croaked out one word. "Mom?"

Piper stood frozen in place, her knuckles turning white as she clutched the door knob and stared at her mother, a woman she hadn't seen in three months.

"Surprise," her mom said, a sheepish grin on her face.

Surprise didn't even come close.

Neither did flabbergasted.

And dumbfounded wasn't even in the ballpark.

Disbelief, shock, and astonishment might work.

"What are you doing here?" Piper asked, which was better than what she wanted to say. The question on her tongue had a few more expletives.

"I'm here about the apartment. I'm the one who answered your ad."

A ripple of dread flowed through as Piper glanced down at the rolling suitcase and battered duffle bag at her mother's feet.

"Oh no. No way."

Claire Denton put a hand on her hip, and Piper noticed the way her faded jeans hung loosely around her previously curvy waist. "I thought you might be at least a little happy to see me."

"Why? The last time I saw you was when you dumped me on Aunt Cassie's doorstep and went riding off on the back of a motorcycle."

Her mom raised an eyebrow. "Yeah? Well, the last time I saw you, you had black spiky hair, a piss-poor attitude, a pierced nose, and you were wearing clothes out of a vampire fashion magazine."

Piper touched her shoulder-length blonde hair. She had gone through a bit of a Goth stage in high school.

When she'd moved in with Cassie and started school in Pleasant Valley, her hair and her whole wardrobe had been black. She'd made a few friends in the Goth crowd, but then she'd started dating Drew and made new friends, and new fashion choices. Cassie had taken her shopping, and she'd dyed her hair back to its original color and let it grow out.

"I've changed."

"I can see that. So have I."

Her mom did look different. Rougher, somehow. Like the life she'd been living hadn't been kind. She'd always had full naturally wavy hair, but now her too-blonde bleached hair hung limp and seemed thinner. And an inch and a half of dark roots gave away her natural color. The pale blue top she wore drooped on her shoulders, and her black motorcycle boots were scuffed and worn.

But Piper wasn't about to feel sorry for her. She'd made her choice. A choice that hadn't included her daughter. "How is Spider, by the way? Is that his first name or his last—I never was sure. Should I call him Mr. Spider?"

Claire shrugged. "I'm through with that guy so you can call him whatever the hell you want. I call him a dirty cheatin' bastard."

Interesting. "So, what are you really doing here?"

"I told you. I answered your ad. I'm your new roomie."

Piper reread the emails in her head, searching for any kind of clues that they had been from her mother. "You said your name was L. Penny."

Claire chuckled. "I know. Pretty clever, right? Don't you remember? It was the name of that first dog we had, back when you were little. Her name was Penny but we always called her Lucky Penny because of the way she'd just turned up on our doorstep. So, I borrowed her name and got L. Penny. I thought it was hilarious."

She remembered now. "Yeah, hilarious."

"What does it matter what name I used? I fit the requirements you laid out. You said you were looking for someone who was semi-tidy, easy-going, and had a sense of humor. And I always could make you laugh."

That was a long time ago. And she wasn't laughing now. "It also said 'non-smoker'."

"That's good. Because I quit."

Piper glanced down at her mom's hands. Before she ran off with the motorcycle gang, Claire had been a beautician and had always prided herself on her hair and nails. Now her mom's nails were unpainted, and appeared dry and brittle. But they didn't carry the tell-tale yellow stains nicotine could often leave.

"Look, Pip, I already paid the landlord my share of this month's rent, so you're stuck with me for now. So, are you going to invite me, or what?"

She winced at the old nickname and the fact she now was indeed stuck. If Claire had already paid the rent, she couldn't very well turn her out. Especially if she'd just saved her bacon, and her apartment. She took a step back. "Fine."

Her mom picked up her bags and stepped into the room.

Piper peered out into the hall. "Where's the rest of your stuff?"

"This is it. I travel light."

"I know. That's because you usually travel without your kid."

Claire raised a penciled eyebrow. "I can see you still have the attitude."

Piper ignored the dig and closed the door. "The place is kind of small. Two bedrooms and we have to share a bathroom."

Claire looked around the apartment. "This is nice. I like the set-up of the kitchen and the living room together. And it's bigger than that place we had over on Water Street. Remember the one-bedroom apartment we had with the electric blue carpeting?"

Piper remembered. She remembered everything. And she'd actually loved that small apartment. Even loved the blue carpet. It reminded her of Cookie Monster. But she especially loved the way she and her mom felt like a team—like it was them against the world. But that was before. Before her mom went off the rails. Before she started having her nightly rum and cokes—just to take the edge off and help her get to sleep.

Piper pointed to the door to the left of the kitchen. "That's your room."

Claire lowered her voice and lifted her chin toward the bedroom. "Is that where it happened? Where the girl was…?"

"Murdered?" Piper shook her head. "No. She was killed pretty much where you're standing right now."

Claire leapt away from the spot, high-stepping her feet as if she were walking on hot coals. She stopped on the other side of the table and smoothed her hair, as if trying to compose herself. "Poor thing. Have they heard anything? Made any progress in the case?"

"No. Not that I know of."

Claire narrowed her eyes and studied her daughter. "You okay? This has got to freak you out a little."

"Your concern is touching." Although it was about three years too late. "I'm fine."

Her mom held up her hands. "Okay. I was just asking."

"You don't need to worry about me."

Claire shrugged then picked up her bags and carried them into her room.

Piper stood still, listening as her mom walked around the bedroom and flung the suitcase on the bed. She could hear the whisper of the zipper, the flop of the lid, and the soft slide of the dresser drawers.

She should go to her own room—let her mom have some space. It's not like she cared what she was doing in there.

But her feet carried her forward, as if they had a mind of their own. Only to the threshold, though. She couldn't make herself actually enter the room.

She leaned against the door jam and watched her mother unpack her meager belongings. The suitcase was stuffed full of a hodgepodge of items that looked like they'd been thrown in at the last minute.

Claire lifted a small stack of clothes from the suitcase and dumped it into the drawers, then pulled out a couple bags of toiletries and tossed them on top of the dresser. Piper recognized the slim green bag which held her beautician tools, easily capturing memories of haircuts and her mom fixing her hair.

A lump formed in Piper's throat as Claire took a framed photo from her bag and tenderly brushed the side of the frame before setting it up on the nightstand.

Piper recognized the photo—it had sat on their mantel for most of her life, and had always been one of her favorites.

It had been taken when she was about seven or eight, and before her dad had died. Back in the days when their life was good—when they were happy. The three of them had been goofing around at a summer barbecue in Cassie's backyard, and her aunt had snapped the picture. It showed her mom and dad with their arms wrapped around Piper, who was beaming up at them, a happy smile on her face, her lips ringed with pink from the red Kool-Aid she'd been drinking.

James (Denny) Denton had been the rock of their family, and their world had crashed down around them when he'd died—as if their life had been one more piece of collateral damage his motorcycle accident had taken.

For Piper, she'd lost both of her parents that night. After Denny died, her mom changed and nothing was ever the same. It was like she fell into this pit of despair and never could pull herself out. Piper tried to help—tried everything she could to reach her, to drag her from the pit. But no matter how many ropes Piper threw in to save her, she couldn't, or wouldn't, ever grab one.

But that picture had been taken before—before the crash, before the devastation of their lives.

The photo exuded love and joy, and it hurt her heart to look at it.

She swallowed the emotion—cleared her throat as if she could cough away the pain and grief. Why was her mom even carrying it around with her? It's not like she cared about any of that now. Now she seemed to only care about herself.

The room still seemed bare, even though Claire had apparently finished her unpacking.

Piper gestured to the bare mattress. "I've got an extra set of sheets for the bed, if you need them."

"Thanks. That would be great. I left in a bit of a hurry and didn't get to grab all my things." Claire let out a bitter laugh. "And there were some things I left behind on purpose." She dumped the rest of the bag's contents into the next empty drawer then closed the suitcase and pushed it under the bed, mumbling to herself, "Like my pride."

Piper noticed she'd pushed the duffel bag under the bed as well. Why hadn't she unpacked it?

Was there something in it she didn't want Piper to see?

Geez—she was starting to sound like Edna—looking

for suspicion and mystery in everything. It was probably just her bras and undies.

"I'll figure out what all I need and go shopping later this week," Claire said, offering her a smile.

Piper couldn't smile back. It was as if her face were trapped in a permanent scowl. "Sure. It's your life. You can do whatever you want." That's what she'd been doing the last several years anyway. Ever since Denny had died.

Claire pulled her smart phone from her pocket and held it up. "I didn't forget the third roommate requirement. I have a subscription to Netflix—just got it today. Do you want to order a pizza and binge-watch a series or something?"

Yeah, right. Maybe she and her mom could cuddle up on the sofa and binge out on *The Gilmore Girls*—that sounded just peachy.

"No. I'm good. I've got homework tonight."

"Okay, sure. That's smart. School always come first." She stood next to the bed, chewing on her bottom lip—a sign Piper knew meant she was either nervous or going to ask her a favor. Like to borrow twenty bucks.

"Was there something else?" She tried to keep the annoyance out of her voice, but failed. Miserably.

"No. Not really. Just talking about pizza made me hungry. How about you? Do you want me to order one, or maybe I could make us something? I didn't have time to get groceries, but if you have some bread and cheese, I can make you one of Mom's Famous Cheesy Melt Sandwiches."

Her mom loved to give ordinary things extraordinary titles, as if calling it a Famous Cheesy Melt made an average grilled cheese sandwich something special.

"I'll pass."

She pretended not to see the look of hurt shadow her mother's eyes.

Too bad. She'd had plenty of hurt. And most of it had been her mom's doing. A grilled cheese sandwich wasn't going to make up for abandoning her.

"I'm not hungry. I'll be in my room. But you're welcome to help yourself."

Claire's shoulders slumped. "I'll pick up some groceries tomorrow."

"Whatever."

❀ ❀ ❀

The next day Claire did indeed pick up groceries. Lots of them.

It was midafternoon and Piper had skipped lunch as she focused on her homework. Claire had taken off a couple of hours ago, and she'd tried to make the best use of the time her mother was gone.

Something about her mom being in the apartment made it hard for her to concentrate on anything besides the fact her *mother* was in the next room. Although she *had* slept better the night before. But she was only contributing that to the fact she wasn't alone in the apartment.

She had a short shift at The Perk this afternoon, then book club was at her place tonight, so she'd been trying to get everything done. The apartment was in good shape since she'd cleaned it the day before in preparation for her new roomie.

She'd just finished turning in the last assignment when the front door burst open, and Claire rushed in, her arms laden with grocery bags.

"I hope you're hungry, because I bought a roast chicken, and I can't eat it all myself," she said, dumping the bags on the counter. "I noticed your cupboards were a little bare, so I thought I could help by filling them up. I may have gone a little overboard." She offered Piper a

39

sheepish grin.

A little overboard? The woman had just carried in eight bags of groceries and a roast chicken. Which Piper would, of course, refuse to eat.

Her stomach growled in protest. Okay, she might eat a little.

"I've got more stuff in the car," Claire said, heading back out the front door. "I'll be right back."

Piper followed her out. Her mother had just bought them a crap-ton of groceries—the least she could do was help her to carry them in.

An older model blue Toyota sat at the curb, its paint so faded it looked almost silver. Claire hadn't had a vehicle when she'd left a few months ago, and this one looked like the kind of car that could be purchased with a handful of cash at one of those corner used car lots.

Not for the first time, Piper wondered what kind of life her mom had been leading in the past several months.

And where had she gotten the money to buy all this stuff?

The back seat of the car was filled with grocery bags and white sacks from Bed, Bath, & Beyond. A new pillow and a purple comforter set in a giant plastic bag filled the front seat.

"Geez, you really went on a shopping spree," Piper said, grabbing a handful of bags.

Claire shrugged. "It looks like more than it is. And you know I've always been a good shopper. Plus, I had some coupons."

It was true. Her mom had always known how to stretch a dollar. In the beginning, before Claire had fallen into the pit, they'd made a game of trying to find great deals or figuring out how to make the best meal for the smallest amount of money.

Her mom used to always do stuff like that. She was

constantly turning menial tasks into games or making the most mundane things fun.

But that was before.

Piper had almost smiled as her mom shook a box of mac and cheese and proclaimed, "Four for a dollar, baby," but instead, she stuffed down those thoughts of fun times and hauled the groceries into the apartment.

It took one more trip to get everything in. Her mom must have filled the whole cart because the kitchen was covered in grocery bags. Thank goodness they were the white ones from Price Mart and not the tan ones from the Spend Thrift.

A shiver ran down her spine as she imagined Brittany's last moments, struggling to breathe through the thin plastic.

"I've always wanted a purple-themed bedroom," Claire said, coming out of the bedroom with another large bag in her hands.

"Why? So you can feel like you're sleeping inside of a grape?"

"Don't be mean," she scolded lightly. "It's just for fun, and the color makes me smile." She pulled a large blue throw rug from the bag and casually spread it out over the area between the table and the kitchen, the area where Brittany's body had lain.

Neither of them said anything about it, but having the gruesome spot covered did make Piper breathe a little easier.

"Speaking of fun, I also got these." Claire pulled a stack of Powerball and scratch tickets from her purse and spread them on the counter with a flourish. "I got a couple of Lucky Sevens for you and a quick-pick ticket for the lotto drawing."

"Are you kidding? Why would you waste your money on this stuff?"

"It's not a waste. And you can't win if you don't play. I play three Powerball tickets a week." She held up three tickets. "One is always a quick-pick, one is your dad and I's anniversary date, and I call this one "The Birthday Card." She laid the last card on the counter and gave it a loving pat. "It's got all three of our birthdays on it—yours, mine, and Denny's—those are always my lucky numbers." Her voice choked a little as she explained the last card.

Piper thought tears may have filled her eyes, but Claire turned away and busied herself with emptying a bag of groceries.

She ran her fingers over the array of colorful tickets. "Is this how you suddenly have money to buy all this stuff? Did you *win* it?"

Claire turned on the radio, and either drowned out Piper's questions or was choosing to ignore her as she opened all the cupboards. Several were completely bare. She touched the empty shelf in the cabinet next to the sink. "Don't you have any glasses or mugs?"

Piper pointed to the deep lower drawer next to the dishwasher. "We keep them down there."

Claire shook her head. "Why? Who keeps their glasses in a lower drawer? I thought everyone kept them in the cabinet above the dishwasher?"

"I know. It's weird. But I guess that's the way Brittany's family does it, and she's the one who unpacked that part of the kitchen."

"Would it bother you if I moved them up here?"

Piper shook her head. "I don't care. And Brittany isn't going to care anymore either."

Claire moved the few glasses and mugs up to the higher cabinet. "Do you have any other preferences or a specific order to your kitchen, or can I just put this food stuff away where I think it should go?"

"Knock yourself out."

"I'm not picky about sharing," she said, filling a shelf with boxed pasta. "You can eat whatever you find. But I will totally respect your food if you don't want to share."

"Brittany and I set aside one shelf in the fridge and one shelf in the pantry for stuff that was just ours. Otherwise, we shared stuff too. We figured it wasn't worth the expense to double up on everyday stuff like having two cartons of milk."

"Makes sense." She tossed Piper a bag of Caesar salad and set a bowl on the counter. "You want to mix this up while I finish putting stuff away? I thought it would go with the chicken."

Piper pushed the lottery tickets to the side, then ripped open the bag and dumped it into the bowl, actually happy to have a task to do instead of just watch as her mom took over the kitchen. She didn't really care about the order of how the groceries were put away—she wasn't really territorial about her stuff.

Which was strange since she was an only child. But there were a lot of things about her and her childhood which didn't fit the norm. And she'd learned long ago to not sweat the small stuff—like which kitchen shelf the canned soup went on.

"So, what's your day look like? Do you have class this afternoon?" Claire asked.

"No. I work from two to five, then I'm having book club over here tonight so I'm coming home to make spaghetti." She glanced at the full cupboards and knew her mom was making a real effort to get along. It wouldn't hurt anything to at least be cordial. "There will be plenty of food. You can eat with us if you want."

The slightest smile crossed her mom's face. "Thank you. I think I will." She took a deep breath. "Cassie doesn't know I'm back yet."

Interesting. "Why not?"

"It was kind of a spur of the moment decision to come back. But it's not a secret. I was going to call her. I just haven't got around to it yet."

"Well, you'll see her tonight."

"I guess so. What's the book you're reading?"

Piper pointed to the paperback on the coffee table. "It's a new psychological thriller. It was Edna's choice—she loves books like that. It was pretty good. But with everything that's happened, it also kind of gave me the creeps."

"I can understand that. Why would you want to read about a mysterious murder when you're in the middle of one yourself?"

Four hours later, Piper rushed up the steps to her apartment. She was so late. The book club was going to arrive in fifteen minutes, and she hadn't even started cooking.

A flash of white drew her eye to the space under the porch, and she caught a glimpse of the scruffy mutt. She leaned over the railing and spoke softly to the dog. "I don't have time to feed you now, but I'll bring you out some food in a bit. You're a good girl."

She didn't know why she now assumed the dog was a girl, as she hadn't gotten close enough to check, but it seemed right to her.

The dog laid down and settled her head on her front paws, as if she'd understood exactly what Piper had said and was prepared to contentedly wait.

Her coworker had been late coming in for her shift, and Piper didn't feel right leaving until she arrived. She knew she smelled like coffee and had hoped to grab a quick shower before the other women arrived.

Now she'd be lucky to get her hands washed.

Running through the recipe steps in her head, she pushed through the front door of the Victorian and stopped dead in her tracks at the scent of garlic in the hall.

Instantly taken back to the day of the murder, her mouth went dry, and she couldn't breathe. What if the murderer had come back?

Oh no. Mom.

She ran forward, fumbling with the key in the lock, then burst into the room. "Mom!"

Expecting to see her mother laid out on the floor, a

plastic sack wrapped around her head, she stopped again and sagged against the door frame as she spied her mom standing at the stove.

Claire turned around, a wooden spoon in her hand. "Good Lord, what's wrong? Are you okay? You're white as a sheet." She tossed the spoon in the sink and rushed to Piper's side. Putting an arm around her, she led her toward the kitchen table.

Piper shrugged off her mom's arm and sank into the chair as she gasped for breath. "I'm sorry. The smell of garlic—it was the same as the day Brittany was killed. I thought you were dead."

"I'm sorry. I didn't mean to scare you." She got Piper a glass of water and set it on the table in front of her. "I started the spaghetti. I was trying to help."

Piper took a big gulp of water as she glanced at the stove and the bubbling pots of water and sauce. Relief flooded her, both at the fact her mom was alive and that she'd already made the meal for that night. "Thank you. You didn't have to do that."

"I know. But I wanted to."

"That was nice of you."

"Why don't you take a minute to wash your face and pull yourself together? I'll finish setting the table. You still have fifteen minutes before they show up."

Piper nodded and headed for the bathroom. She took a quick shower and put on yoga pants and a T-shirt. Pulling her hair into a ponytail, she walked back into the living room, this time inhaling the scent of spaghetti sauce and appreciating the smell.

She really should thank her mom, but she wasn't in the kitchen. She could hear her in the bedroom, but before she could say anything, a knock sounded at the door.

The Page Turners had arrived.

Her nerves were jumpy as she opened the door and let

herself be engulfed by her Aunt Cassie's arms.

Edna and Sunny were in the hall behind her, and they both gave her hugs as they entered the living room.

"It smells wonderful in here," Cassie said, sniffing the air.

"How's the new roommate working out?" Edna said, dropping her coat on the sofa.

"Seriously, did I give you this recipe?" Cassie asked, reaching to hang her purse on the back of the chair. "I swear it smells like my mom's sauce."

"About that…" Piper said as Claire stepped out of her bedroom.

Cassie's purse missed the chair and hit the floor with a thud. Her hands flew to her mouth.

Then she ran to her sister and threw her arms around her in a tight hug. "Oh my gosh. I'm so glad you're all right."

Glad you're all right? Not glad to see you? Why wouldn't her mom be all right?

Claire hugged Cassie back. "I'm okay."

"Why haven't you called me? I haven't been able to reach you in weeks."

"I had to get a new phone." Claire glanced at Piper then squeezed Cassie's arm. "But everything's fine now."

"What are you doing here?"

"I live here. I'm Piper's new roomie."

"You're what?"

Edna chuckled. "That sounds like a bad reality TV show—*Rooming With My Mom*."

Piper groaned. A bad reality TV show that had become her life.

Claire gestured to the table. "Why don't we sit down, and we'll tell you all about it while we eat." She crossed to the kitchen to drain the spaghetti.

Sunny put her arm around Piper's shoulders. She was

always the perceptive one. "Are you okay? I mean, really? This must have been a shock to have her show up out of the blue like this?"

"Not just show up, but move herself in," Edna added, a noticeable huff in her voice.

Piper shrugged. "I'm okay. I didn't have any other options. No one even called about the apartment. And she's already paid this month's rent."

The door to the apartment burst open, and Maggie rushed in. "Sorry I'm late. I had to drop Dylan off at soccer practice." She stopped midway into the room as she saw Claire holding the pot of sauce. "What the hell are you doing here?"

She glanced from Claire to Piper, her maternal instincts obviously firing on all cylinders. Drew might have broken up with her, but his mom still treated Piper like she was one of her own kids. And she didn't have the extra baggage of being related to Claire like Cassie did.

"She's her new roommate," Edna said, arching an eyebrow.

"Like hell she is." Maggie flashed her gaze to Piper.

Piper shrugged again. "I needed the rent money."

"Not this badly. You don't need to go this far. If you need money, I'll pay your rent."

Cassie pulled out a chair and motioned for Maggie to take it. "They were just getting ready to tell us all about it. Let's sit down and eat, and then we can form an opinion."

"Or rip someone's eyes out," mumbled Maggie as she grudgingly sat down.

The rest of the group took their places and spent the next five minutes dishing up the food and digging in.

Piper watched the women eat, wisely keeping her mouth shut, except to shovel in spaghetti and garlic bread. She wanted to hear her mom's story without actually having to ask her about it.

But her mom was the queen of deflection, only giving little pieces of the story, then directing questions at Cassie or Sunny. She tried to ignore Maggie, who had barely eaten anything and who continued to glare daggers at her throughout the meal.

All Piper really found out about the past few months of her mom's life was she'd moved several times, following Spider's motorcycle gang, and things hadn't worked out like she'd thought they would, and in the end, Claire had left. From the few things she'd said the night before and from the way her eyes narrowed when she said his name, Piper gathered Spider hadn't turned out to be such a great guy.

In fact, he sounded like kind of a douche.

"It worked out great that Piper needed a new roomie right when I came back to town," Claire said. "The timing couldn't have been better."

"It didn't work out so great for Brittany," Edna muttered.

Claire ignored her and started to gather the plates. "Why don't I clean up while you all talk about the book? I read it this afternoon. It was quite good."

What? Her mom had read the book? Why? To get closer to Piper? Or just because she was bored and it was sitting on the coffee table?

It made Piper's head hurt to try to figure that woman out.

True to her word, she stayed in the kitchen, loading the dishwasher and washing pans while the rest of them moved to the living room. They talked a little about the book, but it was obvious from the awkward silences and furtive glances toward the kitchen that Claire remained the bleached-blond elephant in the room.

Claire rinsed the last pan and dried her hands on a towel. "I'm going back to cutting hair and have enrolled in some refresher courses to keep up with the new trends," she announced. "We're working on color right now, and I need to practice if anyone wants some highlights or to add some fun color to their hair."

"Fun color?" Cassie asked. "Like what?"

"Like stripes of purple or blue or dyeing the underside or the ends of your hair pink or teal."

"I've always wanted to do that," Piper said. "There's a girl in my class who has the ends of her hair dyed blue, and it looks cool."

"I could do that for you," Claire offered. "Easy. What color do you want?"

"I don't know. Pink, I guess."

"Pink would look adorable with your blond hair. And I could liken you up a little as well. Let me grab my stuff." Claire hurried into the bedroom.

Piper suddenly wasn't so sure this was a good idea. But it was only hair. And she had been thinking about adding some color. This way she could try it and would save the cost of having it done at a pricey salon.

Claire returned with her tools and a bag from the local beauty supply store. She laid a towel on the counter and emptied the contents of the bag onto it. Boxes of colors and hair product littered the counter. She showed them a picture in a magazine of some of the hot new ideas to do with color.

Edna peered at the magazine and touched her silver locks. "I think the teal looks like a lot of fun. Or the royal blue. It would match most of my outfits. I do wear a lot of blue."

"Then you could do both. It's easy to do several shades of one color," Claire said. "That's what I'm going to do with Piper. Her hair will transition from blonde to light pink then get darker pink toward the ends."

"I'm not sure…" Piper started to say.

"Oh don't worry. If you hate it, we can always dye it back. Don't worry. It'll be fun," Claire assured her while pulling on a pair of plastic gloves.

Famous last words.

Two hours later, the ends of Piper's hair were a gorgeous hombre shade of pink, Cassie had a few strands of purple in hers, and Edna's curls were suffused with tints of blue, green, and turquoise.

Claire even colored her own hair, changing it back to the chestnut brown it had been years ago. It looked better than the bleachy blonde—the soft caramel color complementing the skin tone of her face. She'd also cut a few inches of the dry ends off and let Cassie give her bangs. The new cut and color made her look younger, healthier.

"It looks great," Cassie said, stepping back to admire her sister's new look. "You could almost pass for a different person."

Maggie pursed her lips as she gave Claire a cool once-over. "I'm surprised you went darker. I thought blondes were supposed to have more fun."

"I've had enough fun for a while," Claire muttered, as she turned to clean up her tools.

Although Maggie was still wary of Claire, the women did settle into somewhat easy conversation, and they were all laughing five minutes later when a knock sounded at the door.

"That'll be my Johnny," Edna said. "He's picking me up." She threw open the door with a flourish and plumped up her newly colored hair.

Johnny stood in the door, his mouth hanging open as he stared at his new bride. "You look like a mermaid," he finally sputtered.

"Thank you." Edna planted a hand on her hip, narrowing her eyes at her husband, her voice carrying a hint of steel as if daring him to say one negative thing. "And what do you have to say about it, mister?"

His mouth opened and closed again. "I say…"

They all waited, holding their collective breath, the room deathly quiet as they watched Johnny and waited for his reaction.

"I say I've always wanted to kiss a mermaid," he finished with a devilish grin.

"Swoon," Cassie whispered, as they all let out their breath.

Edna laughed and batted her eyes. "I say with that answer, you'll be getting more than a kiss from this mermaid tonight. I might even show you my tail."

"Ew," Piper said. "Get a room."

Edna flashed her a saucy grin then gave her a quick hug. "Take care of yourself. Call me if you need me." She grabbed her coat and purse and followed Johnny out the door.

"Well, aren't they just the cutest?" Claire said.

"They were high school sweethearts who just found each other again," Cassie explained.

"Speaking of high school sweethearts," her mom said, staring pointedly at her. "When are you going to get back on the dating horse, Pip?"

"Uh, I don't know." Her eyes widened, and she gave Maggie a questioning glance.

"It's okay. Drew breaking up with you was his loss, honey," Maggie assured her. "It won't bother me if you start dating again. In fact, I think you should."

"She will, when she's ready," Cassie said, putting an arm around her.

Was she ready?

An image of Fitz popped into her mind. He'd worked a different shift at the coffee shop today, and she hadn't seen him since they'd talked on the phone a few nights ago. He'd texted her a couple of times, but his test was today, so he'd been in full homework mode the night before. She was hoping he'd text tonight. She still hadn't had a chance to tell him about her mom moving in.

"Surely there are some cute guys in your classes." Claire kept going, ignoring her sister, and charging forward like a bull in a conversation china shop. "Or what about online dating? That's all the rage now. I've even done it. Have you tried that?"

The book club shared a glance, smirking at an inside joke. They'd all had some experience with online dating earlier that summer when they'd tried to find a suitable match for Sunny.

"No," Piper declared. "And I don't plan to. I can find my own dates. In my own time. And I'm just not sure I'm ready."

"Maybe you don't know you're ready until you try."

"Maybe we should change the subject."

❀ ❀ ❀

The next afternoon, Piper's new pink hair got rave reviews from her coworkers at The Perk.

"It looks awesome," Sarah told her.

"Wow," Fitz said from behind the counter where he was opening a couple of bags of coffee beans and pouring them into the grinder. His eyes were wide, but a smile played on his lips. "Pretty in pink."

What was that supposed to mean? She'd seen the movie, of course, but was he actually calling *her* pretty? Or was he making fun of her new shade? She couldn't tell.

She twisted the ends of her hair around her finger. "I'm not sure about it yet. It's pretty different."

He shrugged. "Sometimes different is good."

Hmmm. Was that a double entendre? Did he mean a

different guy or was he just making a statement about different in general?

And why was she questioning every sentence out of his mouth? Why did she think every word might have a double meaning?

Sometimes it would make life a whole lot easier if guys wore signs that read what they were thinking. Although that idea could turn disastrous since she'd heard most guys think about something to do with sex every three minutes.

"I think it looks great," Sarah said. "Who did it for you?"

"My mom."

Fitz reared his head back. "Your mom? I thought you hadn't seen or heard from your mom in months."

"I hadn't. But now I see her all the time. Apparently, through some jacked up cosmic joke of the universe, she is now my new roommate."

"You're kidding."

"I wish I was."

She filled them in on the arrival of her mom and their new roomie status.

"You doing okay with all that?" Fitz asked, a note of concern in his voice.

Piper shrugged. "I guess. It's weird. And kinda cool. And kinda awful. I can't really figure out how I feel about it. Sometimes I like it, and sometimes it makes my stomach hurt. It's been a crazy couple of days."

"I figured you must be busy, and that's why I hadn't heard from you," he said as he stabbed the top of the second bag of coffee beans with a small pocketknife then neatly sliced it open. He didn't look at her, but instead kept his focus on wiping the blade of the knife against the corner of his apron then folding it closed and pushing it back into the front pocket of his jeans.

Hadn't heard from her? Had he been hoping she'd call or text?

She'd been waiting for him to get in touch with her.

Ug. Another guy/girl communication breakdown.

Maybe she needed to up the ante—see if he really was interested in her. She could throw out an unmistakable hint and see if he picked up on it.

"Yeah, sorry. We've been getting settled and figuring each other out. It's weird trying to be roommates instead of just mother and daughter. I can tell she's trying, but she still mothers me a little. Yesterday she bought tons of groceries, which was good, but she also tried to get involved with my love life, which wasn't so good." Okay, she'd laid the groundwork, now to subtly drop in the hint. "She thinks it's time I started dating again."

Her timing hadn't worked as perfectly as she'd hoped because Fitz had just turned his back to her to pour the coffee beans into the machine so she couldn't see his face or read his expression. But his shoulders raised in what seemed like an offhand gesture.

"I agree," he said, turning back around. "I think you *should* start dating again. Why not?"

She held her breath, waiting to see if his next question would involve asking her out.

"It was Drew's loss when he broke up with you, and I'm sure there are lots of other guys out there who would be interested in you."

Lots of *other* guys? She let her breath out in a defeated rush.

She wasn't interested in *other* guys—she was interested in Fitz. Couldn't he see that? She'd just laid down the perfect opening.

But maybe he wasn't interested in her. At least not like that. Maybe mentioning Drew had been a purposeful reminder that he'd been Drew's friend—and therefore not a dating option.

An ardent ache squeezed her heart.

What was she thinking? She knew Fitz was totally out of her league. She'd been fooling herself with the idea he was interested in her. So what if he'd called her the other night? One phone call didn't mean anything. And he *was* her boss. Maybe he was just showing concern for her as an employee or to make sure she was okay so she didn't call off and cause a disruption in the schedule.

Before she could respond, the door to the coffee shop opened and several customers flooded in. Which was probably just as well, since she didn't know what to say anyway.

He had pushed her securely back into the friend zone, and she needed to catch her breath and think before she said or did something that made a fool of herself.

But she couldn't think as she dealt with the rush of customers and the complicated orders of lattes and cappuccinos. Plus, every time she brushed against Fitz, her body went all jumpy with nervous jitters.

And in the tight space behind the counter, they couldn't help but bump into each other or brush hands as they both prepared drinks.

In the last few days, whenever she'd swept by him or their hips had bumped, she'd loved it. She'd loved the funny tinglies in her belly and the way her breath caught if his fingers accidentally—or maybe on purpose—skimmed her hand.

But not today—not now. Now her chest was full of ache and doubt, and she chastised herself for thinking he was being anything but nice to her. To one of his friend's exes.

What could he possibly see in her anyway? He was a brainiac, and she'd barely passed high school. He came from a good family, and her home life was a train wreck.

He was ridiculously cute, and now she just looked ridiculous. How had she thought dying her hair pink had been a good idea?

She worked to swallow down the emotions flooding her throat as she pasted on a smile for the last customer in line.

He was a guy around her age, and he smiled nervously at her. "Hi. I'm Brandon. I like your hair."

At least someone liked it. She smiled back. "Thanks, Brandon. I'm Piper. What can I make for you today?"

"Oh yeah, um…" he studied the menu board. "I'm not much of a coffee drinker. What do you recommend?"

What was he doing in a coffee shop if he didn't drink coffee? "We also have sodas and hot chocolate."

"Okay, sure. I'll have a hot chocolate and one of those banana muffins." He pointed to the display case and knocked over the daily special sign. His face colored as he righted the sign. "Sorry. I'm just on my way to class and needed a snack."

"This should do it then. Bananas are supposed to be good brain food." She rang up his order and gave him the total.

He pulled out his wallet. "You look familiar. Don't you go to the college too? I think we have English Comp together. Wednesday morning with Profession Reardon?"

"Oh yeah. I am in that class. I just finished my paper this morning."

"Me too." He rubbed his hand along the back of his neck and kept his gaze focused on the counter. "We should study together. Or go out for coffee sometime. We could talk about English."

She narrowed her eyes. "I thought you just said you didn't really like coffee."

He shrugged. "I don't. But I like you."

"Oh."

"And I'd like to go out with you. I mean, if you want to."

She studied him. He looked normal—average height, average build, average brown hair. He was wearing a shirt which had Han Solo and Chewbacca on it, so he had to have a few nerdy tendencies. But he was attractive, in a cute nerd kind of way.

And he had liked her hair.

She noticed Fitz was standing closer than normal, and she glanced over him, surprised to see the scowl on his face. A scowl directed at Brandon, the cute nerd who'd just asked her out to coffee.

What was that about? Hadn't he just made it clear that he wasn't interested in going out with her?

Well, this Brandon guy apparently was.

And if Fitz didn't want to go out with her, she might as well go for coffee, or whatever, with this guy. And maybe Fitz would realize what he was missing.

"Sure, why not?"

"Yeah? Great. How about tomorrow? After class?"

"That sounds good." She quickly jotted her number on the back of his receipt. "You can text me the details."

He smiled and stuffed the receipt in his pocket, juggling the muffin and the cup of hot chocolate Sarah had just handed him. "See ya tomorrow then."

A tiny smile crept across her face. Maybe she wasn't so bad after all.

Her small victory didn't make up for the fact that Fitz ignored her for the next hour.

Not that they had time to talk. The coffee shop was crowded with customers, and they were both focused on getting through the mid-morning rush.

The rush finally ended, and Piper grabbed a cloth and hurried around the lobby, trying to get all the empty tables straightened and wiped down.

A cute guy with brownish hair had been studying in the corner, and he looked up and smiled as she passed. "Hey, I like your hair. It's cool."

She smiled back, restraining her urge to check behind her in case he was talking to someone else. "Thanks."

"It reminds me of strawberry ice cream." His tone held a flirty note, and he made the words 'strawberry ice cream' sound the slightest bit sexy.

And she had absolutely no idea how to respond. "Is that a good thing?"

"Yeah. It's a great thing. I love ice cream. Don't you?"

"Of course."

"We should go get some together."

"Excuse me?" What was happening today?

He shrugged. "I was asking you if you wanted to go get some ice cream with me. I've spent the last thirty minutes trying to figure out how to ask you."

"Why?"

He chuckled. "Because you're cute and seem nice. I've been watching you with the customers, and you have a great smile. And I figure anyone who dyes their hair pink has got to be fun. So, what do you say?"

"Um…okay." She glanced at the counter and saw Fitz watching her. "Yes. That sounds fun."

"Great. It's a date. I've got class this afternoon, but I could meet you around four."

"Today?"

"Why not? Have you been to Campus Cones? It's on the west side of the college."

"I've seen it, but I've never been there."

"It's cool. They make these really over the top milk shakes. You'll love it." He stuffed his laptop into his backpack and pushed back from the table. It was then she noticed his t-shirt and the images of R2-D2 and C3PO and a funny caption about which droids someone had been looking for. "I've gotta get to class, but I'll see you there then. Around four?"

Her hands hung limp at her sides, the cleaning cloth all but forgotten. What was going on? Two guys had asked her out in the same day? And both were science fiction fans? Evidently guys who liked space stories were also attracted to girls with pink hair. "Okay."

He flashed her another flirty grin. "I'm Clay, by the way."

"Piper."

"I know."

"How did you…?"

He pointed to her nametag as he headed for the door. "See ya later."

"See ya." She wiped down his table, lost in thought. Her new hair must really be attention-getting.

She jumped, startled, as a presence loomed next to her.

"What was that all about?"

"Geez, Fitz. You scared the crap out of me." She pressed her hand to her chest.

"Sorry." He grabbed the empty cups off the table in front of her. "So what did that guy want?"

She shrugged. "To ask me out for ice cream, I guess."

"What? Do you even know him?"

She shrugged. "I do now. And weren't you just the one telling me I should start going out with other guys?"

"I didn't mean *all* of them," he muttered, then turned away, carrying the trash he'd cleared from the table to the trashcan.

Piper leaned against the counter, trying not to check the clock again. She had ten minutes left of her shift, and she was ready to go.

It had been a weird day, and Fitz had been acting strange all day and frankly, she was just over it.

The weather had been screwy too— cloudy and overcast and generally dreary. Which was a little how she felt. She should be excited—she'd been asked out on two dates today. But neither one was with the guy she wanted to go out with.

She let out a sigh. Maybe one of them might turn out to be a great guy. A guy who could make her forget all about the Brilliant Barista.

The door to the coffee shop opened, and a brown-haired guy strode in. He walked to the counter, his eye on the menu board as he unzipped his jacket to reveal a faded green t-shirt with Darth Vader on the front.

You have got to be kidding me.

Was today *National Wear Your Star Wars Shirt Day*, and she just hadn't gotten the memo?

Maybe she should test her theory—see if sci-fi guys really did dig chicks with pink hair. She offered him a smile. "Hi, I'm Piper. Nice shirt."

He smiled back. "Thanks. Nice hair."

Seriously? It worked.

"Thanks. What can I get you?"

"Caramel latte with an extra shot. And your number."

She raised her eyebrows. What was happening? Was this guy for real? Was this day for real?

She planted a hand on her hip. "Why would I give you

my number?"

"I don't know. I just aced a Calculus test, and I'm feeling lucky."

Another smart guy. "I don't even know you."

"True." He held out his hand. "I'm Aaron. And I'm having a great day. I aced my test, and I finished a huge project and turned it in today, and I think you're cute so I'm taking a chance and hoping you'll give me your number and agree to have coffee with me sometime."

She studied him as she made his latte.

He was tall and stocky and wore wire-rimmed glasses. He had a nice smile and straight white teeth which had to be the product of braces.

His smile faltered just the slightest. "Come on. What could it hurt to have coffee? And I'm on a winning streak here. In fact, if you say yes, I may even go buy a lottery ticket."

She laughed. What *would* it hurt to have a coffee? "Okay, fine. But if you win any money on that ticket, you have to split it with me."

His grin returned, splitting across his face. "Deal."

She handed him his coffee then grabbed a page from a stack of flyers which sat next to the register and jotted down her number.

He passed her a five-dollar bill. "There's a cool coffee bar downtown that has live music after seven. It's called Java & Jams. How about we check it out tomorrow night? I could pick you up."

"Tomorrow night?"

"Hey, I told you I was feeling lucky."

As long as he didn't think he was going to *get* lucky. "Why don't I meet you there?"

He shrugged. "That's cool. Say about seven?"

"Sure."

He grabbed his cup and offered her a wave. "See you

tomorrow."

She let out a laugh and turned to see Fitz standing in the doorway of the stock room, another scowl on his face. "I just wanted to tell you your shift's over. You can go home now."

"Okay. I was just ringing up the last customer."

"Yeah, I saw." He turned back to the stock room as Sarah came out to take over the counter.

Geez. What was he so grumpy about? Was he actually bothered by the guys who had asked her out today? He's the one who had told her to get out there and try her hand at dating.

Although she hadn't expected her hand to be so full so quickly.

She didn't have time to worry about it. She had an hour and a half to get home, get changed, and then walk to her afternoon class. She had two classes still today then her 'date' with Clay for ice cream.

She grabbed her purse and jacket from the back and headed out the door, waving to Sarah and Fitz.

Ignoring the stab of pain to her heart. It was his choice if he wanted to act that way.

She flipped back her new pink hair and headed toward campus.

❀ ❀ ❀

Piper peered around the ice cream shop, spotting Clay sitting in a booth in the back. It was a cute shop—kitschy with pink and white checked tablecloths and sit-down service. All the desserts had cutesy names which followed the campus theme like Brainy Butterscotch and Chemistry Crunch.

"Hi," she said, sliding into the seat next to him.

"Hey. Glad you made it." He gestured to the glasses

on the table. "I got us some water, but I didn't know if you wanted something else to drink."

"Water's fine."

"I was just waiting for the waitress, and I was going to order us some chocolate shakes."

She blinked. "Why would you order for me?"

He shrugged. "Sorry, I just assumed everyone likes chocolate."

"Actually, I prefer vanilla."

"Are you sure? You don't seem like a vanilla kind of girl."

What the heck does that mean? "Well, I am."

He held up his hands. "Okay, no offense intended. I guess I thought a girl who colored her hair pink was a little more adventurous." He raised an eyebrow as if daring her to deny it.

"I am adventurous," she retorted, her back bristling. "I just happen to like vanilla."

This was why she didn't like going out on dates. She was terrible at it. Drew had been her first real boyfriend so she had no experience with all this flirty chatter, and she totally sucked at small talk.

But they hadn't even ordered yet, so it was probably too soon to try for a quick getaway.

Thankfully, a waitress approached the table and took their order, saving her from having to continue to defend her 'adventurous' status.

She settled into the back of the booth after the waitress left. "So did you grow up around here?"

"Nope."

She studied his face. Something about his eyes seemed familiar. "Me either. But I graduated from high school here. I can't believe it was only a few months ago. I feel like I've already changed so much since high school."

He let out a hard laugh. "Yeah, me too."

Their ice cream arrived, and they settled into an awkward silence as they dug in. Piper kept sneaking glances at him as she tried to think of something clever to say.

Coming up short, she focused on finishing her ice cream instead, the consequences of a brain freeze preferable to more of her clumsy attempts at conversation.

He was watching her, and he licked a drop of chocolate from his spoon as his gaze dipped unmistakably to her breasts.

She wore a loose white V-neck T-shirt under an open blue and gray checked flannel and suddenly felt the urge to draw the edges of her flannel together to cover her chest.

He leaned toward her ear as he slid his hand onto her upper thigh. "What do you say we get out of here?"

Get out of here?

This was moving way too fast for her. She *did* need to get out of here, but *not* with him. She shifted her leg away from his hand. "I thought we were just meeting for ice cream," she stammered.

He pulled his hand back into his own lap. "Sorry. My mistake. I just thought—" He raised his eyes to her head.

Seriously? The hair again. How did adding pink dye to her tips suddenly make her seem like an adventurous chocolate-loving slut?

"I'm actually meeting my mom for dinner, so I should probably go."

"Hey, listen. I'm sorry if I got the wrong idea."

"I just got out of a relationship, and I'm not ready to jump into all that again."

"I get that. But I'd really like to see you again."

"I don't know." She pulled a crumpled five-dollar bill from her pocket and tossed it on the table.

"Hey, don't worry about that. I invited you."

"It's okay. I've really got to go."

"Can I call you? Or text you, maybe?"

"Sure, I guess," she muttered then turned and made her way around the tables toward the door.

She didn't really want him to call her. She wanted Fitz to call her.

Clay had seemed nice enough, except for that whole grabby hands/hook-up assumption, but maybe that's how dates went in college. Once again, she felt like the clueless dork who didn't know what she was doing. She felt her cheeks warm and was glad he couldn't see her face as she pushed through the door and out into the cool autumn air.

❀ ❀ ❀

Her mind was full of conflicting thoughts as she walked across campus.

Was she really ready for this dating thing? And why had she agreed to go out with *three* different guys when there was really only one guy who she was interested in?

Oh yeah, because apparently, he wasn't interested in her.

And what did all of this even matter when poor Brittany was never going to go out on a date again? She hadn't heard anything more on the girl's murder and some days she could almost pretend it never happened.

Thinking about it made her head hurt and her stomach feel queasy.

The light rain that had started as she walked across campus turned into a downpour, and she was drenched by the time she made it back to her apartment.

Hurrying up the sidewalk, she almost missed the blur of white under the porch.

She leaned down and saw the scruffy dog, its thin body drenched and trembling as it cowered against the rail.

Oh no. Poor thing.

Her heart broke for the miserable-looking little mutt. She knew what it was like to feel alone and unwanted, to be hungry and scared and not know who to trust.

It didn't matter how long it took—she wasn't leaving this dog out here to freeze in the rain. No way.

She crouched down, the moisture of the cold wet ground soaking through the knees of her jeans. She didn't care. "Come here, pup. I'm not going to hurt you," she cooed, wiping her sopping bangs from her eyes.

Holding out her hand, she spoke gently to the dog, coaxing it from the back corner of the porch.

It took several minutes of cajoling, but it finally inched forward enough for her to pet its small wet head. She'd only seen it under the porch the last several days, but it appeared to be malnourished and had probably been out here longer.

"Come on, sweetheart. Come with me, and I'll get you something to eat." The dog crept a little closer, almost— but not quite—touching her knee.

A flash of lightning lit up the sky, followed by a loud clap of thunder and the dog scrambled up her legs and into her lap, pressing its trembling body against her chest.

She wrapped her arms around it, ignoring the trails of muddy paw prints it left across her jeans. It didn't matter. Her clothes were already wet, and she was soaked to the skin—a little more mud wouldn't hurt anything.

Cuddling the dog to her, she whispered soft encouragement to it as she carried it into the house.

Her mom was sitting on the sofa, and her eyes widened when Piper walked into the apartment, her shoes squishing with each step. "Wow. What happened to you?"

"I got caught in the rain on my way home."

"Where'd you find the drowned rat?"

"It's not a rat. It's a dog."

"Whatever it is, you're not bringing it in here."

"Yes, I am. The poor thing is freezing and starving, and I'm not letting it stay out there in the rain. This dog is our new roommate, so get used to it."

"I will not get used to anything of the sort." Her mom put down the book she was reading and pushed up from the sofa. She planted a fist on her hip. "I'm serious, Piper. That thing is hideous. I'm not about to let it move in here with us. So, it's your choice, it's me or the mutt."

Piper pushed her shoulders back, standing her ground as she looked Claire in the eye. "Well, it was fun while it lasted. Don't let the door hit you on the way out." Like she ever did. She knew her mom wasn't going to stay long anyway. Frankly, she'd been surprised she'd lasted the week.

Claire's mouth fell open. "You're kidding, right? I'm the one who has actually *paid* the rent."

Piper shrugged. "Then I guess you'd better get used to the dog."

Her mom arched an eyebrow, a smile tugging at the corner of her lips. "You've changed, kid—toughened up. I like it." She took a few steps closer and peered down at the little dog. "Fine. It can stay. But you're giving it a bath."

Her heart swelled in her chest. Not that she needed her mom's permission for anything anymore, but she'd still felt like a little kid standing in front of her mom asking her if she could keep the stray dog she'd found on the way home.

But she wasn't a little kid. She was a grown woman, and she'd just been the one to tell her mom what they were doing.

It felt good. Like maybe their relationship was shifting—morphing into something new, something different. Which was great, because what they'd done before hadn't always worked.

Not that Piper was letting her guard down. Their

relationship hadn't changed *that* much. And she still expected Claire to pack up her few things and leave any day, but it felt like they had made a small crack in the wall between the them, the tiniest fissure, but a crack just the same.

"Fine," she said. It would need a bath anyway. It was covered in mud, and its fur was matted with dirt and grime. "But let me try to feed it first." The dog wiggled in her arms, almost as if it understood food was on its way. She struggled to get a better grip and ended up cradling it like a baby. She rubbed its tummy and saw her intuition was right about the dog being a female.

Her mom peered at the dog's exposed belly, and her scowl softened. "She does look half-starved." She crossed to the kitchen and dug out a couple of the disposable plastic take-out bowls they kept in the drawer. She filled one with water and set it on the floor. Reaching into the pantry, she pulled out the bag Piper had bought a few days before. "I noticed we had a bag of dog food in the pantry and wondered what it was for. Now I know."

"She's been under the front porch for several days. I've fed her a few times, but it obviously hasn't been enough." The dog was still cowered against her chest, but raised its head at the sound of the dry dog food Claire was pouring into the bowl on the floor.

Piper set the dog down, and she cautiously approached the bowls, sniffing at the food. Her small pink tongue took a couple laps of water, then she peered uncertainly up at Piper.

"It's okay, girl. Eat up," she encouraged.

The dog turned back to the bowl and greedily gulped the food down.

Her mom gestured to the bathroom. "Go get out of those wet clothes, and I'll figure out how we're going to give her a bath."

It only took Piper a few minutes to shed her wet clothes and blot the rain from her hair. She put on yoga pants, a big comfy sweatshirt, and a thick pair of socks. Grabbing a few extra towels, she returned to the kitchen, surprised to see her mom stirring a sudsy concoction in one of their glass measuring cups.

"What the heck is that?"

"It's a mixture of deluded dish soap and some apple cider vinegar."

"And what do you plan to do with it?"

"Use it to wash your new dog. We don't have any dog shampoo, and I heard using people shampoo isn't good for their skin, so I Googled it and this is supposed to be a good substitute until we can get the real stuff."

"Weird. But okay."

"I already rinsed out the sink and laid down a washcloth so its feet won't slip on the porcelain."

"Smart." Where had her mom come up with that idea? They'd never had a dog, or any pet for that matter, so she wasn't sure how Claire knew these good tricks. Maybe she Googled that too.

Piper had a few tricks of her own. She pulled a jar of peanut butter from the cupboard and spread a thin layer on the edge of the sink.

Her mom's eyes widened. "What in the world are you doing?"

"You're not the only one who knows how to use the internet. I saw this on Facebook," she said, picking up the dog and setting it in the sink.

It must have been familiar with peanut butter because it immediately started licking it. All its focus remained on licking the sticky stuff, and she didn't even flinch when Piper turned on the warm water and sprayed it down her back.

"See, it works. All she cares about is the peanut butter

and isn't even bothered by the water." She nodded to the measuring cup. "Now pour some of the soap on her."

Claire held up her hands. "I just made it. I wasn't planning on getting roped into helping with the actual bath."

"You said you were working on getting your beautician skills back. Consider this practice."

Claire shrugged and pushed back her sleeves. "Fine. I guess I have had some clients who have been real dogs."

Piper chuckled as her mom poured some of the soapy mixture onto the dog. Her fur was so light, she could see her pink skin. "At least she doesn't have fleas."

The peanut butter worked like a charm, keeping the dogs focus while she and her mom worked together, lathering up and rinsing out the dog's matted and filthy coat.

Her hands were slippery with suds as she tried to maneuver the sprayer. It slipped from her hands, hitting the bottom of the sink and flipping around, spraying both the women with water as the hose coiled.

Claire let out a shriek.

Piper froze, ignoring the shock of water that just doused her shirt, her heart thudding against her chest as she waited for her mom to yell or get angry. "I'm so sorry."

Claire's eyes were round, her face registering shock at the splash of water that had missed her chest and instead had sprayed across her face and hair. She blew the drips of water from her lips, then broke out into laughter.

Piper's tense shoulders loosened, and she laughed along with her mom. It felt good to laugh together.

It felt good to be together.

Too bad it wouldn't last.

It wasn't that she didn't love her mom or love being with her. She did. She just knew she couldn't count on her

71

to stick around—couldn't trust her to stay.

Claire didn't always leave by riding off on a motorcycle. Sometimes her demons took over, and she left emotionally, closing herself off from everyone and everything as she tried to deal with the grief of losing Denny and the life they'd had planned.

Piper swallowed, trying not to think about her dad—or about her mom leaving. Her dad would have loved this dog. He'd talked about letting her get a puppy when she was old enough, but it had never happened.

Well, she had one now. Not one she'd necessarily found, but one who had found her. Or maybe they'd found each other.

The dog looked up at her, almost as if it knew what she was thinking. Its eyes were huge and dark brown and full of trust, and Piper knew she wasn't ever going to leave this dog.

She would still call the Humane Society to see if anyone had lost it, but she wasn't wearing a collar and had obviously been on her own for a while now. Piper had been watching around the neighborhood and checking bulletin boards around campus to see if anyone posted about a lost dog, but hadn't seen anything yet.

And somehow she knew this dog was now hers—felt it in her heart they were supposed to be together.

Piper turned off the water and wrapped the dog in a towel. She scrubbed the moisture from its coat before cuddling it against her. As she dried it, little white and tan curls sprang up in the dog's fur.

"I didn't realize how white she was," Piper said, setting her on the floor.

The dog wiggled out of the towel and shook her body, sending sprays of water into the air.

Claire held up her hands to deflect the mist and studied the little dog. "I'll bet she doesn't weigh much more than a sack of flour. We need to fatten her up a little. You can see her ribs."

Piper sat on the floor and pulled the dog gently into her lap. She plucked at the curls on her back. "She's really kind of cute, now that she's clean."

Claire raised an eyebrow. "Cute is subjective."

"True," Piper said with a chuckle. "She is pretty sweet, though."

"I wouldn't think the word 'pretty' is used very often when describing this one." Her mom plopped down on the floor next to her and stroked the dog's head. She was rewarded with a tiny lick to her hand. "She's kind of like that one friend you have who you just love so you're always trying to set her up with people but when they ask what she looks like, your reply is always something about her having a great personality."

Piper winced, but a small grin played at the corners of her lips. "Ouch."

Claire laughed. "It's true."

It was good to hear her mom laugh. She hadn't realized how much she'd missed it. "Ugh. I know how that feels. I think I've *been* that girl."

Her mom nudged her arm. "You have not. You've always been much prettier than you've ever seen yourself." She reached up and brushed Piper's bangs from her forehead.

Piper leaned toward her, her body instinctively craving the touch of her mother's hand. Then she pulled back as she realized she was doing it and gave a small, hard laugh. "Thanks. I'll be sure to add that to my dating resume." She made air quotes with her fingers. "My mom thinks I'm pretty."

"Dating resume?" Claire arched an eyebrow, either not noticing the way Piper had pulled back or choosing to ignore it. "So are you thinking about dating again now?"

She considered telling her mom about the three dates she'd been asked on and sharing the details of her ice cream outing with Clay, but something held her back. They might be having a good time taking care of the dog, but she wasn't quite ready to forgive everything and spill her guts in a heart-to-heart girl chat.

Things were going well with them, but not that well.

"I don't know." She shrugged, setting the dog on the rug and pushed up from the floor. "I do know we need to get this stuff cleaned up, and then I have homework to do."

"I was thinking of making some tacos for dinner. Want some?"

They'd been having a nice time and her mom had been trying. She might not be ready to jump back into heart-to-hearts, but she didn't have to keep giving her the cold shoulder either. And tacos did sound good. "Sure. That would be nice."

Her mom smiled.

If she *was* pretty, it was because she looked like her mom. They had the same facial structure and similar noses.

It had only been a few days, but Claire looked better than she had when she'd first arrived. Some of the luster had come back to her freshly-colored hair, and her cheeks didn't look quite so gaunt. She was still too skinny, but her eyes didn't have that haunted bruised look of too much stress and not enough sleep like the first day she'd arrived.

It would seem they were both settling in to this new life together.

🐾 🐾 🐾

The next day, Piper sat in her English class, her palms starting to sweat as the professor finished up the lesson for the day.

She'd spotted Brandon, aka Date #2, across the lecture hall when she'd first arrived at class and had offered him an awkward wave.

Then she'd tried to ignore him for the rest of the hour and focus on the lesson. But it had been crazy hard to concentrate when she knew she had a "date" after class. Well, a get together for coffee anyway. If she didn't call it a date, maybe it would make her less nervous.

She'd tried to keep her gaze trained on the professor, but had given Brandon a few furtive glances, studying his profile as he listened attentively to the lecture.

Today he was wearing faded jeans and running shoes. His blue button-down oxford was untucked but appeared fairly wrinkle-free—versus some of her other classmates who looked like they may have plucked their current wardrobe selection from a pile of laundry on the floor.

Brandon seemed to be a good student. Or at least he appeared to be listening and taking notes as the professor spoke. But who knew? She couldn't see his laptop—he could be typing up notes for a Dungeons & Dragons game or emailing his grandmother. Hmm…she wasn't sure which would be better…or worse.

But he seemed like he was paying attention, anyway. Unlike her, who alternately listened then snuck quick glances at Brandon then spaced out as she worried about her newest new roommate.

How did she keep collecting this odd assortment of roomies? Although she was pretty sure her latest addition was going to be the easiest to get along with.

The little dog had slept at the end of her bed the night before and had devotedly followed her around the apartment all morning as she got ready for class.

She was so sweet, Piper had considered skipping class so she could stay home and play with her all day. But she'd worked too hard to get here and was paying too much for these classes to consider cutting even one.

Her mom had appeared in the kitchen before she'd left and grudgingly agreed to keep an eye on the dog while she was gone that morning, but Piper couldn't help but worry about how they were getting along.

The professor finished the lecture, and she eyed the exit, wondering if it was too late to make a quick getaway. She could always text him and say she'd suddenly gotten ill.

It wouldn't be too much of a stretch. She did suddenly feel a little queasy.

She stole a quick glance in his direction.

Too late.

He was already heading her way.

Piper crammed her notebook into her backpack and pushed back from her chair. "Hi," she said, feeling her face warm as he finally reached her.

"Hi." He grinned and nodded toward the exit doors. They had been so inviting a moment before when they'd been her escape route, now the thought of walking through them only inspired dread.

"You still up for coffee?" he asked.

"Yeah. Sure."

"I thought we could just go to the coffee shop in the student center. If that's okay?"

"Yes. Fine with me." Wow. She was really killing it with her amazing conversational skills. Hopefully the coffee would kick her brain into a higher gear.

They made small talk as they walked to the coffee shop and ordered their drinks, chatting about their English class, the latest assignment, the book they'd been assigned, and of course, the weather.

Because when you've never talked to someone before, it somehow always boils down to a discussion about the weather.

Brandon secured them a table in the far corner, and Piper chewed her lip as she walked behind him. She couldn't think of a single other topic to discuss as they sat down with their cups.

Brandon didn't seem to have that problem. "So, I heard something about you being the one who lived with that girl who was murdered. Is that true?"

She almost spit out her coffee. *Way to ease right into that one.* Had she missed the segue cue that had led from "when do you think it might snow" to "let's talk about the murder that happened in your apartment"?

"Uh, yeah, I guess. I mean, yes. That was my roommate."

"Wow. What a trip. Were you guys pretty close friends?"

"No. Not really. We'd just met each other a few weeks before."

"Have they caught the guy who did it?"

"Not yet."

"I heard you were the one who found her."

"Yeah."

"Whoa. What was that like?"

What was that like? How was she supposed to answer a question like that? "It was…like awful. How do you think it was?"

He dipped his chin. "Sorry. Of course, it must have been awful. I just meant like how did you find her? Was she still alive? Did you give her CPR?"

"No. It was too late."

"Bummer."

Yeah, it had certainly been too late for Brittany. But Piper wasn't sure if Brandon hadn't meant it was bummer she had already been dead or a bummer Piper hadn't had a chance to fail at her life-saving skills.

"Could we talk about something else?" She took a sip of her coffee and grimaced. It was too sweet. She'd ordered a pumpkin spice latte but they made them better at The Perk.

Oh great. Now she was thinking about The Perk, which meant she was thinking about Fitz. And wishing it was him sitting across from her instead of Brandon.

At least Fitz didn't pepper her with rapid fire questions about the murder.

She tried to think back to if he'd even asked her a

single question about it. He'd asked her several times if she was okay or how she was feeling about being back in the apartment, but she couldn't remember him asking about any of the actual details. And certainly not in rapid-fire succession like Brandon was doing.

"Yeah, totally," he said. "It's just interesting. I've never had anything like that happen to me."

"I hope you never do."

He looked down at the table. "You're right. Sometimes I say stuff out loud before I really think through how it's going to sound to other people."

She offered him a small smile. "It's okay. I do that too."

"It's just that I can't help wondering how she looked when you found her. Was she on her stomach or her back? How did you know she was dead? Did she leave any kind of clues as to who her killer might be?"

Seriously? "I *really* don't want to talk about it." She made a show of looking down at her watch. "In fact, I should probably get going. I promised my mom I would have lunch with her, and I don't want to be late."

Her relationship with her mom might be iffy lately, but she sure came in handy as an excuse to get out of a date.

"Already? Can't you stay a little longer? We've barely had any time to talk."

You mean I've barely had time to answer all your questions.

"Yeah, sorry. I really do need to go. But this was fun." She swallowed the last of her coffee and grabbed her backpack, making her escape before he had a chance to stop her. She waved as she weaved between the tables. "I'll see ya in class."

Thoughts of the murder filled her head as she walked home, and her anxiety was high as she approached the apartment.

At least the door wasn't partially open today.

She hated to think it, but she was actually thankful, for the moment, that her mom was her roommate. At least someone else was in the apartment with her, and even if she didn't like to admit it, it was kind of nice to come home to someone.

But her mom wasn't there. And neither was the little dog.

"Hello?" she called out as she pushed the door shut behind her. But the apartment was empty.

Too empty, she thought as she dumped her jacket and backpack on the kitchen table. She'd made an odd habit of walking around the area where she'd found Brittany. The throw rug her mom had bought to cover the spot helped, and she wasn't sure she really even thought that much about the section of floor anymore.

But now her mind was swimming with the details of the murder.

Why hadn't they caught the guy yet? Did they have any leads? Any suspects in custody? Any suspects at all?

Or was the killer just walking around free, thinking he got away with it, and looking for another victim?

That thought sent a cold chill down Piper's spine.

A knock sounded at her door.

She jumped, letting out a tiny shriek and automatically scanning the room for a weapon. Where was the Mace Edna had given her and all the other book club members for Christmas last year?

"Who's there?" She grabbed a knife from the kitchen and approached the door warily, her imagination filling with all sorts of images of the killer coming back to finish off the other roommate.

Mac hadn't told her much, but he had said they thought Brittany had known her assailant.

Had the murderer knocked at the door and Brittany unknowingly let him in and offered him a cup of tea?

She shook her head. That was stupid. She didn't think they even had any tea. And who offered someone a cup of tea anyway? It's not like they lived in *Downton Abbey*.

"It's Fitz. I brought you a sandwich," a voice called through the door.

Fitz? What was he doing here?

Bringing her a sandwich, apparently.

She leaned over, checking her teeth in the mirror which hung by the door—a trick her mom had taught her. They'd always had a mirror by the front door to do one last glance before heading out. A memory of her mom at that mirror, laughing and dabbing on lip gloss as she readied to leave on a date with her dad flashed through her mind. She pushed it away, not needing to add one more distraction to her already anxious nerves.

She pulled the door open, and her breath caught at the sight of Fitz standing in the doorway, a white bag from her favorite sandwich shop held aloft in his hand.

"Surprise," he said.

Was it ever.

"What are you doing here?" She stepped back and let him in.

He crossed the room and set the bag on the kitchen counter. "I told you. Bringing you a sandwich."

"But why?"

"Because I knew you had a couple of classes this morning, and I thought you might be hungry."

"Wow. That was really nice of you."

"So, are you?"

"Am I what?"

"Hungry?"

JENNIE MARTS

"Oh, yeah." She blinked. "I mean yes, I am. Hungry."

He eyed the kitchen knife still clutched in her hand. "I hope you're going to use that to cut the sandwich."

"Sorry." She dropped the knife on the counter then flinched at the loud clatter it made. "I'd been thinking about the...about Brittany. And I guess I got spooked."

He took a step closer and rested a hand on her shoulder. "I'm sorry if I scared you. This whole thing has got to be really rough on you. I should have called or texted you or something."

"No. This is perfect." She looked up at him, losing herself in the navy blue of his eyes. "I'm glad you're here." Her voice came out as a whisper.

He kept his gaze locked on hers, not moving and not shifting his hand.

She could feel the heat of his palm through the thin cotton of her sleeve.

Hell, she could feel the heat of his body as he stood close to her. Only a few inches separated them, and she wanted to reach out and touch him—to press a hand against his chest or brush her fingers across his perfect cheek.

She swallowed, afraid the click in her throat echoed in the quiet room.

He leaned his head toward hers, just the slightest movement, but it was enough to have Piper's heart pounding in her chest and her mouth go as dry as a cotton ball.

Her lips parted, anticipating—hoping, praying, dying, for a kiss.

His gaze dipped to her mouth as his grip tightened on her arm.

That one quick glance sent a flurry of flutters through her stomach and caused her head to swim with dizziness. She was thankful he was holding her arm because her knees had suddenly gone weak.

She wet her lips and held her breath, thinking if he didn't kiss her in the next two seconds she might faint.

He leaned closer still, and she could smell the spearmint scent of his gum.

Closer still...then the front door banged open, and the little dog raced into the room, circling her legs and crying as she pawed her feet.

Claire burst into the room, her arms filled with shopping bags. She stopped, eyed Fitz, then a slow grin crossed her face. "Sorry. Did I interrupt something?"

"No." Piper took a quick step back and knelt to pick up the dog. She buried her face in the dog's fur, feeling the heat in her cheeks. "This is my friend...er, I mean my boss, Fitz. From the coffee shop."

Fitz winced. "I'm both, I think. And I'm not really your boss. I'm just the shift leader."

"Well, whatever you are, how about you help me with these bags?"

"Of course." He rushed forward, taking the bags from her hands.

"What is all this stuff?" Piper asked, tilting her head to read the logo on the side of the bag. It was of the pet superstore, and she spied colorful food bowls through the plastic.

Claire blew up her bangs. "I don't know. I went to get a bag of food and ended up buying half the store. I made the mistake of telling the floor guy we just got this dog, and he started listing off all the things we would need. Before I knew it, my cart was full of food and water bowls, a collar, a leash, and some dog treats. Oh, and I got some real doggy shampoo and some weird thing called a Kong."

Piper pulled an assortment of stuffed animals and squeaky toys from one of the bags. She held up a plush alligator. "Was this on the required list of things a dog needs?"

Her mom grinned. "No, I just thought it was cute. I'd brought the dog into the store with me and had her in the cart, and when I stuck that in there, she laid her head on it. So, I had to get it." She held up a small pink dog bed with a glittery silver tiara embroidered on the front. "This however, might have been a bit overboard."

"I didn't know you had a dog," Fitz said, reaching out to pet its head.

"We didn't," her mom answered. "Until yesterday when Pip decided to rescue this one from under the porch."

He raised an eyebrow. "Pip?"

Piper rolled her eyes. "It's a mom-thing. Don't you dare call me that."

He laughed then scanned the array of bags. "Well, it looks like she's your dog now. What are you going to call her?"

"I haven't even thought about it." She shook her head, still in awe of the fact her mom had done all of this. She'd figured she'd come home and find the dog curled up on her bed and her mom anxious to pass doggie-duty back to her. Never did she expect her mother to embrace the scruffy little mutt. Claire had even said 'we' when she recounted how she'd told the sales guy they got a new dog.

Still, leave it to her mom to take the dog out on a shopping spree.

And what a spree. She must have spent a fortune.

"I can help pay for some of this with my next paycheck." She peered at the bags again then looked over at Fitz. "And by the way, can I have a raise?"

He chuckled. "It looks like you're going to need it."

Her mom waved a hand away. "Don't worry about it. It wasn't really that much. Most of this stuff was on sale, and besides, I had a coupon."

Hmmm. It must have been some coupon.

"I also got her a crate and a bag of food. Would you guys mind grabbing those from the car?" She held up the keys.

"I've got it," Fitz said, taking the keys and heading for the door.

"Thanks, hon. It's that fancy blueish Toyota parked at the curb—the one with the dog crate in the back."

"He'll find it," Piper said. "I'm sure he can deduce the right car. He's an engineering major."

Claire sauntered toward Piper, a knowing grin on her face. "He looks like he's majoring in Hottie-Town 101."

A warm flush heated Piper's neck, and she turned her attention to the bags on the counter. "Don't be weird. He's just a friend."

"According to you? Or him?"

Before she could answer, the subject of their conversation walked back into the room, holding the dog food in one hand and the handle of the small hot pink crate in the other. He set them against the wall and shut the front door.

Piper turned to her mom. "You got her a hot pink crate *and* a pink fluffy bed?"

Claire shrugged. "What? You've always loved pink."

"Did you get her a tiara and a dog tag that says Princess too?"

"Close," she answered, digging through the bags then holding up a pink sparkly rhinestone collar.

Piper rolled her eyes again, but she secretly loved all the things her mom had bought. And she really loved the fact her mom was spoiling the dog. It made her feel all warm and fuzzy inside. "It looks like you thought of everything."

"Not everything. I should have picked up lunch. I'm

starving."

"I've got that covered," Fitz said. "I brought over sandwiches, and they're huge. We can easily split them into thirds."

"That's nice of you, but I can heat up a can of soup. I don't want to impose on your lunch."

"You're not imposing. And really there's plenty of food in that bag."

"Okay, if you insist. Piper, you want to grab some paper plates from the pantry. Fitz, I'll get some sodas if you want to grab some glasses." She pointed toward the sink.

Fitz stepped into the kitchen and pulled out the drawer by the dishwasher. A funny look crossed his face, then he closed the drawer and reached up to open the cupboard next to the sink. He grabbed three glasses and set them by the refrigerator then turned to wash his hands. "What else can I do?"

Piper had been heading toward the pantry when she'd noticed Fitz's movements and had stopped to watch him. A look passed between her and her mom, then she turned back to the pantry to search for the paper plates.

"I've got it from here," Claire said. "You can sit down."

He pulled the sandwiches out and grinned at Piper as she set the plates on the table. "Any chance you've still got that knife?"

"Uh, yeah." Piper picked up the knife from the counter and passed it to him.

He cut the sandwiches in three equal portions. "I wasn't sure what all you liked but I know you've brought turkey sandwiches to work before so I got turkey and cheese and had them wrap some fixin's on the side."

"It's perfect," she said. *You're perfect.* Or at least she'd thought he was. Up until about a minute ago. Now she wasn't so sure.

"Let's eat," Claire said, motioning them all to sit down. "Piper, how was your morning? Anything exciting happen?"

"She went on a date," Fitz said.

"A date? With who?" Her mom raised both eyebrows. "I didn't know you had a date."

Piper glared at Fitz. "It wasn't a date exactly. I just met someone for coffee."

"And you're meeting someone else 'for coffee' later tonight, aren't you?" He shook his head. "That seems like a lot of coffee for one day."

Was he really talking about the coffee or was he implying something about her and the fact she was seeing two guys in one day. Well, three if you counted Fitz. And she had been counting him. Although now she wasn't sure. Especially since he'd just thrown her under the Too Much Information For Her Mom Bus.

"That's a funny statement coming from a guy whose job *depends* on people drinking a lot of coffee," she countered.

"Wait, back up," her mom said. "I didn't even know about one date, let alone two. And you already met with one? I hope it was in a safe place."

"It was. And it wasn't a date. We have English class together, and we walked from the lecture hall to the student union. It was no big deal."

"Is that where you're meeting the guy tonight?"

"No. We're meeting downtown at Java & Jams. Not that it's any of your business." She'd already said more than she'd wanted to.

"Okay, sorry. We'll drop it."

Sure she would.

"This is good." Piper held up the sandwich in an effort to change the subject. "This is actually from one of my favorite sandwich shops."

"I know," Fitz said. "I pay attention."

So did her mother. And she was paying a little too much attention to her conversation with Fitz. "I really appreciate you bringing the food by," she told him. "But I should probably get going. I've got class in half an hour."

"Oh, yeah. Sure. I've got class this afternoon too." He shoved the last bite of sandwich in his mouth, then carried his trash to the bin.

"I'll walk you out."

"It's okay," he said, leaning down to scratch the dog's head. "I'll see you at work tomorrow."

"Thanks again." She pushed up from her chair, but he'd already slipped through the front door.

Her mom was watching her as she sank back into her seat. "How well do you know this guy?"

She shrugged. "Pretty well, I guess. We work together, and he went to my same high school. He was friends with Drew, my old boyfriend. They played soccer together."

Which reminded her of why she shouldn't even be thinking about the guy. Mixing work and friends of old boyfriends seemed like a recipe for disaster.

Claire tapped her finger against her chin. "Has he been over here before?"

"Not with me."

"What about with your roommate? Brittany? Did he know her?"

"Not that I know of." She searched her mind for anything he might have said that would have given her that implication. "I've talked about her several times, and he's never said anything about knowing her."

"If he's never been here…" Claire started to say, and Piper knew she was going to say before the words came out of her mouth. Knew it with a foreboding sense of dread and apprehension.

"...then how did he know to look for the glasses in that weird spot next to the dishwasher?"

Piper walked into Java & Jams promptly at seven o'clock. She peered around, searching for Aaron, both praying he was already there and that he wasn't going to show up at all.

If he wasn't there, she'd have to sit alone in the coffee shop and wait for him, which totally sucked. She hated going to places and sitting at tables alone. No one probably took notice of her at all, but she always felt like everyone around her figured she couldn't even find *one* friend to come out and eat with her.

If he didn't show up, she could chalk this up to another dumb idea then go home and cuddle on the sofa with the dog. Who she still hadn't thought of a name for.

Add that to her list of things to do.

Along with stop accepting random coffee requests from guys who came into The Perk.

A single guy sitting at a table in the back raised his hand and waved.

Shoot. He did show up.

I mean yay, he's here.

She pasted on what she hoped looked like an enthusiastic smile and made her way to the table.

He watched her approach and smiled as she dropped into the seat next to him. "Hey, you made it."

Wait. Did she have a choice? Could she have backed out at the last minute?

Ugh. This dating business was tough.

But she was here now so she might as well make the best of it.

And who knew, maybe this date would turn out to be

fabulous.

She just had to think of something clever and witty to say to start the conversation ball rolling. "So, it turned out to be a nice day today."

Okay, maybe not rolling, but at least wobbling a little.

He nodded. "At least it didn't rain again. I got drenched in that downpour yesterday."

"Me too." She looked around the room. "This place seems nice."

Oh yeah, that would do it. Lob out a little comment about the decor. And she couldn't go wrong with awesome descriptive adjectives like 'nice'. Any second now, they were going to make a real conversation-connection.

"I like it. The musician is on break right now, but he's pretty good. It's just a single guy tonight with an acoustic guitar." He nodded to the counter. "Can I get you a coffee? Or something to drink?"

"Sure. I'll have a peppermint hot chocolate. Just a small one."

"That sounds good. I'll have one of those too. Be right back," he said over his shoulder as he headed for the counter.

Piper watched him walk away. He had on jeans and wore a red flannel shirt open in the front with a black T-shirt underneath. He'd smelled like laundry detergent and Axe body spray. Which wasn't a bad combination.

She hoped the drinks took a long time to make so she'd have a few minutes to try to up her chatting game. Holding her phone in her lap, she quickly Googled 'conversation starters' so when he got back, she'd be armed with some killer questions like, "What's your biggest fear?" and "If your life had a music soundtrack, what songs would be on it?"

She scanned a list of questions before stuffing her phone in her pocket as Aaron made his way back to the table. "Just checking my email," she said as he set the cups on the table.

"Did you get anything good?" He slid into the chair next to her, and his knee brushed hers.

She wasn't sure if he'd done it on purpose or not. "Uh, no. Nothing good," she stammered as he scooted his chair closer to hers and now not only his knee, but most of his thigh was pressed against hers. Yep, definitely did that move on purpose.

"Figured I could see the musician better from over here," he said with a wink, then picked up his mug and took a sip.

She nodded and wrapped her hands around the warm red ceramic cup. A frothy dollop of whipped cream swam in the middle of the chocolate and she took a sip, mainly for something for her mouth, which had suddenly gone dry, to do. "It's good."

"Yeah, I like this place. It's chill."

She nodded, staring into her cup as she desperately tried to ignore the warm pressure of his leg and remember the list of questions she'd just read. "What was the best Halloween costume you ever wore?" she blurted out.

His eyes widened then he chuckled. "Wow. Random question. But okay."

"I was just thinking, you know, Halloween is right around the corner."

"Yeah, smart. You're a thinker, I can tell. Even with the pink hair." He lifted his hand and touched the hot pink tips of her hair.

Geez. What was it about this hair color? Apparently she could add the opposite of being a thinker to her list of pink-tressed credentials.

"I guess my favorite costume ever was the year I dressed as a giant Lego. I was in fifth grade, and my dad helped me make this costume out of a cardboard box and some red Solo cups. It was pretty cool."

"Sounds cool."

He leaned forward, lowering his voice and resting his arm along the back of her chair. "I've got a little something for you," he said, nodding to his other hand in his lap.

Horrified, but still curious enough to see what it was, she glanced into his lap, praying it was something great like a puppy and not a gesture involving a one-eyed snake. She let out her breath as she glimpsed the flash of the silver flask he was holding.

"Want me to spice up your hot chocolate?"

She shook her head. "No, I'm good. I've got class in the morning."

"So do I. But you seem kind of nervous, and it's just a little vodka. It might loosen you up." He ran his hand up her back and massaged her neck.

His fingers were warm, but he was acting way too friendly and not in a good way. She held back a shiver. "Thanks for thinking of me, but really, I'm good. I'm not much of a drinker."

"Suit yourself." He shrugged then unscrewed the cap and poured a generous amount into his own cup. He took a drink, then settled back into his seat. "So, tell me about yourself, Piper. What else do you do besides go to class and serve coffee?"

"Not much. I'm actually pretty boring." She leaned forward to take a sip of her cocoa, trying to dislodge his hand from her neck.

He slid his hand down her back and let it rest along the curve of her back, which was not any better. "I doubt that."

Why would he doubt that? Just because she'd been adventurous enough to dip the ends of her hair into pink dye? And she hadn't even done it herself. Her mom had.

Maybe she should tell him she was rooming with her mom. That seemed interesting. Or somewhat pathetic.

She peered around the room again, trying to think of a clever comeback which sounded smart and witty, and almost choked on her sip of cocoa when she spied three familiar women sitting at a table by the hallway to the restroom.

What the hell are they doing here?

Her mom, Cassie, and Edna appeared to all be innocently drinking coffee and nibbling on the giant slab of chocolate cake that sat on the table in front of them.

Piper glared daggers at them, but they all seemed to suddenly have something extremely interesting to look at it and not one would make eye contact. She pushed back from her chair then stood, finally extricating herself from his roaming hand, which he'd started to slowly circle around her waist. "I'm sorry. I need to run to the ladies' room for a sec."

"Sure." He settled back in his chair, his gaze focused on the stage as the musician tuned his guitar and readied for his next set.

Music filled the room as Piper crossed to the hallway. Keeping her eyes forward, she spoke out the side of her mouth as she passed the women's table. "You three—meet me in the restroom. NOW."

She paused a moment before stepping into the hallway, doing a quick double take as she spotted another familiar figure sitting in a corner chair, his head bent forward, seemingly engrossed in the book in his lap. Even with the baseball cap pulled low over his ears, Piper would recognize the wavy blond hair and that strong chin anywhere.

But what the hell was Fitz doing in the Java & Jams? He got *free* coffee at The Perk. Maybe he was here for the music. Yeah, right.

Maybe that's why her mother, her aunt, and their geriatric cohort were there as well. She was sure it had *nothing* to do with spying on her and her date.

She pushed through the door of the restroom and leaned back against the sink.

It only took a few seconds for Cassie, Claire, and Edna to nonchalantly amble into the bathroom.

Edna affected a surprised look on her face. "Well, Piper, what a surprise. What are you doing here?"

"Nice try. The real question is what are you all doing here?"

Claire's attempt at an innocent expression was worse than Edna's. "We were just in the mood for some coffee and heard this place had great cake. And you know how your aunt likes cake."

"Hey," Cassie cried, giving her sister a hard nudge with her elbow. "You're the one who ordered it."

Claire shrugged. "I didn't say I didn't like cake, too."

"It is good cake," Edna agreed. "It's got a mild hazelnut flavor to it."

Piper huffed out her breath. "Enough about the damn cake. Why are you here?"

"Oh fine," her mom said. "We're not here for the cake. We're here to make sure you're okay."

"Why wouldn't I be okay?"

"Because you're going out with a strange guy who you've never met before. Don't you know the first rule of dating someone for the first time is to have a back-up plan in place? You've gotta have a wingman—someone that's watching your back. Someone to make sure you don't get kidnapped by a creepy axe-murderer that's trolling online dating sites for his next victim."

Piper shivered at the word 'murderer'—that one hitting too close to home. But still, she hadn't asked for help. "So what? You three are supposed to be my wingmen?"

"Wing *women*, really," Edna corrected, her blueish green-tinted hair making her look more like a wing-leprechaun.

"And I suppose that's why Fitz is here too? Everyone is just so worried about me. Like I can't take care of myself."

"Fitz? We don't know anything about Fitz."

"I spotted him in the corner as I walked in here. He's in the baseball cap, so not a very ingenious disguise."

Edna frowned. "I told you we should have worn disguises. Next time, I'm wearing that blonde wig."

"The Dolly Parton one you wore at Halloween last year?" Cassie asked. "Yeah, that wouldn't be conspicuous at all."

"It's not that we don't think you can take care of yourself, Pip," her mom said, ignoring the bickering of the other two. "We just wanted to be available to watch your back, in case you needed us."

She sighed and grudgingly offered them a thank you.

"How *is* it going?" Claire asked. "He seems nice, from what we can tell. He bought your drink, at least. And he's cute."

Piper scrubbed her hands across her face. "It's actually going pretty awful. I'm awful with idle chit-chat, and I don't know what to talk about. He seems to think because I have pink hair, I must be kind of wild, and I'm not. I'm really pretty boring. I'd much rather be home on the couch watching a movie than here drinking spiked hot chocolate."

"Spiked hot chocolate?" Edna asked. "I didn't know you could order drink-drinks here."

"You can't. Aaron brought a flask."

"Ah. Well, do you want us to help get you out of it?" Claire asked. "We could act like we just ran into you and need you to come home."

"Yeah, that could work," she answered, sarcasm dripping from her voice. "My mom, my aunt, and a lady from their book club just happened to run into me at a coffee shop and suddenly need my help at home."

"I could pretend to be your aunt too," Edna offered, then pushed back her shoulders at the look Claire offered her. "Okay, maybe your great aunt."

"It doesn't matter. That's still not gonna work."

"You could always pretend to be sick," Edna said. "Tell him the hot chocolate didn't agree with you. You've already been in the bathroom a while. And no one can argue with a sudden case of the Hershey-squirts."

"Ew. The date isn't going great, but I'm not ready to go with the diarrhea-defense just yet. Although I'm sure that would put an excellent spin on our already awkward night." Piper held up her hands before they could offer any other suggestions. "I'll be fine. I got myself into this date, I can get myself out of it."

"Suit yourself," Claire said.

Her aunt Cassie rubbed her arm. "But we're here if you need us."

"I'm good," Piper said, backing out of the door.

"Keep the 'diarrhea ditch' as a backup idea," Edna whispered before the door shut.

Piper shook her head as she made her way back to the table.

Aaron smiled up at her and pulled her chair out.

But before she could sit down, a hand grabbed her arm. "Hey babe, I told you I was sorry."

Piper recognized Fitz's voice but not the term of endearment. *Babe?* Since when did he call her that and what was he sorry for?

A crease wrinkled Aaron's forehead. "Who's this guy?"

Before she could open her mouth, Fitz squeezed her arm and pushed his body between her and the table. "I'm her boyfriend. Who are you?"

Her boyfriend?

Piper whipped her head towards Fitz. What was he playing at?

"I thought I was her date." Aaron gave her a questioning glance. "You didn't tell me you had a boyfriend."

"I don't. I mean, I didn't think I did. I guess I forgot," she stuttered out.

"You *forgot* you had a boyfriend?"

"She didn't forget. We just had a fight," Fitz said, coming to her rescue. "She thought we broke up, but I'm not letting her go." He turned to her, applying pressure to her arm again. "Come on, babe. I really am sorry. Just come home with me, and we can work this out."

She didn't know exactly what was going on, but she knew Fitz was up to something and wanted her to leave with him. And despite the weird thing that had happened that afternoon, she trusted him more than she trusted the guy with the vodka flask in his pants. And she also liked the feel of his hand touching her arm.

"Okay fine. I'll come...home with you." She stumbled on the word 'home', realizing it implied she *lived with* the Brilliant Barista, an idea which had her heart thudding like a hammer against her chest.

She looked down at Aaron and shrugged. "I'm sorry. We've been together so long, I guess he deserves another chance. Thanks for the cocoa."

Before she could say anything else, Fitz put his arm around her and led her from the coffee shop. He kept his arm around her shoulder until they made it out of sight of the window of the coffee shop, then he pulled her into the alley next to the building.

Her heart pounded... but not like before when she'd been excited. This time, her heart was pounding from fright.

But how could she be afraid of Fitz?

Her mind triggered back to the memory of him opening the cupboard drawer today. The one in which only someone who had been in that kitchen, in that apartment, would know to open.

Her mouth went dry while her stomach churned with nausea. Fitz couldn't have had anything to do with Brittany's death. She knew it—knew in her heart he wasn't dangerous.

But something was off about this whole situation. And she wanted—needed some answers.

She stopped, turning to face him and planting her feet, determined to get to the truth. "What is going on?"

He opened his mouth as if to speak, then his back went stiff and his face went pale.

A low voice spoke from behind him. "Think long and hard about how you're going to answer that question, sonny."

Oh brother.

Piper recognized the voice, but Fitz had no idea who was behind him, and she loved the way he circled his arms around her, as if trying to protect her.

"We don't want any trouble," Fitz said. "Just take my wallet and go. Nobody needs to get hurt."

"The only one that's going to get hurt is you, if you don't start talking and tell us why you killed that girl."

"What?" Fitz's voice came out as a strangled cry. "I didn't kill anyone."

Piper peered around Fitz's side at the petite elderly woman holding a Taser gun at his back. "Edna, what are you doing?"

Cassie and Claire burst around the side of the building

and almost ran into them.

Her mom bent forward, putting her hands on her knees as she gasped for breath. "Geez, for a little old lady, you sure can move fast."

"Who are you calling old?" Edna whipped around, now aiming the Taser at Claire.

"Edna, put the Taser down," Piper said as her mom held her hands up in surrender and Fitz took two steps forward and out of the line of fire. She offered him an apologetic look. "Sorry. This is Edna Allen. She's in my book club. And this is my aunt Cassie and you've already met my mom. This is my friend, Fitz."

At least she hoped he was still her friend, after Edna had just accused him of murder.

Fitz ignored the introductions as he gripped Piper's arm and peered down at her, his gaze intense and his eyes filled with hurt. "Do you think I had something to do with Brittany's murder?"

"No, I don't."

"Well, I do," Edna said, and whirled back to aim the gun Fitz's way again.

"Why would you think that?" he asked, disregarding the older woman's comment and keeping his focus on Piper.

"Because you never told me you knew Brittany or that you'd been in my apartment before, but obviously you have been."

"What do you mean by 'obviously'?"

"Because nobody in their right mind keeps their glasses in a lower drawer," Claire said, "yet you went straight for that drawer to find them the other day."

Fitz's shoulders slumped. "Just because I knew the odd place that Brittany kept her glasses doesn't mean I killed her."

"But you knew her," Claire accused.

"So? I know a lot of people."

"A lot of people who have been murdered?"

He let out a sigh. "Look, I met Brittany through Kyle, her boyfriend. Kyle and I played soccer together in high school." He ignored Claire and spoke only to Piper. "Drew knows him too. He was on our same team. I've only been to your apartment one time. It was right after you guys had moved in, and I dropped by to pick up Kyle. It was a hot day, and Brittany offered me a glass of water. I saw her get the glass from that drawer. I thought it was weird at the time, weird enough that I must have remembered it the other day. But not weird enough to *kill* her for."

Piper let out a shiver—which could have been a reaction to the cool night air or the idea of Fitz hurting her roommate. She peered up into his eyes, so intense as if he were trying to convey the truth to her through his gaze. "I believe you," she whispered.

"A smoldering look might be enough to sway Piper," Edna said. "But I'm still not convinced."

Fitz turned to the other women. "Would it help if I told you I had an alibi? I was at The Perk that whole day. I worked an eight-hour shift, and it was the first day of classes, so we were slammed the whole day. Any number of people can attest to the fact that I was behind the counter making coffee all day."

"Well, hell, why didn't you say that in the first place?" Edna shoved the Taser gun into her huge shoulder bag.

A frown tightened his lips. "I didn't think I had to."

Piper laid a hand gently on his arm. "I'm sorry."

He shook his head and let out another sigh. "Don't be. I have no idea what it's like to be in your situation, and it's got to be hard to know who to trust. I just wish you would have trusted *me* more and that douchey guy you met in the coffee shop less."

Her shoulders bristled. "He didn't seem so bad. Besides the fact we didn't really have anything to talk about."

"That's because he wasn't interested in talking."

"What do you mean?"

"I think he was interested in something else. I can't be a hundred percent sure, but I'm almost positive I saw him slip something into your drink when you were in the bathroom."

Piper's knees threatened to buckle. In all the confusion and talk about Brittany, she'd almost forgotten the real reason they were all standing in the alley together. "That's why you came over to our table, why you pretended to be my boyfriend? To rescue me?"

"Yeah, of course. I know it was lame, but it was all I could think of to get you out of there."

It hadn't seemed lame to her at all. "Thank you."

"Somebody needs to go back in there and teach that guy a lesson," Edna said, digging in her bag again for the Taser gun.

"I would have done just that if I would have known for sure," Fitz said. "I would have knocked the guy out, but like I said, I wasn't positive, and I thought the easiest thing was to get you out of there."

Piper held up her hands. "Can everyone just stop for a minute? My head is spinning, and I really just want to go home. I don't even like going out on random dates in the first place, I don't know why I agreed to go out with these guys. Maybe I thought guys wearing *Star Wars* shirts would be safe because they are nerdier, but going out with three guys in two days was too much for me."

"*Three* guys?" Claire asked. "There were only supposed to be two."

Piper glared at her mother. "What do you mean, there were only supposed to be *two*?"

"Well, um," Claire stammered. "I just meant that surely there couldn't be more than two guys wearing *Star Wars* paraphernalia who would ask you out in one day."

She narrowed her eyes. "Mother, did you have something to do with those guys asking me out?" How could her mom possibly have anything to do with these three random guys? "Were you standing outside of the coffee shop offering them money or something to ask me on a date?"

"No, of course not." Claire stared at a puddle of greasy water on the ground of the alley.

Piper didn't believe this innocent act for a second. "Mom? What did you do?"

"Nothing. Really. I just might have built you an online dating profile and pretended to be you and talked to two guys who looked cute and nice and arranged for them to come into the coffee shop and compliment you on your hair and then ask you out." Her words came out in a rush. "But I was just trying to help. And I only talked to two guys, not three."

Her mouth opened and closed, but no words came out. She was stunned and could think of absolutely nothing to say.

"Then how did *three* different guys know to follow the same pattern?" Fitz asked. He looked down at Piper. "I know they were all wearing something that had to do with *Star Wars*, but that could be a weird coincidence. Did they all say something nice about your hair?"

She nodded.

"So, who's the third guy, and how did he know those specific details and where she worked?" Cassie asked.

"More important than *how* someone did it," Edna said, "is *why* they did it. Why would someone pretend to be one of Piper's profile matches?"

A chill ran down Piper's back. She couldn't think of any reason that wasn't strange, creepy, or downright terrifying.

"There's one way to find out," Claire said. "Let's go check out the online site. Piper should be able to look at the profile pictures and easily figure out which one is the imposter."

❀ ❀ ❀

Thirty minutes later, the whole group was back at Piper's apartment and clustered around Claire's laptop.

Piper couldn't help but notice the computer looked brand new, but she had more things to worry about right now than her mom's peculiar financial affairs.

Like why someone would want to go out with her and keep their identity a secret. Or why someone would want to go with her at all. But that was a different therapy session.

"What are the names of the three guys you went out with?" Claire tapped the keys to get to the dating site.

"Brandon, Clay, and Aaron," Piper said. The dog was snuggled around her socked feet, and she was surprised by the comfort she took in the weight of its small body against her legs.

"What about their last names?" Cassie asked.

"And are you sure those are their *real* names?" Edna asked.

Piper shrugged. "I don't know. I never asked any of

them what their last names were, but I assume those are their real first names. I didn't ask for their ID's."

"Maybe next time you should," Edna stated.

"Yeah, right. Next time I'll be like, 'Oh sure, I'd love to grab coffee with you, but first, I'll need to see some ID.'"

Not like there was going to *be* a next time.

Piper was done with dating. She snuck a glance at Fitz who was staring intently at the laptop screen. Well, maybe not done with dating entirely. But done with dating random guys who she didn't know.

"Sounds like a good idea to me," Fitz muttered, not taking his eyes off the computer.

Claire shook her head in frustration. "I don't get it. They're all gone."

"What do you mean they're all gone?"

"I mean they are *all gone*. All the profiles which had shown interest in you were on the side of the screen, and now they aren't. They've been deleted. And when I go back in to search for matches, none of them come up."

"How can that be?" Piper asked, groaning at the picture her mom had chosen to use on her profile page. She'd never seen it before, but it was recent enough that it had her new pink-colored hair in it. The background showed the kitchen cabinets of the apartment, and she recognized the side of Cassie's arm and the purple sweater she'd been wearing the last time the Page Turners had been over for book club. Her mom must have taken it that night and uploaded it from her phone.

It wasn't a terrible picture of her. In fact, it captured a rare moment of her laughing. But if anyone saw that picture they'd assume that was her natural state—that she spent her life in joyous laughter—that, heaven forbid, she was actually *fun*.

The profile pic was just setting her up for failure. It

wouldn't take but ten minutes of actually spending time with her to realize she wasn't fun at all. She was plain and boring and generally preferred spending time in the company of a good book over spending time with actual company.

"Why would they all be gone? And *how* are they all gone? No one has access to this profile except for me." Claire repeatedly clicked the cursor on the side of the screen as if the profiles would magically reappear if she just clicked it enough times.

"Someone had access to it," Fitz said. "Whoever hacked into it in the first place obviously went in again and deleted all the profiles so Piper wouldn't be able to figure out which guy was the fake."

"But you saw them, Mom," Piper said. "Can't you just try to describe them and we can figure out which one doesn't fit the description."

"I can try," Claire said. "They both had kind of brownish hair."

"That doesn't help. All three of the guys I went out with had brownish hair. But one wore glasses. Did any of them wear glasses?"

"I don't think so."

"That doesn't prove anything," Cassie said. "Lots of people take their glasses off for pictures or he could have been wearing contacts."

"True."

"Have you ever seen any of the boys before?" Edna asked.

"No, but one of them, Brandon, is in my English class. And I saw him there today."

"That doesn't mean anything either," Fitz said. "Not if you had English in one of the huge lecture halls. Anyone could go in there and pretend to be in the class. It's not like they take roll."

"But he was taking notes, and he knew about the assignments."

"Did you *see* the notes? Or just see him typing? He could have been updating his Facebook status."

"Or his serial-killer files," Edna added.

Piper raised an eyebrow at the older woman. "Not helping."

Edna shrugged.

"Think about your conversations with him," Fitz continued. "Did he actually tell you about the assignments, or did he just ask you general questions which could be about any assignment."

She shook her head. "I can't remember. He mainly asked me questions about Brittany's murder."

Edna smacked her hand on the kitchen table. "Well that seems suspicious, right there."

"Why? You ask me about the murder all the time? Does that mean you did it?"

"Touché," she grumbled.

"We need to start from the beginning." Cassie headed toward the kitchen. "I'll make us all something to eat while you tell us everything. Start with the first second when you met each one and tell us what they said and what happened on each date. Claire, you grab some paper and make a note of anything that seems suspicious."

While Cassie put together sandwiches and set out chips, Piper relayed every detail she could think of about each of the three guys. They had seemed so ordinary, but after scrutinizing each one, it seemed like they each had at least one thing which could be deemed as questionable behavior.

Clay had seemed way too handsy for a first date, Brandon had asked too many questions about the murder, and Aaron had possibly tried to slip something into her drink.

Piper ran a hand through her hair and let out a frustrated sigh. "This isn't doing any good. All of these things can be explained. Plenty of people treat those online dating sites as places to find hook-ups and plenty of people ask me questions about Brittany and what happened. It's not that unusual for people to be curious."

"But what about Aaron? Drugging someone is not ordinary behavior." Cassie pressed the last of her potato chip crumbs onto her finger then sucked them into her mouth.

"It is for some people," Claire muttered.

Wait…what? What was that supposed to mean?

Before Piper could press her mom on what she meant by that, Edna barged ahead with the conversation.

"As deplorable as the idea is, we don't know for sure that Date #3 did, in fact, try to slip something into her drink. We only know what Fitz thought he saw, and that's all circumstantial."

"Circumstantial? We're not in court."

"Not yet."

Claire had written each boy's name at the top of a sheet of paper and had jotted down pertinent details as Piper had talked. She taped the three sheets to the wall above the dining room table. "This seems like a measly list of suspects."

"We don't even know if they are suspects," Piper said. "This whole dating thing is weird, but we don't really have anything which connects this situation to what happened to Brittany."

They studied the pages, each of them looking for any kind of clues or connections.

A hard knock sounded at the door, causing them all to jump at once.

"Holy hiccups," Edna said, pressing her hand to her chest, as the group stood up from the table. "I think I might have just had a heart attack."

Cassie crossed to the door, shouting, "Who is it?" as she walked.

"It's Mac," a deep voice answered.

She opened the door, and the tall police officer strode in.

He scanned the room, seemingly taking in all the details. He pointed to Fitz, who was standing next to Piper. "Who's this?"

She put her hand on Fitz's arm. "This is Fitz. We work together at The Perk. And he's also my friend. Fitz, this is Officer McCarthy. He's a friend of the family."

"Nice to meet you." Fitz stuck a hand out to shake Mac's.

"Well, I'm family, and you're not a friend of mine," Claire said, giving him a cool once-over with her eyes and offering him a flirty smile. "Not yet."

Gag.

Piper had seen her mother do this routine a hundred times.

"Down girl," Edna said firmly. "Mac's taken. By my granddaughter, Zoey."

Zoey was the newest member of the book club, but she'd been spending a few weeks at her parents' farm helping them with the fall harvest so Claire hadn't had a chance to meet her.

Piper nodded her head toward her mother. "This is my mom, Claire Denton. She's my new roommate."

Mac raised an eyebrow, glancing between her and her mother as he shook Claire's hand. "Nice to meet you. I'm glad to see you spending time with your daughter." He knew their history and how Claire had abandoned her at Cassie's.

His eyes narrowed as his gaze swept over the table and landed on the sheets of paper taped to the wall. "I see the Page Turners have been doing my job for me again."

"Now don't get your knickers in a twist," Edna said. "We're just doing a little investigative digging. We're not stepping on anyone's toes, and we haven't found out much of anything yet."

He sighed, a grim frown tightening his mouth. "I wish you had. We're racing against the clock right now, and I'd take any ideas you had."

"Why? What's happened?"

"I'm afraid there's been another murder."

Piper's stomach clenched, and she doubled over as if she'd been punched in the gut. "Oh no."

Fitz wrapped an arm around her and settled her back into her chair. "It's okay. Put your head between your knees if you feel like you're gonna hurl."

She did feel like she might hurl. A hot sweat broke out across her back, and her chest felt tight. She was nauseous. And shocked. And terrified to her very toes. "Who was it?"

"I can't release the victim's name yet, but I can tell you it was another student at the college and around the same age as Brittany."

"How was she killed?" Piper asked, although she felt like she already knew the answer. Otherwise, Mac wouldn't be here.

A crease wrinkled his forehead. "Strangulation and asphyxiation. Same as before."

"Then the two are definitely related."

"Again, I can't confirm or deny any details, but I can warn you to be careful and tell you not to go out alone or off with someone you don't know or trust. The campus has added extra security measures as well. I don't think they're putting out any kind of official statement just yet, but they are aware of the situation and doing what they can."

Edna narrowed her eyes at Mac. "Other than the obvious means by which they were killed, are the girls connected in any other way? Same color hair? Same neighborhood? Same classes?"

Mac shrugged. "I wish I could tell you more, but I

can't."

"We appreciate you letting us know," Cassie said, laying a hand on his arm.

He looked down at her, his expression softening. "Keep an eye on Piper. All of you need to keep a close eye on her."

"We will." She lowered her voice to a whisper, but they all heard her. "Do you really think she's in danger?"

"I wouldn't be here if I weren't worried about her. She could be in danger in a lot of ways. The more people who find out about this, the more amateur sleuths come out of the woodwork. People could see Piper as the next victim. Or as a suspect."

Claire gasped. "A suspect?"

"The first murder *did* happen in this apartment."

The apartment that was supposed to be her doorway to freedom, to living on her own and finally being able to control her own life.

The apartment which now felt more like a prison, a heavy weight dragging her down instead of lifting her up.

Edna had moved to Mac's other side, and she pointed to the sheets of paper on the wall. "Are any of these guys on your list of suspects?"

Mac took a step closer and studied the pages. "Why, do you think they should be?"

Piper gave him a quick rundown on the events of the last few days and the strange extra date.

"Hmm. That does seem weird," he said, pulling his notebook from his pocket and jotting down the three names. "I'll add them to my list of things to check out."

Edna stood glued to his elbow, craning her neck as she tried to read the notes on the pad.

He frowned down at her and snapped the notebook shut. "You all have my number if you need me."

"Thanks, Mac," Piper said, walking him to the door.

He bent forward and drew her into a hug. "Watch yourself, kid."

She held on for just a second, savoring the feel of Mac's protective arms around her. His shirt was crisply pressed, and he smelled like aftershave and starch. She gave herself one moment to remember the feeling of being safe and sheltered in her dad's embrace, one tiny beat of time to let down her wall and miss her father.

Then she let go and swallowed back the emotion burning her throat. "I'll be careful," she whispered.

She pushed the door shut and took a second to compose herself before sucking in a deep breath and turning back to the group. "What do we do now?"

Cassie put an arm around Piper's shoulder. "I think we all go home and let you get some rest. You've had a heck of a day."

She nodded, her body feeling the exhaustion, as if it had been suddenly overwhelmed with the stress and trauma of the day.

"We're not done investigating," Edna said.

"We're done for tonight," Cassie said, overruling her. "We can get back together tomorrow and talk some more. Why don't I bring over some lunch, and we can invite Maggie and Sunny too?" She tenderly brushed the hair from Piper's forehead. "Why don't you stay home tomorrow? You can take one day off."

Piper knew her aunt well enough to know when she was just being nice. She was using the offer of staying home and bringing over lunch as a way to follow Mac's direction and keep an eye on her. "I can't. I have class at eleven, and I can't miss it."

"Oh." She pursed her lips as if the suggestion had a sour taste. "Surely you can miss one class. Just this once."

Cassie was suggesting she miss a class? Who was this woman? Not the task-master PTA President who considered an absence a mark on your character. "No, I can't."

"I have the day off tomorrow," Fitz said. "I can walk you to class in the morning then wait for you and walk you back home."

Why would he do that? Why would he give up his morning to babysit her? "I appreciate the offer, but what are you going to do, stand in the hall and guard the door while I'm in class?"

He shrugged. "If I have to. If it will make you feel safer."

The thought of Fitz standing guard over her both appalled and appealed to her. "I can't ask you to do that. I'll be fine. I'll be on campus with lots of other people around me."

"You're not asking me. I'm offering. And it's no big deal for me to wait. I can bring a book and study while you're in class."

"Just let him do it," Claire said. "It will make us all feel better."

"Fine," she grumbled.

"And I'll feed you lunch for your trouble," Cassie said, then picked up her and Edna's purses. "Now we're all going to get out of here and let you get some rest."

"Fine." Edna snatched her bag from Cassie, her tone just as sulky as Piper's had been a second ago. "But first, I have a question. Who is Kyle Hammond?"

Fitz paused, his arm partway in the sleeve of his jacket. "That's Brittany's boyfriend. The guy we went to high school with. Why?"

"Because Mac had his name circled in his notebook."

Claire grabbed another sheet of paper and wrote Kyle's name at the top then taped it to the wall next to the others. "What do we know about this guy?"

Cassie sighed. "We know we've done enough

investigating for one night. You can all look into this Kyle kid tonight, and we can share what we find out tomorrow at lunch. But for now, we're leaving and letting Piper get to bed."

She wrapped an arm around Cassie's waist and rested her head on her aunt's shoulder. Piper loved the way Cassie took charge of a room and could be both dictatorial and maternal at the same time. "Thanks, Cass."

Her mom busied herself picking up the plates and cups, and Piper wondered if her daughter's closeness to her sister actually bothered Claire. Too bad if it did. She should have thought of that before she'd dumped her in Cassie's lap and taken off to live her own life.

❀ ❀ ❀

Fitz kept his word and walked Piper to and from class the next morning. They didn't talk much as they walked, but she was okay with that. She was just happy to walk beside him, content in the feeling that he cared enough about her to give up his morning to spend chaperoning her to campus.

A couple of times, the back of their hands brushed as they walked next to each other, sending a thrill racing up Piper's spine, but he never took her hand or linked his fingers with hers.

He did press his hand to the small of her back as he guided her into the building in front of him, and she felt the heat from his hand, as if it had branded her skin, all through her class.

Fitz did it again now as they walked through the door of her apartment building. She'd spied her aunt's minivan out front and also recognized Sunny's practical blue compact SUV.

The Page Turners had arrived.

Fitz had experienced a small measure of the book club the night before, but she wasn't sure he was ready for the full impact of the Page Turners when they were all together.

The sound of their laughter could be heard in the hallway as she unlocked the door and entered the apartment.

The little dog raced across the room, and Piper scooped it into her arms. She laughed as it licked her face and squirmed its body to snuggle closer to her chest. She really needed to come up with a name for it. Add that to the list right after figure out who killed her roommate.

Priorities.

Scents of grilled meat and fresh bread filled the room, and her stomach let out a growl. She glanced at Fitz. "You sure you're up for this?"

He grinned. "Bring it on."

Sunny and Edna were at the table, paper and markers spread out in front of them. The sheets of paper from the night before had been replaced with poster boards, color-coded for each suspect. Sunny was a teacher, and Piper was sure the new system was her doing.

Claire and Cassie were in the kitchen setting out plates and glasses.

"I brought pulled pork for sandwiches, and there's chips, and potato salad," Cassie said, pointing to the counter full of food. "Grab a plate and something to drink."

Fitz's eyes widened. "You made all this food this morning?"

Cassie beamed. "It was nothing. This is what I do. I also made a chocolate cake and some oatmeal cookies."

"Cassie's chocolate cake is so good, it's to die for," Piper said, then immediately regretted her words. That's what they were all here for, because someone literally had died. And it hadn't been due to chocolate cake.

The group filed through the kitchen, piling food onto their plates then settled at the table where Sunny had pushed their work to the center.

"It looks like you all have been busy," Piper said, pulling out a chair and sitting down. The dog jumped into her lap, and she absently stroked its back. "Have you found anything out?"

Edna nodded. "We've found out plenty. But not enough to figure out who the killer is."

Sunny tapped the papers. "We did find some correlations between the girls, though."

"How? We don't even who the second girl is. Mac wouldn't tell us her name."

"Mac's not the only connection we have in this town," Edna said. "I've got a friend whose grandson works at the police station, and he gave us a few details of the murder, including the girl's name." She spoke with her typical dramatic style, doling out the information with the flair of a circus master introducing each act. *In this ring, we've got one college freshman recently suffocated with a plastic sack, and in this ring...*

Piper sighed. "Just tell us. What was her name, and how was she related to Brittany?"

Edna harrumphed, obviously insulted her showmanship was going unappreciated. "Fine. Her name was Lisa Clark."

"Lisa Clark?" Piper repeated the name, turning it over in her mouth as she searched her mind for any recollection of it. She shook her head. "I don't know her."

"You should," Sunny said. "Because apparently, you went to high school with her."

"I went there for like a month and a half. And that school has hundreds of kids in it. There's no way I could know all of them."

Even though the town of Pleasant Valley was small, the school served a number of the surrounding small towns, and each class had several hundred kids in it.

Cassie pointed a finger at Fitz. "You went there too. Do you know this girl?"

He shook his head. "The name doesn't sound familiar. But maybe I would recognize her if I saw her. Do you have a picture?"

"Not yet."

"I can get my yearbook and bring it over later. If she went to our school, there should be at least one picture of her in there."

"Good idea." Edna tapped the poster board titled with Kyle's name. "I think we need to focus more on this kid. There's a reason Mac had his name circled in his notebook. Besides being the victim's boyfriend, he also went to both high school and college with the girls."

"I don't think that's reason enough to kill them, though," Piper said.

"No, you're right. And that's what we're missing. Motive." The older woman wrinkled her brow in concentration. "The motive for murder usually boils down to a few key reasons—passion, money, revenge, lust, greed."

"I don't think she had much in the way of money, and our apartment wasn't robbed," Piper pointed out. "And I can't imagine anyone wanting revenge on Brittany. She was super nice. Everyone liked her."

"Not everyone. And if this guy was her boyfriend, then maybe this was a crime of passion."

"Then he would've had to have some kind of passion with the other girl, too."

"Unless these girls are just a substitute for what he's really passionate about. Like a vendetta against his mother."

"Oh Lord, Edna," Claire scoffed. "Where do you come up with this stuff?"

"I watch television. A lot of television. And I stay informed."

"Let's stay focused," Sunny said, using her teacher voice. "We need to figure out a way to talk to this kid. To get him to let his guard down and open up to us."

"How are we going to get him to let his guard down to us? Invite him to our book club and get him drunk on Moscato?" Piper scoffed.

"I don't know what Moscato is," Fitz said. "But if you're looking to get him drunk, I can probably help with that. His uncle runs this dive bar on the south side of town, and we go over there sometimes because we don't always get carded. I could call him, and see if he wants to meet up there tonight. He's probably pretty broken up over Brittany already. Maybe I could get a few beers into him and get him to talk to me."

Edna nodded. "Not that I condone underage drinking, but in this case, I'll make an exception. Only because it's the only plan we've got. But it can't just be hearsay of what you tell us. You've got to record the conversation."

"I can do that with my phone."

"Good idea. But I still think we need to be there as well."

"What do you mean? You all want to come and have a drink with us? I don't think he'd talk to all of us."

"No. We won't be *at* the bar with you, but I think we need to be *in* the bar with you. You know, undercover."

Sunny groaned. "Oh no. Not another Edna Undercover Idea. Why do we have to be there?"

"I *want* to be there," Piper said. "I want to see his face and hear what he has to say."

"Well, if Piper's going to be there, I want to be there too," Claire said. "That police officer told us last night we needed to keep an eye on her."

"We can all be there," Edna said. "It's not that big of a deal to go into a bar and have a drink."

"It is with this bar," Fitz said. "It really is kind of a dive. It's not the kind of place where a group of middle class women would stop into for a glass of wine."

"Then we won't look like middle class women. That's the point of going undercover," Edna explained. "We wear disguises. This isn't our first rodeo, young man."

"Exactly what kind of clientele *does* usually frequent the place?" Sunny asked, chewing on her bottom lip.

Fitz shrugged. "All sorts, I guess. But usually a little more of a rougher crowd. Mainly bikers and some construction worker type guys, you know, the kind of people who all have concealed carry permits and actually carry. Or have multiples guns in their trucks but aren't planning on going hunting. The kind of guys who think the word 'militia' sounds like summer camp."

"Oh yeah, it sounds like we'll fit right in," Sunny said. "I didn't much like actual summer camp."

"This sounds too dangerous," Cassie added.

"Really? It sounds like fun to me," Edna said, a familiar mischievous twinkle sparkling in her eye. "And what could be safer than being surrounded by a bunch of armed men?"

Cassie rolled her eyes. "My living room. That sounds much safer."

"You don't have to come," Edna said. "But I'm going. I'm not afraid of a little riff-raff."

"Count me in, too," Claire said. "I've been to plenty of bars like this, and I'm not worried about me, but I'm not letting my daughter go into one on her own."

Now she gets maternal.

"What about the women?" Edna asked. "What are the women like? How do we need to dress if we want to fit in?"

"Like bar-flies," Claire said. "I don't think any of you could pass as biker chicks, unless you have some secret stores of leather, but you might be able to pass for bar-flies if you cake on some makeup, wear some faded jeans, high heels, and show some cleavage."

Sunny peered down at her boringly B-cupped chest. "I'll have to rely on the makeup and tight jeans. My cleavage department is somewhat lacking."

"That's what push-up bras are for," Edna told her, palming her bra cups and giving her chest a little lift.

"We all know you carry more in your bra than your meager amount of cleavage," Sunny replied.

"Darn tootin'. And you know my brassiere will be fully loaded tonight. I'll have mace, brass knuckles, and I'll make sure my stun gun is charged."

Fitz's eyes went wide. "I feel a little like I fell down a rabbit hole. Or have been allowed behind the curtain of the 'woman' club. Is this the kind of stuff all women talk about?"

"You have no idea, son," Edna said with a chuckle. "This is a tame night for us."

Piper lifted her shoulders. "I tried to warn you."

"I like it. Well, not the cleavage comments so much." His face pinked with the mention of cleavage. "But the rest is kind of funny. Where do you even get brass knuckles?"

"Oh, you can order anything online these days," Edna said.

"Before we get all worked up creating our disguises, why don't you text Kyle and see if he'll even agree to meet you," Piper said.

"Good idea." Fitz pulled his phone from his pocket and sent a quick text.

The room was uncharacteristically quiet as the women watched Fitz's phone.

It buzzed a few seconds later with a message from Kyle agreeing to hang out. Fitz messaged back a time and the place, and Kyle replied with a simple 'K'.

"We're on. He'll be there at nine."

"Nine? I'm usually in bed by nine," Sunny said. "Or at least in my pajamas and headed that way."

"You don't have to go," Edna said.

"I'm not going to miss this. I can stay up if there's a chance I'm going to get to see Edna going incognito as a bar-fly."

The group planned to meet at Piper's around eight, but Cassie had arrived earlier and Claire had spent the last thirty minutes turning her into a bar-fly. Well, a middle class suburban mom kind of bar-fly. Claire had darkened her makeup, giving her eyes a smoky shadow effect with deep tones of purple and gray. She'd poofed out her hair a little with extra spray and product and slicked a thin layer of red gloss on her lips.

"It wasn't hard for me to find a pair of tight jeans," Cassie said, patting her ample rump. She held out her foot, now encased in a black high-heeled boot. "But I haven't worn these boots in years. Thankfully Matt and the kids are at the movies tonight. Otherwise, I never would have been able to get out of the house in this." She smoothed the black jersey knit Henley she wore. "And this has been in my closet for years. I should have gotten rid of it. It's way too tight. I feel like everything I have is on display."

Claire reached out and popped the top button of her shirt. "There. Now everything you have is on display." She laughed at Cassie's horrified face, then slapped her on the rump. "You look great, Cass. Men love curves. I wish I had your body."

Piper had been watching her mom and her aunt, and she glanced at her mom's thin frame. She'd put on a little weight since she'd moved in, at least she didn't have that unhealthy half-starved gaunt look to her, but her mom still looked pretty great for her age.

She'd put on a faded pair of jeans, thick-soled black boots, and a snug white tank top with the word "Angel" surrounded by a set of wings emboldened across her chest. She had her hair plaited in two braids and captured the look of an authentic biker chick.

That's right. Because for the last six months, she'd *been* an authentic biker chick.

But Piper hadn't seen this side of her mom since she'd been back. She'd mainly worn jeans and loose sweaters and sensible little tennies, or yoga pants, T-shirts, and flip-flops if she were hanging around the house.

The sight of her mom in this get-up was a hard reminder of the life she'd abandoned Piper for.

She swallowed the hurt burning her throat and was thankful for the distraction of the knock at the door. "Who is it?" she called before opening the door.

"A bar-fly and a biker babe," came the muffled response.

Piper opened the door, and her mouth dropped open at the sight of Edna Allen decked out in full leather, from the cute hat perched on her fluffy green and blue-tinted curls to the set of full leather chaps wrapped around her legs.

Piper clapped a hand over her mouth and pinched her lips together to keep from busting out laughing.

"Oh. My. Gosh," her mom said as Edna sashayed into the room, followed by Sunny, who wore a zipped-up sweatshirt and carried a large tote bag over her shoulder. "What in the world are you wearing?"

Edna spun in a circle worthy of any runway model. "This is what all the well-dressed biker babes are wearing. I *Googled* it." She had on a pair of pink sweat pants under the chaps, the word "Juicy" visible across her petite rear-end.

"Please tell me you didn't have those chaps in your closet," Cassie said, her eyes wide and blinking at Edna's outfit.

"I'm not telling you all the things I have in my

closet," Edna declared, with a lewd wink and a racy lift of her shoulder.

"Ew." Piper gave a shudder as she covered her ears. "I do not want to know."

"If you must know, I got this outfit at a costume shop," Edna explained. "The bag said 'Authentic Biker Babe' right on it."

"I'm not taking any responsibility for this," Sunny said. "She looked like that when I picked her up." She dumped the over-stuffed tote on the sofa and unzipped her sweatshirt, revealing a tight T-shirt with an American Flag printed across her chest. Her hair was more curly than usual and hit her shoulders in bouncy waves. Long, feathered earrings hung from her ear lobes and a thick silver bangle bracelet circled her wrist.

She pulled a pair of high-heeled boots from her tote and kicked off her tennis shoes. "I usually wear these with a dress, but figured they might look the part if I tucked my jeans into them." She nodded at Edna. "Not that anyone is going to notice I'm even in the bar with 'Biker Babe-elicious' in the room." She peered at Cassie, then let out a low whistle. "Speaking of babe-elicious. Wow, Cass, you look amazing. Check out those curves."

Cassie's cheeks went pink, and she hugged her arms around her chest. "I feel silly."

"Don't," Piper reassured her with an encouraging smile. "You really do look great, Aunt Cass."

"Where's Maggie?" Edna asked.

"She couldn't make it," Cassie explained, the pinched expression on her face relaxing at the change of subject. "Her son had a soccer banquet or something at school she had to go to. She said she's sorry to miss this, but I'm not sure she said it with much sincerity."

Piper wished she could miss it. She'd much rather spend the night curled up on the sofa with the still-nameless dog and a good book.

But that didn't look like it was going to happen. And if any of this helped to figure out who killed Brittany, this crazy scheme would be worth it. "So, what's the plan?"

"We need to stick together, or at least in pairs of two, so no one is on their own," Cassie said.

"Why don't I stick with Piper and you three get a table and work the room," suggested Edna.

"How the heck are we supposed to do that?" Sunny asked.

"Ask questions. Talk to people."

"And say what? Anyone have any clues as to how this girl got murdered across town?"

"I'd suggest going for a little more subtlety," Edna explained. "See if anyone knows this kid Kyle or can tell us anything about him. If he hangs out there a lot, maybe someone knows something about him. And nobody needs to worry. I'm packing tonight." She patted the front of her chest.

Cassie gasped. "You're carrying a gun in your bra?"

"Not an *actual* gun, but the next best thing." Edna reached down the front of her shirt and pulled out a small pink rectangular-shaped item that resembled a cell phone. "They call this little baby *The Terminator*."

"What is it? It looks like a mini-tape recorder." Sunny reached a hand toward it, but Edna snatched it away.

"It's a stun gun. And it's got five hundred and fifty megavolts of power packed into this little pink box."

"Where in the world did you get a pink stun gun?" Claire asked.

"Where I get everything," she answered with a shrug. "On Amazon. Only cost me eight ninety-five."

Claire shook her head. "Just don't stun yourself with it. We don't need to add an electric boob-blunder to this night. It's crazy enough as it is."

Edna harrumphed and stuffed the pink stun gun back into her blouse.

"Fitz said he would try to grab a spot at the bar with Kyle," Piper said, trying to deflect any more attention aimed at Edna's bra baggage. "I'm going to try to sit on his other side, and hopefully I can listen in on their conversation."

"Good plan. I'll try to get the bartender talking," Edna said.

"I think you'd better stay at the table in the back of the room," Cassie said. "I'll sit at the bar with Piper and chat with the bartender. People tend to talk to me. I think I remind them of their mother, and I'm a good listener."

"You don't look like anyone's mother tonight," Claire said. "I say we show up and get the lay of the land and wing it from there. We'll all have our phones so we can text each other if the plan changes."

"Sounds good," Piper agreed. She wore a simple outfit of jeans, her favorite pair of Chucks, and a slouchy black hoodie over a gray T-shirt. Her plan was to blend in, but with the bar, not the patrons. Let the other women serve as distractions, her plan was to fade into the background and not draw any attention to herself. "We should probably go in separately so as not to draw attention to ourselves." She gestured to Edna. "Well, any *more* attention to ourselves."

Claire grinned. "I guarantee no one in that bar will notice us once Ms. Authentic Betty Biker Babe walks in."

Edna held up her hand. "That reminds me. We all need code names."

"Code names?" Claire raised an eyebrow at Piper, who shrugged. She was used to Edna's elaborately hare-brained schemes.

"Of course. We can't use our real names. That's the point of being *undercover*," Edna explained. "I think I'll go with Ginger. Ginger Lafayette. I always wanted to be a fiery redhead."

"I thought you said *code* names, not stripper names."

"Hmm. I see your point." Edna tapped her chin. "Okay, I guess I'll go with the one you suggested. You all can call me Betty tonight."

Piper shook her head, amused Edna didn't see the irony of the nickname. "How about if we just agree that no one talks to me at all."

"Let's make it easy and go by Phoebe, Monica, and Rachel." Cassie pointed to herself, Sunny, and Claire as she assigned each one a name then looked at Piper. "And you can be Joey."

Piper rolled her eyes. "Thanks."

"Nobody is going to be anybody if we don't get over there," Claire said, pointing toward the door. "I'll drive my car with Cass and Piper and we'll follow you two over. Cassie and Piper can go in first then we'll wait about ten minutes and I'll come in with Monica and Sweet Cheeks Lafayette."

"Now that sounds like a stripper name," Edna said, following Sunny out the door.

❀ ❀ ❀

Twenty minutes later, a socially-awkward college freshman and a smoky-eyed middle-aged mom in tight jeans walked into a bar.

Unfortunately, that wasn't the beginning of a joke, although Piper felt an odd compulsion to giggle as she and her aunt crossed the room toward the long bar where she spotted Fitz and Kyle.

Fitz was right, the place was kind of a dive. Dark and dismal, a few neon beer signs adorned the wood-paneled walls. Four or five tables sprawled across the concrete floor with a few booths lining the wall. A juke box softly played a classic rock ballad and the smack of a pool ball cracked through the air as three burly guys in flannel played a game at one of the two pool tables at the far end of the room.

The scents of stale beer, peanuts, and disinfectant warred with each other in the stuffy air.

The bar was fairly quiet, only one other guy sat nursing a beer at the other end of the bar.

Piper took the seat next to Fitz but didn't acknowledge him, and Cassie…er, Phoebe, took the seat next to her after subtly brushing a few crumbs from the bar stool.

The bartender, a tall, muscled bald guy with a thick mustache and salt and pepper goatee, ambled toward them and slapped a couple of cardboard coasters on the bar in front of them. A snake tattoo curled around his huge muscled bicep, just visible under the sleeve of his white T-shirt. He wore a black leather vest and eyed Piper with a shrewd appraisal. "What can I get you ladies?"

Cassie smiled and peered behind the bar. "Do you have a drink menu?"

Piper dug an elbow into her side. "She's kidding. She'll have a rum and coke, and I'll just have a coke." She offered him what she hoped was a casual shrug. "I'm driving."

And under-age, but she appreciated the bartender's slight nod and the fact he didn't point that small issue out.

She snuck a quick glance at Fitz's glass and was glad to see it looked like he was drinking soda as well. A half-empty glass of beer sat on the bar in front of Kyle, who looked like he'd slept in his clothes and hadn't combed his hair in days. He held his forehead in his hand as he leaned against the bar, as if the weight of simply holding his head up was too much for him to bear.

Piper felt a pang of sympathy for him, until she

remembered he might be a murderer, and her empathy dried up faster than a cheetah with its tail on fire.

"Here you go," the bartender said, clunking down their drinks in front of them. He eyed Cassie appreciatively and offered her a flirty grin. Or the closest thing Piper could imagine to flirty from a giant muscled tattooed biker dude. "I'm Snake," he told them, which explained the reptilian ring of tattoos. "Holler if you need anything."

"Thanks, Mr. Snake. I mean Snake," Cassie stuttered, as she raised her glass and took a tentative sip.

Piper was impressed when she held it together and swallowed the sip, especially after the grimace she made.

Luckily, Snake's attention was elsewhere. His eyes had gone round as he stared at the door, and Piper had a feeling Monica, Rachel, and Sweet Cheeks had just entered the building.

Spinning slightly in her chair, Piper, and the rest of the bar watched the three women walk in.

Edna paraded through the room, followed by Sunny, who stared at the floor and looked like she wanted to sink into it. Claire sauntered behind them, her gaze coolly assessing the room as if it were an everyday occurrence for her to accompany a second-grade teacher and an old lady dressed as biker chicks into a trashy bar.

A waitress, presumably the only one in the bar, sidled up to their table in a tiny skirt and cowboy boots. A grin covered her face as she walked away from their table, then leaned over the bar next to Cassie to relay their order. "The ladies at the booth in the back would like a pitcher of Coors Light and three glasses. You should have heard that little granny talk. She was cracking me up. She told me her 'hog' was in the shop then she asked me if I knew where she could score some weed. The skinny one mouthed she was her grandma and didn't get out much. They're a hoot."

It took all of Piper's willpower to keep her eyes from rolling. So much for Edna staying low key and blending in. But hey, whatever it took. Who knows, maybe Edna would become best pals with this waitress, and she'd finagle a piece of key information from her. Piper had seen Edna do it before—the woman might be a little wacky, but she had skills.

Speaking of skills, Piper needed to focus on her own part of this scheme. She pulled her phone from her pocket and laid it on the bar next to Fitz's arm. He had his back to her, but his elbow rested casually on the bar.

She set her phone to record then turned it upside down and pushed it as close to Fitz as possible without seeming to be too obvious.

He shifted on the bar stool, just the smallest amount, but enough to slightly brush his arm against the side of her hand—just enough to send a spark of heat darting up her spine.

She could almost feel the warmth of him radiating off his body, and she wanted to nestle against his back, but they were here to do a job and she had her part to play, which was being the back-up recorder.

Letting the phone do its job, she leaned forward on the bar, sneaking an occasional glance at Kyle as she tried to nonchalantly listen to Fitz's conversation with him.

"I know it's gotta be tough, dude," Fitz was saying as Kyle threw back the rest of his beer and signaled for another. "How are you really holding up?"

Kyle drew his hand through his already messy hair. "Not very well. This shit is messing with my head. I mean, first Brittany, and now Lisa. I don't understand what's happening."

"I knew about you and Brittany, but I didn't know you knew the other girl, too."

"Yeah, she went to high school with us. I only knew her a little back then. I met her this one time at a party, but that night turned into a shit show of the highest order, and I didn't really talk to her again at school. Then I saw her here on campus at the beginning of the school year, and we'd started talking again."

"What do you mean by a shit show?"

Kyle shook his head, and his eyes went teary. "Oh man. I don't know if I can even talk about it."

"It couldn't have been that bad."

"It was. I did some stupid shit. It was a bad night. Brittany and I were in a fight, and I'd been drinking. A lot. I met this girl. Lisa. She was different than anyone I'd ever known."

"Different how?"

"Just different. You know, not someone we would ever even talk to at school. She hung out with a different crowd. Kids we would *never* be seen hanging around. I don't even know why she was at that party."

"I get it. So, what happened? I take it you did talk to her."

"I did. She was cool. And like I said, Brittany and I were fighting and this girl, she was a good listener. And really pretty, under all the makeup and junk she wore. At least I think she was. I was already pretty messed up then we did some shots and one thing led to another, and we ended up in one of the bedrooms. Then this kid, he must have been a friend of hers because they looked the same, he walked in on us and caught us together, her half-naked and me with my pants around my ankles."

"Oh dang."

"Yeah, that wasn't what I was thinking. Actually, I wasn't thinking at all. I was just reacting. I was drunk, and I'm ashamed of myself."

"We all do stupid stuff when it comes to girls."

"That wasn't all I did that was stupid." He lowered his voice, and Piper leaned closer, straining to hear him. "The girl was an idiot move. I never should have fooled around on Brittany. But like I said, this girl wasn't someone we would ever even talk to. It was bad enough Brit was going to kill me, but now everyone in school was going to make fun of me for hooking up with this girl. I had to shut that kid up, and make sure he didn't tell anyone what he saw."

"So, what did you do?"

Kyle shook his head again and scrubbed his hands across his face. "It all happened so fast. And the details are a little blurry. But I was pissed, and the kid knew it. He just stood in the doorway, like he was frozen or something. I remember the way his mouth opened and shut like this stupid goldfish my little sister had when we were kids. I yanked up my pants and started yelling at him that I'd kill him if he told anybody. Then he ran. The stupid kid ran."

Kyle made a funny sound—a cross between a hiccup and a burp and stared miserably into his beer. "I think about that night sometimes, and I always wonder what would have happened if he hadn't run."

"What *did* happen?"

"I took off after him. I don't know what I was going to do. Try to talk to him or scare him. I don't know. He just took off, and I started chasing him. I chased him through the house, and he ran out the back door and past a couple of my buddies who were standing at the keg. They saw me running after him and joined in the chase. The house was over off Brookdale, you know the neighborhood with all those trees and the forest service land behind it?"

Fitz nodded.

"Well, he ran into those trees, and we ran after him. It still seems like something out of a dream. I think I've blocked out a lot of what happened that night. It was like we were crazy cannibals or something, chasing after this kid like we were going to eat him. All three of us guys were acting nuts, screaming and running through the trees like we were hunting a wild animal."

"Did you catch him?" Fitz's voice was low, and Piper could feel his back bristle and his muscles tense as he listened. She realized her own hands were clenched in fists.

It was hard for her to listen to Kyle's story without wanting to punch the guy. The way he described going after that kid, who hadn't done anything except been in the wrong place at the wrong time.

"Yeah. We did. He must have tripped or something and hurt his leg because he was lying on the ground next to this big tree, curled up against it like he was trying to disappear into it."

"What'd you do?"

Kyle's cheeks sagged, like his whole face was melting with the misery of telling the story. His voice was barely above a whisper now. "We taught him a lesson, I guess. We roughed him up and made him swear not to tell anyone. He was scared shitless. I'm pretty sure he pissed himself. But we didn't care. We were beyond caring. It was like that mob thing they talk about happening where the motions of the crowd take over."

She was pretty sure Kyle was crying now. She couldn't see his face around Fitz's shoulder, but his voice had that husky scratchy sound, and he sniffed a couple of times.

"We left him out there. We left that kid out there all by himself."

"Then what happened?"

"Nothing. Nothing ever happened. I never saw the kid again, and us guys never talked about it. We just showed up at school on Monday and acted like it never happened. I saw Lisa in the halls a couple of times, but I pretended not to know who she was. I know it was a dick-move, but I was a high school senior, and I *was* kind of a dick. And I didn't know what else to do. I was ashamed of myself, and I just wanted it all to go away and pretend it had never happened. Brittany and I made up and everything went back to normal.

"Except now Brittany's gone, and so is Lisa. Two women murdered, and I've been with both of them."

Kyle was still talking, but Piper didn't hear what he said. She turned as the commotion of a group of six or seven rough-looking bikers entered the bar. They were loud and burly, and the sound of their laughter and swearing filled the bar. Their very presence seemed to take up all the air in the room.

They moved as one toward a grouping of tables, shuffling chairs and pushing three of the small tables together then settling in around them. One of the guys whistled for the waitress, who clomped over in her cowboy boots.

Piper had been so engrossed in Kyle's tale, she hadn't noticed what the other women were doing. Peering around the room, she took stock of her fellow undercover cohorts. Her aunt had turned away from her and seemed captivated by a story Snake was telling her.

A perky personality and smoky eyes must be his thing because he'd been flirting with Cassie and trying to talk to her all night. Piper hadn't been paying much attention to their topics of conversation, but she recognized the 'listening' mode of her aunt.

Cassie *was* a great listener—she asked real questions and had this way of making a person feel like everything they had to say was valuable and important. She'd always thought her aunt could charm a snake. Evidently, it was true. Even a menacing six-foot four bearded biker snake.

Although he didn't seem as scary when he was laughing and playfully flirting with Cassie. Piper noticed the way he looked up and scanned the new group of patrons, and she caught the quick frown he made before his attention returned to her aunt.

Edna was playing pool with three guys who looked like they worked construction for a living, all of them in jeans, long-sleeved undershirts, and flannel. They were laughing at the funny little old lady now, but she had a feeling Ginger Lafayette was hustling those boys out of their hard-earned cash.

'Rachel' and 'Monica' were still in the booth, but Piper's muscles tensed as she watched her mom.

Something was wrong.

She could tell from the way her body had sunk inward, her shoulders hunched down, and her chin almost touched her chest. She'd pulled up the hood of her jacket and stuffed her hands into its pockets.

Before Piper could get up to check on her, Claire slid from the booth, gave the room a furtive glance, then slipped out the door of the bar.

What the heck?

Where was she going?

Sunny scooted from the booth and headed toward the pool tables. She had to pass by the tables of rowdy newcomers, and one of the men grabbed her as she walked by and pulled her into his lap. He wore sunglasses and a black doo-rag wrapped around his head, a silver skull emblem in the center of his forehead.

Why did he need sunglasses? The sun hadn't been out for hours.

But Sunny had other things to worry about besides his choice of eyewear. She struggled to get up, her expression showing signs of panic as she pushed against his chest. Her motions only egged on the other guys at the tables who whistled and cat-called.

Piper jabbed Cassie in the side with her elbow as she pushed off the bar stool.

Snake looked toward the turmoil and grabbed a baseball bat from behind the counter. He leaned toward Cassie. "I think it's time for you and your friend to be going. It gets a little rough around here after ten." He nodded toward Sunny. "And you need to take your pals with you. I wouldn't want anything to happen to you all."

Huh. So much for their undercover op. They hadn't even fooled the bartender.

He made his way toward the group, but Sunny had regained control of the situation and was glaring down at her captor.

Her teacher voice could be heard all the way to the bar. "Take your hands off me right now."

"Ewww. This lady's a tough one," Skull-head said, but he held his hands up in surrender.

Sunny pushed up from his lap, smoothed down her shirt, raised her chin, and continued toward the pool tables.

Piper shook her head. She would have been scared to death. But Sunny handled herself like a champ. She was tougher than she looked.

Still, Piper agreed with Snake. It was time to get out of there.

Sunny reached the pool tables, then turned toward her and Cassie, her expression of panic back. But this time it had nothing to do with the bikers.

She looked scared for the same reason a jolt of fear was skittering up Piper's spine.

Edna was gone.

Piper hurried toward Sunny, Cassie on her heels.

How could an eighty-something year old woman wearing pink sweats and leather chaps disappear?

The bar wasn't that big. The basic layout was one giant room with a hallway which led to the restrooms. An emergency door lit by a green EXIT sign was on the back wall behind the pool tables. Had someone snatched Edna and pulled her through those doors? Had she hustled the wrong flannel shirt-wearing guy and he was teaching her a lesson?

That was crazy. Who beats up an old lady?

The thought sent terror streaking through Piper's veins as she practically tackled Sunny. "Where is she? What happened to her?"

"I don't know. She was here a minute ago. I just saw her." Sunny dragged her fingers through her hair, her head snapping left to right as she searched the bar for signs of the mermaid-colored head.

"She couldn't have just disappeared," Cassie said, dropping all pretense of them being strangers. "Wait, where's Claire?"

Sunny shrugged, her voice climbing a shrill octave. "I don't know. We were just talking. Everything seemed fine. Then that big group came in. Her face went pale then she took off."

"She left on her own," Piper said. *What else is new?* "But I don't think Edna did. Let's focus on finding her and then we can look for my mom."

A loud bang sounded from the hallway, followed by

heated shouting then an eerie silence.

Sunny, Cassie, and Piper stared at each other, similar wide-eyed expressions on all their faces, then they turned as one and raced toward the hallway. Snake and his baseball bat followed in their wake.

The men's room door was propped open by a jean-clad leg and a steel-toed Timberland-booted foot.

Piper pushed open the door, holding her breath as she prayed Edna was okay. Sunny and Cassie squeezed in next to her.

"What the hell happened in here?" Snake asked, peering over Piper's head.

Two of the flannel-shirted pool players lay sprawled out on the floor. One sagged against the corner, his head leaning against the white ceramic front of the urinal, and the other lay sprawled in the middle of the floor. It was the second guy's leg sticking out the restroom door.

Edna stood next to the sink, her cute leather hat missing and her hair sticking up in disarray like little blue-green clouds floating around her head. Her arm drooped at her side, her pink stun gun clutched in her fingers.

A sizzle of electricity seemed to float on the air, and Edna's eyes sparked with fury. "These boys said they were going to introduce me to somebody named Jane. I couldn't figure out what she was doing in the men's room, but I thought she might need help." She pointed to the men on the floor and offered them a sniff of disgust. "Turns out they were just trying to offer me some drugs."

The guy leaning against the urinal wrapped his arm around his chest and let out a groan. "I'm sorry. We just thought it would be funny to get the old lady baked."

Edna planted a fist on her hip. "For your information, young man, the only thing I bake is cookies and cinnamon rolls."

Cassie held out her hand to Edna. "I think we'd better

get out of here."

Edna took her arm and stepped over the man sprawled in the doorway. She dropped her pink stun gun back down the front of her shirt and smoothed her 'pleather' vest. "Didn't anyone tell you boys you should 'just say no' to drugs?"

Snake gave Cassie a wide-eyed look of amusement. "You've got your hands full with that one."

"Don't I know it?" Cassie chuckled then gestured to the bat in his hands. "Thanks for having our backs."

"Anytime. You ladies made my night. Consider your drinks on me." He dipped his chin. "And I'm here most days after three if you want to come back in. We can continue our conversation."

Piper glanced at her aunt and shook her head at the flare of pink coloring Cassie's cheeks. "She'll keep that in mind. Thanks for the drinks." She hustled the group down the hall and out the bar, pressing her lips together to keep from laughing as Snake called out, "Take care, Phoebe."

Claire's car was missing from the parking lot so they all piled into Sunny's sedan. Fitz and Kyle had still been sitting at the bar when they'd hurried past, and Piper filled the others in on the story Kyle had told.

"It sounds like Kyle was a jerk, but nothing about his story gives him a motive for murder," Sunny said. "It seems like he came out of the whole deal pretty unscathed."

"Except for the fact both the girls he was involved with are now dead," Edna pointed out.

"Yeah. Except for that."

Piper slumped back against the seat. "Did anyone else find out anything useful?"

"I don't know how useful it is," Cassie said. "But Snake told me he knows Kyle through his uncle, and he's been in the bar quite a bit lately. He said he's been worried about him because he looks so depressed, and he doesn't think he's been going to his classes."

"Again, that could be due to the fact his girlfriend was just murdered. In which case, his behavior doesn't seem too out of the ordinary."

"I still find it interesting he had a connection to both girls," Edna said.

"Me, too."

They spent the remainder of the drive tossing around ideas and their thoughts about the undercover operation.

"Do you want us to come in with you?" Cassie asked Piper, as they pulled up to the curb in front of her apartment.

She was going to make a comment about how they wouldn't be able to protect her if someone were in the apartment, but she'd just seen a little old lady drop two construction workers with a pink stun gun, so that argument didn't hold much weight.

"No, I'll be fine," she said. "It's only ten steps to my door. You can watch me walk in if you want, and I can flash the lights when I get safely inside."

"Okay. We'll talk more tomorrow. Tell your mom I'll call her later."

Claire's car was not on the street, and Piper had a sudden fear her mom was gone again, this time for good. Pain ripped through her chest, and she dug her nails into her palms as she clenched her hands into fists.

She knew she never should've let her guard down, should never have let herself get close to her mom again.

Standing at her door, her hand on the knob, she paused to take a deep breath, reluctant to open the door and face the evidence of another one of her mom's betrayals.

Screw it. She had to face it sometime.

The sound of sharp toenails on the hardwood greeted

her as the little dog raced across the floor to meet her. Dropping her bag, she scooped the puppy into her arms and grinned as it frantically licked her ear. "Hi girl. I'm glad to see you too."

Peering around the apartment, she saw no signs of her mom. With a sigh, she flashed the room's light twice then heard Cassie's car drive away.

Her feet carried her toward her mom's bedroom, a discouraging sense of dread filling her chest as she wondered if all her mom's belongings would be gone.

Her breath caught in her throat as she saw Claire's things still lined up on the dresser and scattered across the room. The blue sweatshirt she'd been wearing earlier hung from the side of the bed and her favorite pair of running shoes still lay on the floor, a set of low-top socks carelessly tossed across them.

So, she hadn't left.

Or if she had, she'd left all her things.

But if she hadn't left, where was she?

The dog let out a whine then ran to the front door and scratched to be let out.

"Good dog," Piper told it as she grabbed a plastic bag then opened the door and followed her outside. She didn't bother with a leash, because so far, the dog had been very good about going out, getting its business done quickly and running back inside.

Apparently tonight was going to be the exception. The dog ran into the front yard, sniffing the grass as it looked for the perfect spot to relieve itself. But then she stopped and lifted her head, her nose sniffing the air as her ears perked straight up.

She let out a small whine then ran under the porch.

A chill of unease skittered up Piper's back, and she anxiously searched the yard for signs of whatever had frightened the dog.

Nothing seemed out of the ordinary, but suddenly every shadow, every dark corner of her neighbor's yards seemed to hold something sinister.

The forgotten rake leaning against the side of the shed took on the darkened shape of an assailant. The silhouette of an evergreen bush became the hunched figure of a man.

Piper scurried down the stairs and knelt beside the house, peering under the porch. "Here, girl. Please come out," she pleaded with the dog, her voice a frantic whisper.

It was too dark to see much of anything under the porch, but Piper could hear the rustling of dirt and an occasional whimper.

Her heart pounded against her chest, and she peered around the yard again, feeling suddenly exposed and vulnerable.

But what could she do? She couldn't leave the dog out here.

She shoved the plastic bag in one pocket and pulled her phone from the other, then tapped the flashlight app. Shining the light under the porch, she spotted the dog cowering in the far corner.

"Come on, girl," she coaxed, trying to keep her voice calm while everything in her screamed for her to run, to get back inside.

She patted her pockets, hoping to find a forgotten morsel of food, an unfinished power bar, a mint, anything she might be able to use to persuade the dog to come out. There was nothing. Not unless the dog could be enticed by a wadded-up tissue and a tube of lip balm. "Hold on. I'll be right back."

She stood and felt the sudden shift of movement behind her. The hair lifted on the nape of her neck, and her body went stiff.

She held her breath, trying not to make a sound as she took a cautious step back—right into the solid chest of a man.

Before she could move, strong arms snaked around her, one hand covering her mouth and the other gripping her throat.

Piper tried to scream, but no sound came out.

She struggled to take a breath against the dense fabric of the gloved hand pressing against her mouth. Her mouth went dry, and fear curdled her stomach.

Her body seemed frozen, immobile with terror.

Fight! her brain shouted.

Twisting against the constraints of her assailant's arms, she tried to break free, but he was too strong.

She gulped down a breath, her heart racing, feeling like it would explode out of her chest with every frantic beat. She tried to think, to remember the self-defense tips Edna was always drilling into their heads.

Flinging her head back, she tried to smash his face, but he was taller than her and held her too tightly against him, so her head merely thudded against his shoulder.

He had her arms pressed securely against her sides so she couldn't elbow him.

She squeezed her eyes shut and shook her head. No. This couldn't be happening. This couldn't be real.

But the pressure against her throat was real. The foul smell of onion on his breath was real.

And the slight rustling sound of plastic was real.

"No. Please no," she whimpered.

Images of Brittany's body sprawled on the floor, the grocery bag covering her face, filled Piper's mind, and her knees went weak.

What had she been thinking—coming outside alone? How could she have been so stupid? How could she have let herself get into this situation?

More importantly, how could she get herself *out* of this situation?

She wasn't dead yet. And she wasn't going down without a fight.

Think.

The sound of her heartbeat thrashed against her ears as she tried to sharpen her concentration and focus on the details.

But her efforts failed her as he dragged her around the side of the house and into the darkened shadows. He was strong. She could feel the tightened muscles of his arms as he kept her body flush to his. It didn't seem to take much exertion from him to move her, but she still felt the hot moisture of his quickened breathing against her neck.

Was he breathing harder because it took more effort than she thought or was it due to excitement?

That thought had a tremor racing through her body, and she fought to keep her teeth from chattering.

She had to get away.

She struggled against him, trying to free herself, but his hand tightened on her throat, making it harder to even breathe, let alone concentrate.

Why wasn't he saying anything?

The only sound she'd heard from him was a slight grunt when she'd tried to head-butt his shoulder.

The eerie fact he hadn't said anything scared her more than if he'd been yelling threats into her ear.

Why wasn't he speaking?

Was he afraid she'd recognize his voice?

Would she?

His hand moved from her throat and dipped into the neck of her shirt.

No. Please no. Brittany hadn't been sexually assaulted, but maybe he was upping his game.

The rough fabric of his glove scraped against her skin

then she felt him press something smooth and soft into the cup of her bra.

His cheek pressed to the side of her head, and he finally spoke, his voice a gravelly whisper in her ear. "It was supposed to be you. Now everyone will know it was supposed to be you."

Her eyes went wide as the meaning of his words hit her with the force of a strong wave in the ocean, knocking her down and tumbling her around, her body disoriented and unable to gain her footing.

It was supposed to be me?

He pulled his hand out of her shirt, and she let out a gasp, tears of relief pricking her eyes. Until she felt him reach behind her shoulders and heard again the unmistakable sound of plastic crumpling in his hand.

He whipped his arm out, shaking loose the plastic grocery bag he must have pulled from inside of his jacket or a shirt pocket.

Another whimper escaped her throat, and she couldn't take her eyes off the tan bag as he drew it closer to her face.

"Hey, what's going on back there?" a deep voice called from the front of the house.

Her assailant tightened his grip on her. "I'll be back," he growled into her ear, the threat even more menacing in an eerily whispered voice.

Then he let her go and took off, sprinting further into the back yard and hurtling himself over the cedar fence. She heard scrabbling in the gravel as he landed on the other side of the fence then the sound of his feet running down the alley.

Piper's knees finally gave way, and she crumpled to the ground.

"Are you okay?" The man who had called out a moment before hurried toward her.

She cowered against the side of the house, letting out another soft whimper, as his dark shadow loomed over her and his big hands reached toward her.

"Hey now, it's okay. I'm not going to hurt you. Remember me? We met the other day. I do maintenance on this house."

She blinked, bringing the man's face into focus as she finally recognized his voice. Lester Grimley—the handyman who'd been in her apartment. She'd been afraid of him then, even wondered if he might have been the one who'd killed Brittany.

But now he'd saved her from the real killer.

He reached out a hand to help her up, but another dark shape came rushing toward them from the front of the house and rammed into Lester, knocking the handyman to the ground.

"Get the hell away from her!" the shape yelled, planting his feet defensively in the space between Piper and the fallen man.

She knew that shape, knew that voice.

"Fitz?" She croaked out his name, her voice coming out rusty and hoarse, and she touched her throat, the skin tender and raw where her assailant's hand had been gripping her.

What was he doing here? And where had he come from?

"Don't you touch her," Fitz threatened Lester, his voice trembling with rage as he clenched his fists at his sides.

Piper reached for his hand. "Fitz, it's okay. Lester wasn't trying to hurt me. He was saving me."

"*Saving* you? From what?"

"From the guy who killed Brittany."

He whipped his head back and knelt on the ground next to her, his hands tentatively touching her shoulder.

"What happened? Are you okay?"

She nodded, then lifted her chin, trying to control the tremble that threatened it. All she really wanted to do was curl into a ball and shut out the memory of the coarse gloved hand which had been covering her mouth. She could still taste the dust and saltiness of the fabric. "I'm fine. Shaken up and scared, but I'm fine. He didn't hurt me." Not yet.

"Where is he? Where did he go?" His head turned from side to side as he wildly stared into the darkness of the yard.

Piper pointed toward the back. "He went over the fence, and I heard him running down the alley toward the campus."

"Watch her," he instructed Lester, then sprinted to the fence. He pulled himself up, locking his arms and balancing on the top as he peered down the alley in both directions.

"I don't see anyone," he called over his shoulder then dropped down and hurried back to Piper. He wrapped his arm around her and gingerly lifted her from where she still sat huddled on the ground. He tipped his head at Lester. "You'd better come with us. We've got to call the police, and I'm sure they're going to want to get a statement from you too."

"What about the dog?" she cried, trying to pull away as they walked around the front of the house. "My dog is under the porch."

Fitz guided her up the stairs and toward her apartment. "I'll go back and get her. She'll be fine for another few minutes. I'm more worried about you. You're shivering, and I think you're probably in shock. I just want to get you inside."

They entered her apartment, Lester dutifully following behind them.

Fitz sat Piper on the sofa, then grabbed a throw blanket from the chair and wrapped it snugly around her shoulders.

She wished he would sit down, wished he would keep his arm around her, but her concern for the dog was too great. She pointed a shaky hand toward a bowl of snacks which sat on the kitchen counter. "Please go get my dog. Take a granola bar to lure her out. She likes those."

"Got it. I'll be right back." He gave her shoulder a reassuring squeeze, then grabbed a granola bar from the bowl and ran out the front door.

Lester stood awkwardly inside the door, his back pressed against the wall as if he were trying to physically hold it up.

In less than a minute, Fitz was back, a dusty squirming dog in his arms. A swath of dirt ran down the front of his jacket as if he'd laid on the ground to pull her out. He smiled as he carefully placed the dog in Piper's lap. "Good call with the granola bar. She wasn't coming out until I offered her the treat." He pulled Piper's phone from his pocket. "I found this on the ground in front of the porch. I figured you must have dropped it. I think it's time we called the police."

She squeezed the dog to her chest, taking comfort from her small, warm body as the memory of being grabbed from behind overtook her. "Call Mac. His number's in my phone."

It took less than ten minutes for the tall policeman to arrive. He strode purposely through the door and knelt next to Piper. He rested a hand gently on her knee. "You okay?"

She nodded. The dog was curled by her side, and she clutched a warm cup of tea Fitz had made her. He sat back down on her other side, his thigh pressed to hers. Other than the few minutes it took him to make the tea and answer the door, he hadn't left her side.

Lester stood in the same spot, still holding up the wall.

"Tell me what happened," Mac instructed. "I've got a couple of officers checking around outside, but I need you to start from the beginning and tell me all of what you remember."

She relayed everything she could think of, starting from the time she got home.

Her body recoiled when she got to the part about him sticking his hand down the front of her shirt. Her voice trembled as she said, "I thought he was going to rape me. Even though Brittany hadn't been attacked like that, it felt so creepy. Something on his glove scratched my skin, but it also felt like he had something soft in his hand."

A shiver raced along her spine as she had a sudden thought. She took one hand from the cup and pulled out the front of her shirt. Peering down, the air left her lungs as she saw the scrap of blue fabric crumpled inside the top edge of her bra.

"What is it?" Mac asked gently. "Did he leave a mark? Are you bleeding?"

She blinked back tears as she carefully plucked the scrap of fabric from her bra and held it out to Mac. "Worse. He left me a souvenir. I'm sure this is from my sweater. The one Brittany was wearing when she was..." She swallowed, her throat tight. "When she was killed." She dropped the piece of fabric into his hand as if it carried a disease.

Her hands were shaking so badly now that some of the tea sloshed over the side of the mug. Fitz took the cup from her and set it on the coffee table, then clasped both of her hands tightly in his.

Mac pulled a plastic evidence bag from his pocket and dropped the fabric inside.

Piper's whole body was shaking now. "He said..."

She choked on a sob. She normally wasn't a crier, but tonight she couldn't seem to get her emotions under control. Her voice was raspy as she whispered, "He pushed this into my shirt then said it was supposed to be me. I was supposed to be the one who was killed, not Brittany."

"What? No way," Fitz said, taking one of his hands away and wrapping his arm around her shoulder again. "Why would someone want to hurt you?"

"I have no idea. But that's what he said." She shook her head and leaned into him. His body was warm, and she wanted to curl into his lap.

"Is there anything else you can think of? What he smelled like? How tall or broad he was? What kind of clothes he was wearing?"

She shuddered. "He smelled like onions. And sweat. He was taller than me because when I jerked my head back, I hit him in the shoulder. It was dark, but I'm pretty sure he was wearing jeans, and he had on a sweatshirt. The fabric was like forest green or maybe gray—I'm not sure what color, but it had a camouflage pattern on it, like a hunter would wear." Had he worn it because he was hunting her? Another hard shiver ran through her.

"That's good. Those are all good details. You're doing great." Mac gave her knee an encouraging pat. "I'm going to talk to Lester and go out and check in with the officers to see if they found anything. I'll be back."

She nodded, and he stood, gesturing for Lester to follow him outside.

Fitz didn't move, didn't take his arm from around her, and she curled into his side, fighting the ball of emotion burning her throat.

"I'm so sorry this happened to you," he whispered into her hair. "I wish I could make it go away. And I wish I would have been here to protect you."

She didn't know what to say. His words touched her,

but she was afraid if she tried to speak, she would start bawling.

He tipped her chin up to look at him, and the simple gesture combined with the sincere care in his eyes had a single tear escape from her eye and roll down her cheek.

Lifting his hand, he cupped her cheek and swiped the tear away with his thumb.

She thought for a second he might kiss her, even imagined the feel of his mouth against hers, and for some reason, the thought had her lips trembling and the emotion swelling inside of her like a tidal wave ready to burst.

"I know you're strong," he whispered. "But it's okay to cry. I've got you."

Oh.

The wave burst, crashing into her with the force of a tsunami. She wrapped her arms around his middle and buried her head in his shoulder as the tears came.

He held her tightly as her body shook with each sob.

She let out the tears of terror and frustration, of pain and fear, of every fragment of sorrow and desperation which had been hiding in her soul. She was pretty sure there were a few tears in there for her mom, a few sobs which came from that deep hidden place reserved for her feelings about being abandoned by her mother and the fear Claire might be gone again.

Something about Fitz made her feel safe. She fit perfectly against him, fit like she was made to be with him, and she clung to him as her body released all the sadness and fear she'd been carrying inside.

He stroked her hair and murmured soft words into her ear, but his strong arms never left her. His hold on her didn't waver, and she could almost feel his strength pouring into her, filling the empty spaces her tears left behind.

Her sobs finally ran out, and she heaved a deep

shuddering breath into his shoulder. Her fists clutched handfuls of his shirt, and she squeezed him tightly then let go, pulling back as she took another deep breath.

"You okay now?" he asked, not letting her completely go. "I can take more. You can give me all you got."

She offered him a brave smile. "I think I just did."

He reached one hand toward the coffee table and plucked a Kleenex from the box, then handed it to her.

"I may need the whole box." She blew her nose—so attractive, then grabbed another tissue to wipe her face and brush the makeup she was sure had smeared under her eyes. She glanced with horror at the mess of mascara she'd left on the shoulder of his shirt. "Oh my gosh, I'm so sorry. I messed up your shirt."

"Don't worry about it. I don't care. I've got plenty of other shirts. But I've only got one you. I would have died if anything more would have happened to you tonight—if that bastard would have hurt you. Or worse." He leaned in and laid a soft kiss against the spot on her cheek where her tears had been.

Her breath caught as he kissed the other cheek, his lips so tender her heart twisted in her chest.

Another gentle kiss, this one lower and the edge of his lip overlapped the corner of hers.

Her lips parted, and she turned into him, just the slightest movement, but it was enough.

His next kiss landed directly onto her lips, his mouth slanting against hers as he pressed three tender kisses against them, each one pressing harder, increasing with just the slightest pressure.

It was as if he thought she was fragile and didn't want to break her.

But she wasn't fragile, wasn't broken, not anymore. He was healing her, one sweet kiss at a time.

He brought one hand up to cup her cheek while his

other hand pulled her tightly against him.

This time she could feel his emotions as he held her. She dropped the soggy tissues and curled her arms around his waist, her palms flat against his muscled back as she pressed closer to him.

He deepened the next kiss, lingering longer, as if tasting her mouth.

How could this be happening?

How could she be wrapped in Fitz's arms? How could it be he was kissing her with such tenderness? And such passion?

Quit thinking about it.

She didn't want to think, didn't want to analyze the how and why. She just wanted to feel, to experience this moment, to surrender to the swirl of heat and emotion. She felt, and tasted, and smelled everything at once—from the warm pressure of his hand on her back, to the minty sweet taste of his spearmint gum, to the musky scent of his masculine cologne.

He was everything.

And she didn't want this moment to end.

She forgot about everything else, let all the fear and pain and sadness go, and focused only on this man, this moment in time.

The sound of footsteps running down the hall and then the doorknob rattling and the front door flinging open had them pulling apart, both of them struggling to catch their breath as Claire burst into the room.

Piper blinked, her chest tightening with relief at seeing her mother and frustration at Claire's poorly timed entrance.

Her mom rushed toward her. "What the hell is going on? There's two police cars out front, and Mac said you'd been attacked. Are you okay?"

The events of the night crashed into her, the bliss of Fitz's kisses overshadowed by the darkness of murder and assault.

She wanted to spring from the sofa and throw herself into the comfort of her mother's arms, but Piper hadn't found comfort there in a long time. She was usually the one offering the solace as her mom cried into her lap. Piper was the strong one, the one who rubbed her mom's back and cooed soothing words.

As much as they'd mended some of their brokenness in the last few weeks, Claire's actions tonight had torn them back apart, had shattered the thin line of trust Piper had started to let herself feel.

So, she didn't go to her mom, didn't move.

To her surprise, her mom came to her, arms outstretched.

Piper flinched, her body going rigid as Claire drew closer.

She must have read her daughter's body language because Claire dropped her arms, her shoulders sagging as she sank into the chair next to the sofa. Her expression seemed sincere, her eyes brimmed with tears as she leaned forward. "Did he hurt you?"

Piper shook her head, swallowing at the wad of emotion settling in her throat. How could she be so emotional again? She'd thought she'd cried herself dry on Fitz's shoulder, but she must have had a few tears left. "I'm fine."

Claire reached out her hand, not quite touching Piper, but resting her fingers on the edge of the seat near her leg. "I'm so sorry."

"Where were you?" The question came out harder than she'd intended. Or maybe not. Maybe that ball of emotion had more anger than sadness in it.

Her mom pulled her hand back as if Piper's words had burned her. She collapsed against the back of her chair and let out a heavy sigh. "I'm sorry. I really am. But I had to go. I had to get out of the bar."

"Why? Because you wanted a drink?"

Claire shook her head, letting out a weak chuckle. "No. Not at all. I was surprisingly fine with that part of it. It didn't even bother me to see Sunny and Edna drink. And that old lady had me in stitches."

"Then why did you leave?"

"Because of the men who walked in." She kept her eyes trained on Piper's, ignoring Fitz as if he weren't even in the room. "They were from Spider's crew. And I couldn't let them see me."

A chill of foreboding skittered down Piper's spine.

"Let's just say that I didn't leave Spider under the best of terms." She turned her gaze to stare at a spot on the floor next to Piper's foot. "More like escaped in the dead of night after the crew had gone on a solid five-hour bender," she muttered.

"So what would they have done if they'd seen you? It's not like they could make you go back to him."

Claire raised an eyebrow at her daughter. "Are you sure about that? Because I'm not. Spider's guys aren't the kind of men you want to mess with. And the ones we saw in the bar tonight—those were the nice ones."

What had her mom gotten herself mixed up in?

"If these guys are so dangerous, do you think they could somehow be responsible for Brittany's death?"

Claire shook her head. "No, I didn't leave until after she'd been killed. There's no way they could be connected to that. But I am worried about what they would do if they find me or if they try to use you as a way to get to me. Do you think the guy who attacked you tonight could have been one of the guys in the bar? A lot of those guys smoke and I'm sure most of them were drinking tonight. Did the guy smell like booze or leather or cigarettes?"

"No. He smelled like onions. I never saw his face, but I don't think he was wearing leather. Besides, I'm sure the guy who attacked me was the one who killed Brittany."

"How can you be so sure?"

She told her about the scrap of fabric and the ominous message that it should have been her.

Her mom's face paled as she clasped her hand over her mouth.

Before she could speak, a knock sounded on the front door, and Mac poked his head back in.

"We're finishing up out here," he said. "The guys did find a tan grocery sack in the yard consistent with the type used to suffocate both victims, but we can't conclude it belonged to your assailant. Didn't you say you took a grocery sack outside as a doggie bag?"

Piper reached down and pulled the bag she'd had from her pocket. "Yeah, but I still have it. And I know the bag the killer had was tan. I saw it and remember thinking it was the same kind that was used with Brittany."

"That's good to know. Unfortunately, there are a million sacks like that. But we bagged it anyway. Not sure if we can get DNA from it, but we'll hold onto it for when we catch the guy to see if we can get any comparisons."

The radio on his shoulder crackled, and he tilted his head and spoke into the mic in sharp, clipped words. "Adam Twelve. Go ahead."

The dispatcher responded with a series of codes and an address.

"Twelve. Copy that. I'm en route now." He narrowed his eyes at Piper. "I've gotta go, but I want you to stay inside, lock the doors, and don't let anyone in you don't know well or aren't related to. I'll check in on you tomorrow, but you can call me if you need me."

"Thank you," she said, but he was already gone, the door shutting behind him with a click.

"I'm not going anywhere," Claire assured her.

"I'm not either," Fitz said. "I can stay all night if you want. I'll sleep on the couch."

"You don't have to do that," Piper said. "I know you have a test tomorrow. You need to study."

"I don't care about the test."

She took a hold of his hand. "I care. You've already done enough for me. I'll be okay here with my mom." She really wanted him to stay—wanted it with everything in her, but her mind was in a tailspin, and she needed time to process everything that had happened that night.

If this thing with him were real, and she prayed it was, that him kissing her tonight wasn't just a fluke or a moment he felt sorry for her, then they would have time. One night wouldn't change that.

"I haven't done anything," he said. "And I don't feel right leaving you two here alone."

"We're not alone," Claire told him. "I've got my bodyguards, Smith and Wesson, in my bedroom. They'll protect us."

"You've got a gun?" Piper gawked at her. "Here? In the apartment?"

"Dang straight I do. There's a killer on the loose."

"Where is it?"

"Under my pillow."

"You sleep with a gun?"

"It's better than some of the things I've slept with."

Ew.

"I'm not sure if I feel better or worse." She gazed back at Fitz. "But I do know I will feel terrible if you mess up your test because of me and this stupid drama in my life."

"Having someone attack you isn't drama. And it isn't your fault," he replied. "I'll go home, but my test is at eight and then I'm coming right back over. I mean, if that's okay with you."

"That's very okay with me. I would love it." She would love it so much that her resolve over him leaving now was starting to weaken. In her head, she knew it was best if he left and they both had time to think, him about his test and her about her life and all the things which had happened the last few days, including kissing him. But her heart was crying out with a different kind of plea, one that had nothing to do with logic or what made sense. Her heart only wanted to have him near, to touch, to hold, to kiss him again.

She took a deep breath then let go of his hand and pushed up from the sofa. "You'd better go if you're still going to get in some study time tonight."

He looked like he was going to argue again, but instead followed her lead and stood as well. "At least let me take the dog out for you before I go."

She peered down at the little dog. She should probably go out one more time, but Piper had no desire to repeat her earlier attempt to let the dog outside. "Thank you. That would be nice. But this time, take her leash."

"Good idea." He grabbed her leash from the hook by

the door and snapped it on her collar. "We'll be right back."

"I'm going to get ready for bed." Claire stood and headed to her room.

While Fitz was outside, Piper quickly brushed her teeth and ran a cool washcloth over her face. Her eyes were still swollen from crying, but at least the black smudges of makeup were gone from under her eyes when she went back to answer his knock.

"All good," Fitz said, unclipping the leash and hanging it on the hook.

Piper loved the way the dog ran around her legs and acted so excited to see her, even though she'd only been gone for a few minutes.

"Thank you," she said, suddenly feeling shy and awkward and not sure where to put her hands.

He resolved her problem by stepping close and wrapping his arms around her.

Snuggling against him, she slid her arms around his back. She rested her head against his chest, loving the way her cheek fit perfectly into the depression of his shoulder. "Thank you. For everything."

"You don't have to thank me. I'm just glad to finally be here. With you. Like this." He squeezed her tighter to him.

She tipped her head back and looked up at him. "Finally?"

A smile tugged at the corners of his mouth. "I have thought about this so many times. You have to know that I've liked you forever."

"No. I didn't know that at all. If I would have, I never would have gone out with those three other stupid guys."

Including the one who might be trying to kill me.

"I thought you just did that to make me jealous. Like you were playing some kind of 'girl game.'"

"I don't play 'girl games'. I don't play games at all. I only agreed to go out with them because you said you thought my mom might be right and I should start dating again."

"I did say that. But I meant dating *me*."

Oh.

He shook his head. "I was too nervous to come right out and ask you, then I thought I missed my chance."

"What would you have to be nervous about?"

He narrowed his eyes. "Are you kidding me? Have you looked in the mirror lately?"

"Yeah, I just did. And I saw a girl with red, puffy eyes who looks like she's just been on the losing end of a fight with a tornado." She reached to smooth her mussed hair.

He caught her hand and pressed a kiss to her palm. "I see a beautiful girl who is smart and funny and has the biggest heart of anyone I know. I see a girl who always puts others ahead of herself, a girl who had her heart broken by an idiot who didn't cherish the best thing that ever happened to him, and a girl who is totally out of my league."

"Out of your league? Are you kidding me? We're not even playing in the same game."

"I know."

"No. I don't mean it like that. Geez. I could never imagine a guy like you wanting to go out with someone like me."

"What does that mean?"

"Come on, Fitz. Besides the fact you are gorgeous and all tall and muscle-y. I've also seen the textbooks you study. I don't even understand the *titles* of those books, let alone what they say inside of them. You're practically a genius." A blush of heat crept up her cheeks. "You're the Brilliant Barista."

He grinned. "The what?"

She shrugged, too embarrassed to look at him. "It's just the nickname I call you in my head. I never meant to say it out loud."

"I like it. I think I'll order myself a new name tag for work that declares it." He tilted her chin to look at him. "Seriously, Piper. I do like you."

"Why?" She whispered. "I could never be good enough for you."

"You are *too* good for me." He touched a finger to her lips. "Can't we just agree we like each other? Because I would sure rather be kissing you than wasting another second arguing."

She grinned. "See, I told you that you're brilliant."

He chuckled then slanted his mouth across hers, capturing her laugh in a kiss.

His lips were warm, soft, and she melted against him. Her hands clutched the back of his jacket as she held on, trying to keep her knees from buckling and sinking to the floor.

This felt like a dream, like something that happened to other girls, not her. Not a dorky girl who was awkward and introverted and way too much of a smart aleck. Girls like her didn't get to be thoroughly kissed by hot, brainy guys who could have their pick of whoever they wanted.

But for some crazy reason, the Brilliant Barista wanted her.

And she wanted him. Wanted him with everything in her.

Her heart pounded so hard in her chest, she was sure he could feel it beating against his. Coils of heat shimmered and swirled in her stomach, and she wanted to climb him like a monkey. Okay, so maybe that wasn't the sexiest comparison, but it was all she could think of as she clung to him, trying to get closer.

He bent forward, sliding his hands under her butt and

lifting her up. She caught her breath, but wrapped her legs around him as if it were the most natural thing in the world. And a little similar to that monkey-climbing idea.

Licks of fire burned up her spine as she wondered—hoped—he would carry her, like a fireman, to the bedroom and toss her on the bed. But instead of walking toward her bedroom, he lifted her onto the center island, setting her on the counter then laying a trail of kisses across her cheek and down her neck.

Apparently, Fitz would make a terrible fireman, because contrary to the work of an actual fireman who puts fires out, his actions only fanned the flames of her desire.

She tipped her head back, her breath ragged, as her fingers, tingling with the need to touch him, dug into his back.

His hands were everywhere, touching, rubbing, moving up her sides, up her neck to cup her face as he kissed her hard, then around her cheeks to tunnel into her hair.

Her body felt flooded with warmth, her skin flushed with heat, and she arched her back, giving him more of her to kiss, to caress.

A large thud hit the wall in her mom's room, and Fitz pulled back, leaving her breathless and already missing the warmth of his body against hers.

All her nerve endings were stirring and left tingling from his touch, and Piper tried to focus her spinning head as she called out, "You all right in there, Mom?"

"Yep," came her yelled response. "Just wanted to make sure you guys remembered that I'm here."

Fitz's cheeks were flushed and pink as an impish grin spread across his face. "Your mom's a smart one. I completely forgot she was in the next room."

"I completely forgot my own name," she said, fanning

herself with her hand.

Fitz laughed. "Nice. I should probably get going," he said, offering her a roguish grin. "Before I start kissing you again and completely forget to ever leave."

A shiver of longing swirled up her spine, and she peered up at him from under her eyelashes. "Ever?"

"Ever." He deepened his voice, affecting the tone of an English knight. "I'll drag you, my fair maiden, to your bedchamber and keep you holed up in your room for days on end—your luscious body, some ale, and an occasional slab of roast beast the only things I need for sustenance."

She giggled. "Wow. You are a total dork. Is that the voice you use when you play *Dungeons & Dragons*?"

He kept the accent, but added a sheepish grin, as he said, "Possibly. Although I've never spoke of a fair maiden or her bedchamber in any of the rounds of *D & D* I've played. And I don't think I've ever said the word 'luscious' to a woman before. Or ever used it in a sentence."

Piper shrugged and offered him what she hoped was a seductive grin. "I liked that part."

He laughed and pulled her into another hug then lifted her from the counter and set her back on her feet. He pressed a quick kiss to the top of her cheek, then spoke quietly into her hair. "I like you."

His words tickled her ear and sent another bundle of heat swirling through her belly. She hugged him back. "I like you, too."

"I'll be back over tomorrow, as soon as I finish my test."

"Sounds good."

"And I'll bring some food. Donuts or something."

"Not roast beast."

He chuckled. "No, probably donuts. But just so you know, if it came down to it, I *would* slay some roast beast for you."

His words sent a sudden chill skittering down her back. She didn't know why, but something hit her like a fist to the chest, stealing her breath, and sending a wave of dizziness through her.

"Whoa. You okay?" Fitz gripped Piper's arm to steady her. "You looked funny there for a second. I thought you might pass out or something."

She scrubbed a hand across her forehead, the feeling gone.

What the heck was that? It had been strong, but just for a second, like that funny saying about feeling as if someone had walked over your grave.

That was stupid. She didn't even have a grave. Not yet, anyway.

Maybe it was just low blood sugar. When was the last time she'd eaten? She couldn't remember. She was drained.

Did she really even feel something or was her body just mentally and physically wiped out? "I'm fine. I'm just tired."

"You've had a rough day." He tipped his chin and pressed a kiss to her forehead. "Get some sleep. I'll text you in the morning."

"Good luck on your test." She closed the door after him, pressing in the lock and twisting the deadbolt into place.

She checked the latches on the windows and turned off all the lights in the main room. The dog followed her into her bedroom and jumped on the bed as she switched on her bedside lamp and crawled in after her.

It felt good to crawl under the covers and sink into her pillow. Her body felt drained like all her energy was spent.

"Hey," her mom said, poking her head into her

bedroom. "You okay?"

"Yeah. I think so. Just tired."

Claire nodded to the chair piled with clothes in the corner of the room. "You want me to stay in here with you tonight? I could move those clothes and sleep in the chair."

Piper shook her head, surprised—and touched, by the offer. "No, but I appreciate the thought."

"Mind if I sit?"

"Knock yourself out."

Claire settled on the end of the bed. The little dog, who had been curled by Piper's shoulder, got up and crossed the comforter to sniff at her mom's cheek. The dog settled next to her, resting her head on Claire's leg.

She smiled and brushed a hand across the dog's head. "She really is kind of a cute thing. Have you settled on a name yet?"

"Yeah. Actually, I just decided tonight. I'm going to call her Nola."

"Nola?"

"It's short for her favorite snack—granola bars."

Claire chuckled. "Cute. It fits her too." She scratched the dog's ear, a faraway look in her eye. "You know, I really loved your dad."

A lump landed solidly in Piper's throat. What part of left field had that come out of? "I know."

"I'm not sure you do, but I hope you find out. I hope you love someone that much someday. Or maybe not. Maybe you should hope you never do. Because having a love like that, one so strong, one where you feel so connected to the other person, almost as if you are one soul, can consume you. And it can rip you apart when you lose it. Like slash open giant holes inside of you. Holes in you that you don't know how to fill. Holes and rips so deep and painful you don't know how to breathe around them, how to survive the damage of them."

Her mom hadn't talked much about her dad's death, not in a long time, and not with such genuine honesty.

Claire's gaze remained fixed on the opposite wall, and she absently rubbed the back of her hand as she spoke. "When Denny died, I didn't know what to do. I didn't know how to live without him—didn't know how to live at all. I just fell apart. And that wasn't fair. It wasn't fair to you." Her eyes brimmed with tears, but they didn't spill over. "I was selfish and callous. I could only think about myself—about *my* pain and what I was going through. But that was so wrong of me. I see that now. I didn't then. I couldn't see beyond my own suffering. But I see it now. I see how I was so wrapped up in myself that I didn't help this precious little girl who was hurting too—who had just lost her daddy."

A lone tear slipped from Piper's eye and rolled down her cheek.

She didn't wipe it away, didn't move, she barely breathed as she listened to her mom say the things she had always longed to hear.

"That poor little girl. It shatters my heart to think about what I did to her. She must have been so lonely."

I was.

"I never should have left."

No. You shouldn't have.

"I don't know what I was thinking. I wasn't. I wasn't thinking, and I hate myself for what I did. It was negligent and reckless. I was careless with the only important thing I had left in my life—the most important thing. You."

Yes. You were.

Everything her mom was saying was true. But hearing the words and hearing her recognize and for the first time sound regretful, and remorseful, for what she'd done was making Piper's stomach hurt and her chest burn with the emotions battering against it.

"I don't know what to do or how to fix it. I can't go back. I can't change what I did. I can only go forward and try to do better. *Be* better. Be a better mom." She tore her gaze from the wall finally and looked at Piper. Her face was pale, and she bit down on her bottom lip as if trying to keep it from trembling. "And that starts with telling you I'm sorry."

Piper's arms were crossed, and she held them tightly around her stomach, as if trying to hold herself together. She forced herself to swallow over the painful ache in her throat. "Thank you," she whispered. "Thank you for saying that."

"It's true, baby. I'm so utterly, desperately sorry." Her voice caught as she said, "Can you forgive me?"

Piper wanted to. She wanted to hug her, to crawl into her lap like she'd done when she was a little girl—to let her mom rub her back and kiss her hurts away. But she couldn't. Not yet. The wounds from her mom's abandonment were too raw. She'd thought they were scabbed over, dried out, and merely scars by now. But evidently, they were just festering, waiting to be picked open and to bleed again.

She didn't know how to do this. It had been so long— if ever—that her mom had spoken frankly with her, had tried to communicate with her at all. She wanted to tell her everything was okay, that all was forgiven and everything would be great now. But she couldn't do that either.

She wanted to say those things, but the words wouldn't come out of her mouth. Instead, she took a deep shuddering breath and simply said, "I'm trying."

A faint smile crossed her lips, and Claire gave her head a small nod. "Thank you. That's all I can ask for. And that's what I'm doing too."

Nola rolled over between them, splaying out her legs

and offering her belly up for a rub as she let out a funny little groaning sound.

Claire laughed as they both reached to rub the dog's belly. "This little mutt is growing on me."

Piper smiled. "Me, too. I never knew I wanted a dog, but now I can't imagine not having her."

"Life does crazy things sometimes."

"Agreed. And it's sure been crazy lately. You missed it tonight. We actually were asked to leave the bar because Edna used her stun gun on a couple of dudes who were trying to get her to smoke weed with them."

Claire's eyes widened, then she burst out laughing. "Where did that lady come from? She is hysterical." She tilted her head. "Although it might be funny to get Edna baked. She would be hilarious."

"That's what those guys thought. But she told them the only thing she bakes is cookies."

Claire chuckled. "Of course she did."

Piper's hand stilled on the dog's belly. "Are you worried about those guys? The ones from Spider's crew."

Her mom's smile fell, and her shoulders slumped forward. She sighed, the sound filled with a weariness that came from somewhere deep inside. "I'm worried about a lot of things." She rested her hand lightly on Piper's and gave it a light squeeze then stood up. "But right now, I'm worried about you and thinking you need to get some sleep."

Piper scrunched down under the covers.

Her mom started for the door then turned back and leaned down to press a quick kiss on Piper's forehead, just like she'd done when Piper was a little girl.

She squeezed her eyes shut against another sudden prick of tears. Geez, what was with her and all the water works tonight? She must be tired.

Nola curled up against her shoulder as her mom

turned out the bedside lamp.

Claire stopped in the doorway. "Hey, Piper. You were wrong, ya know? With Fitz, earlier. And what you said. You *are* good enough for him. You're good enough for whoever you choose to go out with. *They* are the lucky ones to be chosen by you."

Her mouth dropped open, and she rolled over. "You were listening?"

"Of course."

She rolled her eyes but also let out a soft chuckle. *Of course she was listening.* She was her mother after all. "Good night, Mom."

"Good night, Pip."

🐾 🐾 🐾

The next morning, Piper and Claire went about their morning routines, showering and getting dressed pretty much the same as they'd done every other morning since Claire had moved in, but today felt different. The air in the apartment seemed a little easier to breathe, like the tension had dissipated or some of the anxiety had eased.

They didn't talk about the heart-to-heart chat they'd had the night before, but her mom offered her an open smile and handed her a cup of coffee as she wandered into the kitchen and took a seat at the table.

"How'd you sleep?" Claire asked.

"Surprisingly well," Piper answered, then took a sip of the hot coffee. She'd thought she would lay awake or sleep in terrified fitful spurts and her dreams would have been filled with nightmares of shadowy figures, but her body must have been exhausted because she dozed right off and slept through the night. "Now I need coffee and sugar."

A knock sounded at the front door, and a deep voice called through the wood. "It's me, Fitz, and I come bearing donuts."

Claire gave her a teasing chuckle. "Your wish is his command."

Piper's heart raced as she tried not to run to the door. She said she needed sugar, but she didn't really give a fig about the donuts, she just wanted to see Fitz. She threw the door open and tried to contain the grin spreading across her face. "Hi."

Wow. All that build-up and that's all she had to say.

"Hi." He grinned back, his eyes crinkling at the edges from his smile being so big.

She didn't know what to do—should she hug him, plant a kiss on his cheek, or just stand there and look like a complete dork?

Apparently, she was going with the dork-move because she didn't know how to hug him around the box of donuts and the over-stuffed backpack slung over his shoulder.

"Come on in," Claire said, thankfully breaking the awkwardness of the two of them standing there goofily staring at each other. "Piper was just saying she needed some sugar."

Piper whipped her head back to give her mom one of her trademark "Really, Mom?" glares, but Claire had already turned to the sink, her shoulders shaking with silent laughter at her own joke.

Fitz dropped his crammed backpack inside the door and it hit the floor with a thud.

"Geez, how many books do you have in there?" Piper asked.

"In number or cost-value?" He chuckled at his own joke as he crossed the room and set the donuts on the counter. *Nerd humor.*

Everyone in her apartment thought they were a comedian today.

"How'd you do on your test?" She plucked a chocolate-covered glazed donut from the box and bit into its puffy, sugary side.

"Good, I think. It's hard to tell sometimes. This was more like a quiz, and I was pretty comfortable with the equations we've been working on, so I feel pretty good about it." He pulled a rawhide bone from his jacket. "I brought a treat for the dog, too."

Piper's heart melted like the chocolate on her donut. "Wow. That was nice. You didn't have to do that."

"I wanted to. I think she's adorable." He bent down and held the bone out to the dog. "Come here, No Name. Come and get it, girl."

The dog raced toward him then stopped and tentatively took the offered bone. Once she had it in her teeth, she made cute little growly noises at it as she gnawed on one end.

"She does have a name now," Piper told him, laughing at the dog's funny antics.

"Yeah?"

"Yes, it's Nola."

He grinned. "For the bars she loves?"

She nodded. She knew he'd get it.

"Nice." He scratched the dog's ears. "You're a good dog, Nola."

The dog tore her attention from the rawhide to give his hand a quick lick, earning her a chuckle from Fitz and an "aww" from Piper.

Another knock sounded on the door.

Piper glanced from Fitz to her mom. "You expecting anyone?"

Fitz approached the door. "Who is it?"

"It's Edna Allen," a voice called back. "Who are you, and what are you doing in Piper's apartment?"

Fitz grinned and pulled open the door. "Hi Edna."

She strode in, briefly offering Fitz a small smile and a pat on the arm then heading straight for Piper and threw her arms around the girl. "Oh honey, I heard about what happened last night. I'm so sorry. Are you okay?"

Piper nodded and squeezed the older woman back. "I'm fine. I was a little shaken up last night, but I'm okay today."

"Why didn't you call me?"

She shrugged. "Nothing really happened. He let me go, and he got away. I didn't want to bother anyone, especially since I didn't really have much to say besides I was an idiot and put myself in a vulnerable position by standing right outside of my house in the dark."

Edna took a firm hold of her arm. "This isn't your fault. And it doesn't matter about you calling, I'm here now. And I brought reinforcements. They're parking the car."

Footsteps sounded in the hall, and Fitz, who was still standing by the door, opened it to let Sunny and a tall, gorgeous, muscled guy in.

The guy was Jake Landon, Sunny's boyfriend and a former FBI agent turned private eye.

Their faces were grim, and they both followed Edna's suit and wrapped Piper in a group hug.

"I appreciate all of the love, you guys, but I'm really okay." She glanced from one to the other as a feeling of dread slithered along her spine. "Not that I'm not always glad to see you, Jake, but why do I need reinforcements? Did something happen?"

His mouth was set in a tight line, and he used his 'official' voice to say, "Yes, it did. Last night around zero-one-thirty hours. There was another attack."

Piper's knees gave way.

Jake reached out and grabbed her before she collapsed to the floor. He guided her to the sofa, and she crumpled into it.

Her mom rushed to the sink and got her a glass of water, pressing it into her hands. She absently took a drink then set it on the coffee table in front of her.

She didn't hear him move, but suddenly Fitz was sitting by her side, wrapping his arm around her shoulder. She leaned into him, thankful for the support. He smelled like aftershave, laundry detergent and coffee, and she wanted to bury her head in his shoulder and forget all of this. Forget about murder and assault and being afraid.

All she'd wanted was to go off to college and live a normal, ordinary life. She wanted to date a boy and have all those 'new date' and 'first kiss' kind of experiences with him. Instead, she was having 'walk to class with her so she didn't get murdered' kind of experiences, and they were *not* the same. When she thought about how many times she'd flippantly thought she'd *just die* if Fitz didn't pay attention to her or brush up against her as they worked, or kiss her, she wanted to bury her head in a pillow, because Brittany really had died.

The Page Turners book club had gone through some rough stuff this summer. They'd helped solve murders, and Edna and Maggie had even been kidnapped, but this was somehow different. This time, it was happening to her. *She* was the victim. Or the alleged victim. Or the intended victim. Or whatever she was, she knew she hated it.

She didn't want to be *any kind* of victim.

She'd spent the last half of her life being the 'girl whose dad died in that awful motorcycle crash' or the 'girl whose mom didn't want her' or 'that weird new girl at school.'

She was tired of being those girls, tired of being afraid, tired of always feeling like the stupid victim.

Every part of her screamed she wanted to stand on her own two feet, to take care of herself, to shrug off all this concern, and to stop being weak-kneed and collapsing all over the place.

Well, maybe not *every* part. There was still one tiny part of her that was scared to death. That was terrified to be home alone or to go outside in the dark. One tiny part that reminded her it was okay to be a little afraid—being afraid made her cautious, made her smart, made her think carefully about her decisions.

But being afraid and being weak were two different things. And she hated that this guy, this killer, was making her feel weak.

She took a deep breath and squeezed Fitz's hand. Everyone was looking at her like she'd grown a third eye or something. "It's okay, you guys. I'm not that fragile. And I'm not going to fall apart. I lost it for a second, but I've got it back together."

Jake gave her an encouraging wink.

A sudden thought hit her. "Wait. You said 'attack'. Not murder."

"Yeah, thankfully," Jake said. "The victim was attacked in the same manner as the others, but he somehow survived. Maybe the killer was interrupted in the middle and took off. We don't know for sure. Regardless of what happened, he's still alive. But he's in the hospital and hasn't regained consciousness."

"He?"

"Yeah, this time it was a guy."

"Then how do they know it was the same killer? The last two victims have been girls."

Jake shrugged. "Same MO."

"So who was the guy?"

"His name is David Taylor. Does that ring a bell with you?" Jake asked then stuffed half of a donut into his mouth.

"No, I don't think so. Should it?"

"He's a student here at the college, *and* he went to high school with you."

"I keep telling you guys, there were a lot of kids at that school, and I only went there for a couple of months before I graduated. I didn't meet a lot of people." She turned to Fitz. "You went there forever. Did you know him?"

He shook his head, his brows knit together in concentration. "I don't think so. The name doesn't sound familiar. Maybe if I saw him…"

"Didn't you say you were going to try to track down your yearbook from last year?" Edna asked.

"Yeah, I did. I found it last night and stuffed it in my backpack. I've got it with me." He lugged his bag over, then unzipped it and dug through the stacks of books and folders crammed inside. He pulled free a slim gray book and held it up. "Here it is."

Edna snatched it from his hand and spread it open on the table in front of them. She flipped through the pages until she got to the seniors, running her finger down the lists of names until she found the one she wanted.

She jabbed a picture with her finger. "Here he is. David Taylor. He looks angry, and he's got more holes in him than my colander."

Cassie looked over her shoulder. "Those are called

piercings, Edna. And that's about how Piper looked when she first came to stay with us."

Edna turned the book toward Piper. "Does he look familiar?"

Her breath caught in her throat. "Yeah, I know him. Or I did. We hung out a little bit when I first started there. Except I never knew his name was David."

"How did you hang out with him and never know his name?" Claire asked.

"Because he didn't go by David. I only knew him as Dragon. It was a kind of a thing the Goth kids in that group did—they changed their names and all went by something different, something they felt fit their personality better. It was a name they chose, and his was Dragon."

Edna studied the picture. "He doesn't look like much of a dragon—maybe more like an elephant. What in the world is wrong with his ears? They droop almost to his shoulders."

Piper rolled her eyes. "Those are called gauges. You put them in your ears and keep increasing them in size to make the holes in your ears bigger. It's a style kind of thing."

Edna's eyes went as round as Dragon's gauges. "You mean to tell me he did that to his ears on purpose?"

"Yes." Piper refrained from rolling her eyes a second time, but it was an effort. "Now can we stop talking about his ears and focus on why he was attacked."

"What could he have in common with the other girls? Do you think he knew your roommate?"

Piper's stomach roiled and the few bites of donut she'd taken threatened to come back up. "It doesn't matter if he did or not."

"How can you say that? There has to be a connection to these three kids—something which ties them together and is making this monster go after them."

"That might be, but it doesn't have anything to do with Brittany." She knew she had to tell them, she just couldn't seem to get the words out.

"You lost me," Edna said, staring at her in confusion. "How can it not have anything to do with Brittany? She was the first victim."

"But she wasn't the intended victim. Last night, when I was attacked, the guy told me that killing Brittany was a mistake." Piper swallowed, and her voice dropped to a whisper. "It was supposed to be me."

Edna and Sunny gasped at the same time.

"It was the sweater," Piper told them, fighting back the prick of tears stinging eyes. "We had the same color hair and the same build, and she was wearing my sweater, and he thought she was me."

"Oh honey," Edna said, sitting on the coffee table in front of Piper and rubbing her knee. "That must have been a shock to hear."

She let out her breath in a hard laugh. "Yeah, you could say that."

"Well then, that's even more reason we need to find this bastard and take him out at the knees."

Edna always did have a way with words.

"So if Brittany wasn't the intended victim…" Sunny said, tapping a finger against her chin. "Then we've been looking at this from the wrong angle. We need to throw out everything which connects Lisa and David, I mean Dragon, or whatever, to Brittany, and figure out how these two are connected to you."

"That makes sense," Piper said, glad to have something else to focus on. "But I have no idea what that connection could be. I didn't even know the other girl."

"Are you sure?" Edna asked, reaching for the yearbook. "You didn't think you knew David either.

Maybe you might recognize Lisa if you saw her picture." She flipped a few pages then scanned the pictures. "Hmmm."

"What's wrong?" Piper asked, peering over the top of the book.

"I saw a picture of the girl who was murdered in the paper, and she didn't look like this." Edna squinted at the book. "Well, maybe she did. But in the paper, she had normal hair and was dressed in ordinary clothes. This picture makes her look more like the other boy, with her hair all dyed and spiky."

"Let me see." Piper took the book and glanced down at the picture. The donut made another attempt at returning. "I do know her. But not as Lisa. She introduced herself as Luna, and that's the only thing I ever called her." A fresh wave of grief rolled through her. "She was the first person to talk to me when I started at that school. She sat with me at lunch on my first day. She and Dragon."

Fitz ran his hand along her shoulder. "Sorry. This has got to be tough on you."

She shook her head. "Not as tough as it was on them. I'm still alive." The implication had her head reeling.

"That's right," Edna said. "And that's how you're going to stay. Claire, get a new sheet of paper. We've got to start over and look at this with fresh eyes. Let's go over everything we know about these two and see how we can connect them to Piper. And we can add Jake's input, as well."

The group followed Edna's orders and all moved to the kitchen table.

Claire pulled another giant post-it page from the pad and stuck it to the wall then uncapped a marker and stood ready to write. "Okay Pip, tell us everything you can remember about these two kids. Think of all the times you hung out with them or the places you went with them."

"That's just it. I didn't really hang out with them. I mean, I saw them at school, and I went to the mall with Luna once. We didn't really do anything there except walk around and look in some lame stores. I think she may have lifted a pair of earrings that day, but that wouldn't be enough reason for someone to kill her."

Claire marked a few notes on the paper. "What else?"

Piper scrubbed the heel of her hand against her forehead. "I don't know. It's not like we were besties. We basically just dressed the same. I was pretty angry when I first started that school. I wasn't looking for friends or to hang out with anyone. I just wanted to be left alone. That's kind of the point of the whole Goth thing. Most kids who are into it, especially ones in high school, are mad at the world. They're angry, and they show it through their clothes and their makeup and their hair. And their attitudes. We weren't sitting around having deep conversations. We were all too busy brooding in our own garbage. I wasn't that hardcore, like with all the music and gauges and stuff, but I did feel like the black clothes and dark hair and makeup sent a message to people that I didn't want to talk to them and to leave me alone."

"And the sullen expression helped too," Edna pointed out. "You were one pissed-off kid. I remember when Cassie first brought you to book club. I don't think you said one word the whole night, but the anger rolled off of you in thick waves of resentment and rage."

Memories of that time—those feelings, swirled through Piper, and she avoided looking at her mom. Both of them knew why she'd been so angry and resentful. "The point is, I didn't really hang out or ever *go* out with anyone. I didn't go to parties or school events. I went to school, then came home and shut myself in my room. Until Cassie dragged me to her book club, and I was adopted by a crazy bunch of her friends." She offered a small smile to Sunny and Edna. "And then I met Drew. And everything changed. I changed. I dropped the Goth act, and stopped hanging around those kids. But I still didn't go out much, except to a few of Drew's soccer games."

"There has to be something that connects you," Sunny said. "Could it somehow be the Goth thing?"

"I can't imagine that. We were angry. But I don't think we hurt anyone besides ourselves. We didn't talk to anyone. How could we make anyone upset enough to hurt us? Besides, I was only hanging out with that crowd for a couple of weeks."

"Keep thinking."

"I will." She pushed back from her chair and stood. "Sorry guys, I've got to get ready."

"Get ready for what?" Claire asked.

"I've got class today, and I work this afternoon."

"Are you joking? Do you remember what happened last night? There's no way you're leaving this apartment."

"Of course I remember. But what am I supposed to do? Stay home the rest of my life and hide in my room?"

"Yes," Claire cried. "Yes, that is exactly what you're supposed to do. You're supposed to do whatever it takes to keep you safe…and alive."

Her mom's words struck a chord, but she couldn't just hole up in their apartment. "I can't skip class every day. And I can't hide in my room until this guy is caught."

"We are not saying *every* day for the rest of your life," her mom said, mimicking her daughter's sarcasm. "Just until we feel like you're safe."

"That could be months from now." She planted her fists on her hips. "If I hide, then he wins." She knew her reasoning was sound, she just wished she felt as brave as she was acting.

"I hear what you're saying," Fitz said gently. "But you staying safe is what matters to all of us. I know you want to go to class. I'm happy to walk you to campus again."

"But what about *your* classes? I know you have Computer Science this morning." This was turning into a thing again. And everyone was staring. She hated people making a fuss over her.

"I can miss one class."

"Nobody has to miss any of their classes," Jake said, raising his hands between them. "I have the day off, and I'm planning to walk Piper to class and sit in with her. That's what I'm here for—to be the muscle." He shrugged his well-defined pecs at Fitz. "Sorry dude, no offense."

Fitz shrugged back. "None taken. I know my strength lies in my brain over my brawn."

There was no arguing with Jake's brawn, but still, Piper hated to have him spend his day chaperoning her around. The whole point of her moving out was to show everyone she could take care of herself. "No one has to walk me to class. I can manage on my own."

"Non-negotiable, kiddo." Jake picked up another donut and nodded toward Sunny and Edna. "I've been given my instructions by these two that I'm on bodyguard duty today, and I am much more scared of them than I am of you."

Edna pointed a sparkly pink nail-polished finger at her. "That's right. So, if you insist on going to class, Jake is going with you."

"Fine. But I think we all know who the *real* muscle is around here," Piper muttered.

"I'll be with you at work," Fitz said. "If you still want to come in for your shift this afternoon. Or we can cover for you if you're not feeling up to it."

Piper glared at him. "I'm not an invalid. I can make

coffee drinks and serve some muffins. I'll let *My Bodyguard* walk me to class and will cover my own shift at work. I really doubt he's going to come into the coffee shop and attack me while I'm making lattes."

"Okay. Okay." He offered her a cautious grin. "We get off at the same time tonight, and I'd be glad to give you a ride home. Not because I don't think you can take care of yourself, but because I want to spend time with you."

She begrudgingly agreed, her heart doing a little flip at his words. She wanted to spend time with him too. Just not because of some wacko dude who was out to get her.

"All right, it's settled then," Edna said, resting a hand gently on Piper's arm. "I know you hate anyone making a fuss over you and you want to be brave and independent, but we're doing it because we care about you and don't want to see anything happen to you."

Piper's shoulders sagged, and she gave the elderly woman a quick hug. "I know. I just want this to be over."

"I know you do, sweetie." Edna reached into the front of her shirt, pulled a pink rectangular box from her bra, and handed it to Piper. "But until it is, I want you to take this. Put it in your bra or your pocket—wherever you can get to it the easiest."

"What the hell is that?" Jake asked, peering down at the pink box.

Piper knew what it was, and she zipped it into the front pocket of her hoodie. She recognized it from the night before. Edna had given her The Terminator.

❀ ❀ ❀

Piper kept the pink stun gun in her pocket all afternoon. It made her feel like she had at least a tiny amount of control.

Jake had walked her to and from class and dropped

her off at the coffee shop without even a hint of trouble. She tried not to even think about the fact a killer was out there and might be watching or waiting for her.

Although walking around campus with Jake by her side instigated plenty of other people's stares.

She'd spent the last several hours distracting herself by helping customers, making lattes and cappuccinos, and trying to figure out how to nonchalantly ask Fitz to meet her in the back storeroom to make out.

He'd found plenty of ways to brush up against her or stand so close that their hands or their hips touched. He'd even given her a quick hug when she'd shown up for work, but a quick hug wasn't enough to cut it. She wanted more. She wanted to throw her arms around his neck, to mash her lips against his, to taste the caramel flavoring in the latte he'd just drank, to melt into him.

She wanted to forget about the rest of the world and the psychopath who was hunting her, and just be a girl who ached to be kissed by a boy.

The coffee shop had just emptied, and Piper thought they might have a chance to sneak in a kiss. Then the bell above the door rang again, and she let out a groan as she turned back to the register, already pasting a smile on her face.

Her welcoming smile turned to a frown as she took in the two women who had just entered the coffee shop. "What are you doing here?"

"What?" her mom asked innocently. "Can't I just have a coffee with my sister?"

Cassie feigned innocence as she avoided eye contact with her niece and studied the pastries in the glass display case.

The bell dinged again, and Sunny, Maggie, and Edna walked through the door.

Edna stopped and put her hand to her chest. Her voice

took on her southern damsel imitation as she said, "Well, my heavens, what are you two doing here? What a coincidence."

Coincidence, my foot.

"Seriously?" Piper arched an eyebrow at the Page Turners. "You don't have to babysit me." They were all trying to look so innocent she wasn't about to tell them that a part of her was glad to see them and felt loved by their thoughtfulness.

"That's ridiculous," Edna claimed. "We didn't even know your mother and aunt would be here. Even though I'm sure they are just worried about you and want to make sure you're all right. As for the three of us, we just felt like having some Frack-uccinos."

Piper chuckled. "I think you mean *frapp*uccinos."

"Whatever." Edna waved a hand in dismissal. "I'll take one of those. Chocolate with lots of whipped cream. And do you have any of those little chocolate chips you can stir in there? I'm feeling adventurish tonight."

"Sure." Who was she to stand in the way of a chocolate and whipped cream adventure where a blue-haired old lady was concerned?

Edna jerked a thumb at Maggie and offered Piper a wink. "And Maggie's paying, so you can get one too."

"Thanks." She took their orders as Fitz came out from the back to help make their drinks. He grinned and waved hello to the group.

"No one is trying to babysit you," Maggie said, as she handed Piper her debit card. "We're just worried about you. I know your real mom is back, but you've got four other women who've been filling in for her the last several months and it's hard for us to relinquish that role."

Piper nodded. "Thanks, Mags." She knew Maggie got it, knew she understood. Of all the Page Turners, Maggie was the most fiercely independent. Not only did she have to prove herself in the courtroom as an attorney, she'd been through a pretty rough divorce and tended to have her own fairly significant chip on her shoulder at times.

"Why don't you take a break and sit with them," Fitz said as he handed Maggie her chai tea—no fluffy whipped up coffee drink for her. "Since they did all *accidentally* show up here at the same time and will *coincidentally* end up staying for the next few hours, I'm sure."

"True," she said. "And I could use a break." She looked around the otherwise empty shop. "You could use a break, too. We should be dead for a while. Why don't you come hang out with us?"

They each grabbed a drink and pulled up chairs next to the Page Turners group.

Before they could get too deep in conversation, the shop door opened, and Kyle walked in.

"Hey bro," Fitz said, waving him over to the group. "You look awful."

"I feel awful," he said, slumping into an empty chair next to his friend. "I've got a class in half an hour, and I'm trying to get it together and show up. Otherwise I'm going to flunk out."

Fitz clapped a hand on his shoulder. "You can do it." He gestured to the women around the table. "You remember Piper? And this is her book club. She can introduce you while I make you a drink. What do you want?"

"Mocha latte with a triple shot."

"You got it."

"Um, well, this is Kyle," Piper said, acting like they didn't all already know who he was and hadn't spied on him during an undercover mission at the dive bar. "He dated Brittany, my roommate."

He eyed the women as Piper introduced them. "Some of you look familiar—like I've seen you before."

"Well, I wouldn't presume to know where," Edna said, the southern belle voice back in attendance.

Fitz strode back and handed Kyle a to-go cup. "Here ya go. It's on the house."

"You don't have to do that."

"No worries. You covered our drinks the other night."

He groaned. "Yeah, about that. I wasn't really in my right head that night, and I'm sorry for telling you all that crazy stuff. I get way too chatty when I've been drinking."

"It's okay. It's a rough time." He glanced at Piper, then back at Kyle. "I'm not sure if you heard, but another kid from our school got attacked last night. His name was David Taylor, but I think he went by the nickname Dragon."

Kyle's eyes went wide. "No shit? I knew that kid. He hung around with Lisa." He lowered his voice. "You know, that girl I was telling you about."

"Yeah, Piper knew them, too. And we were talking about them this morning. Trying to find a connection between them. We were wondering if it might have anything to do with them both being Goth. Like a hate crime or something. What do you think?"

"No way," he said, taking a drink of his coffee. "It can't be that. Because Lisa didn't look like that anymore. She'd totally changed, got rid of the black hair and all the makeup. When I saw her on campus, I almost didn't recognize her. And no way could Brittany ever be considered Goth—I don't think she even owned any black clothes."

Piper swallowed and glanced at Fitz. They both knew it didn't matter if Brittany was Goth or not, because she wasn't the intended victim.

"Can you think of any other way in which Lisa and Dragon could be connected?"

"Nah. I never really even talked to the kid. I just saw

him sometimes at school. And he was at that party I was telling you about. I remember seeing him talking to this cheerleader and thinking she was way out of his league, then later he was passed out in this big chair in the living room, and she was curled up in his lap. Everything about that night was crazy." He stared at his cup, twisting it in his hands. "I wish I never would have gone to that stupid party. If it hadn't been the end of the season, I wouldn't have risked it. But it was Senior Sneak Day, and everybody was going."

"Wait a minute," Piper said, a flash of memory sparking at his words. "Did you say it was Senior Sneak Day?"

Kyle nodded.

"Did the house, the one where the party was, did it have a little pond with a cool waterfall in the backyard?"

"Yeah, something like that. I didn't really check it out, but I remember some kid walking around in his boxers because he'd said he'd fallen into a pond."

"I remember that kid. I saw him, too. He had on purple boxers and was wearing a twelve-pack box on his head."

"Yeah, that's right. What an idiot. I told you that night was crazy." Kyle drained the last of his drink then stood. "I gotta get going. Thanks for the coffee. Nice to meet you all." He tossed the cup in the trash as he went out the door.

"See ya around." Fitz absently waved then turned back to Piper with a quizzical look. "I'm confused. How did *you* see that guy? The one at the party in the purple boxers?"

"Because I was at that party, too."

"I can't believe I didn't remember that night." Piper chewed on her lip trying to recall the events of the night. "It wasn't until he brought up Senior Sneak Day that it hit me."

"But I thought you said you never went to parties," Fitz said.

"I didn't. And I didn't really *go* to that one either. Well, I guess I went, but I didn't stay." She shook her head. "I didn't put it together before, but I remember now. It was just a few days after I'd started school, and that week is still kind of a blur. After that first day, I started sitting with Luna and Dragon and a couple of other kids at lunch, and I remember them talking about Senior Sneak Day and how it was so fun because all the seniors skipped class and partied. I didn't care about the partying, but I was all-in when it came to skipping school." She shrugged at her aunt. "Sorry. I was a mess then."

Cassie nodded. "I know. And I knew about Senior Skip Day. I was just glad you'd made a friend and wanted to leave the house."

"I hadn't planned on leaving the house at all. A skip day to me meant hanging out alone in my room, but Luna invited me to some party—insisted that it was going to be the event of the year. I didn't want to go… I was even more antisocial than what I am now. But she wouldn't take no for an answer and came to the house to pick me up. She was driving this fancy black Lincoln. She said it was her dad's car—she probably stole it. I remember it was the nicest car I'd ever been in, all leather and these huge back seats. And it smelled like Old Spice, and money, and just a little bit like stale weed. I never could figure out if that weed smell was from her dad or from the other kids in the car."

"Who were the other kids?" Cassie asked.

"There were four of us. Dragon and I were in the back and…" She searched her memory, trying to recollect the fourth person. "I can't remember the kid's name who was in the front with Luna. It was a guy, but I don't think he said a single word to me. All I can remember is he had this really long, kind of greasy hair, and it hung across one side of his face, like completely covering it, so it looked like he only had one eye. Oh, and he had this tattoo along his arm of a dragon with a sword stuck in his neck, and I kept staring at it and thinking Dragon should be the one with a tattoo of a dragon on his arm. I remember finding that much more amusing than it should have been. It was probably just my way of distracting myself from the torture ahead of me, because the closer we got to the party, the more I was dreading it. I don't like beer and cigarette smoke gives me a headache. I don't like being around people all that much anyway, but I hate being around people I don't know. And I loathe being forced to make stupid small talk."

"Some things never change," her mother muttered.

Considering the heart-to-heart they'd had the night before, Piper hoped that wasn't true. But she didn't have time to think about that right now. Her brain was busy trying to recall a night she'd rather forget.

"We finally made it to the party, and I was right. It was horrible. I didn't know a single person, and I hated being there. But I do remember the pond with the neat waterfall. I found it when I escaped into the backyard trying to find some fresh air that didn't smell like smoke or pot or stale beer. I sat by that waterfall for probably half an hour—just thinking and listening to the water. It was the only good thing about that night so far. I was hating life and hating being there."

"We get the picture, honey. You hated everything," Edna said.

Piper sighed. "I know. I did. I was miserable and depressed, and I just wanted to go home and back to my room. But I couldn't find Luna or Dragon, and I didn't see that other kid either. I figured if they didn't care where I was, then they wouldn't notice if I left, so I just took off. I walked all the way home. It took me almost an hour. I remember I cut through the park, and I saw a fox. It had this jacked-up ear—like half of it had been torn off or something. It's funny, the way your memory works. The details you can recall. I can almost hear the sound of that waterfall, and I can clearly remember seeing that fox with its one messed up ear, but I can't remember anything about the kid who came with us other than the way he wore his hair and some ink on his arm."

"The mind does funny things." Cassie patted her arm.

"That was a great story, kid," Edna said, "but how does it help us figure out who is after you?"

Piper's shoulders slumped forward. "It doesn't, I guess. Maybe we're looking in completely the wrong direction. We keep looking back at high school, but maybe we need to be looking forward. Maybe the connection has nothing to do with high school and something to do with college."

"But I thought the only connection you had with those kids was a few weeks in high school," Claire said.

"That we know of. But maybe there is something we're missing. The lecture halls here are huge, maybe we had a class together."

Edna shook her head. "That couldn't be it, because the first murder happened on your first day of classes. This thing started before you would have had courses with any of them."

"Maybe something happened over the summer," Fitz offered. "Did you see any of them this summer? At the lake or up at High Point?" He mentioned two places popular for kids to hang out, especially in the summer. She noticed he didn't bring up Drew's name, and she wasn't sure if that was intentional or not.

"No. I've never been to either of those places. I told you I'm not big on going out. I mostly hung out with Drew this summer. And these guys." She gestured to the women around the table. "They introduced me to the world of fiction, and if I wasn't working or with Drew then I had my head buried in a book. I spent most of my summer hanging out with a slew of fictional characters. And I'm pretty sure none of them want to kill me."

She let out a sigh. This whole thing seemed hopeless.

It was like they were trying to put together a puzzle but were missing half the pieces.

"Don't worry, honey," Edna said. "We'll figure it out. I'm going to drop by the police station tomorrow. I'll take Mac a plate of my cinnamon rolls and see if I can get any new information out of him. We're not giving up."

She smiled at the table full of her friends. They might be different ages and come from different backgrounds, but she loved these women. And they loved her. She knew they wouldn't give up. Especially Edna. When it came to any kind of mystery, that woman was like a Chihuahua with a chew toy—she held on, barking and growling and yapping until she got what she wanted.

Edna might be in her eighties, but her mind was sharp and she loved a good puzzle. Piper just wished she would hurry up and solve this one.

The bell above the door rang and a group of four teenage girls ambled in, their voices ringing with laughter as they approached the counter.

"I got this," Fitz said, heading for the register. "What can I get you?" he asked the teenagers, eliciting a round of laughter and nervous giggles.

He really was incredibly cute. And apparently, Piper wasn't the only one who thought so. He had the group of teen girls eating out of his hand.

"I should probably help him," she told the Page Turners.

"You go ahead," Cassie said. "We're just going to sit here and drink our coffee. We don't want to bother you while you're working. You won't even know we're here."

She arched an eyebrow at her aunt. "Sure."

She joined Fitz at the counter and helped him make the teenager's drinks. She acted tough, but it was nice to have the women there. They thought they were keeping an eye on her, but this way she got to keep an eye on them as well.

Everyone she really cared about was in the coffee shop at this moment—they were all safe, laughing and together. That was enough. For now.

They stayed until the coffee shop closed at eight.

And even then, it took another fifteen minutes after they'd closed to convince the book club to leave. And then Piper wasn't sure they weren't going to challenge Fitz to an arm wrestling match to see who got to drive her home.

It seemed her mother was the only one who understood. Surprisingly.

"She'll be fine with Fitz. It's a five-minute drive," Claire said, corralling the other women toward their cars.

"Thanks, Mom," Piper told her, then ducked her head, avoiding her mother's eye as she tried to sound nonchalant. "We might take the long way home though."

She looked up as her mom chuckled and offered her a knowing grin. "I know *all* about the long way home. Just

JENNIE MARTS

don't take too long. I'll say I'm not going to wait up, but we both know I will."

It made her happy in an odd way to hear her mom admit to still worrying about her. Granted, it took a serial killer on the loose to get her to say it, but Piper liked it still the same.

Piper waved and called out as she slid into Fitz's car. "Thanks for showing up for coffee tonight." *And for staying for two hours.*

It *had* been a nice gesture though. And despite her grumpy behavior, she did appreciate *all* of her 'moms.'

"I don't really have a long way to get to your house. It's like two right turns," Fitz said.

Okay, so he wasn't always brilliant.

"Then take a left. Take two lefts. I don't care. I just wanted a few minutes alone with you." She gazed at him from under her lashes, blinking out what she hoped was Morse code for 'I'm just making an excuse because I'd really like to kiss you, you idiot.'

"Ahh." An impish grin tugged at the corners of his lips, and he put the car in gear and pulled out. "Then I do, in fact, know of a long way home." The town wasn't that big, so he didn't have a lot of choices, but he drove down Main and turned into the city park. He parked in front of the playground, which was deserted this time of night.

He gave her a sideways glance. "Was this what you meant?"

"Almost." She took his hand from the steering wheel and pulled his arm around her shoulders. Cuddling into him, she said, "This was a little more what I had in mind."

She giggled at his surprised expression. Heck, as long as she was acting bold, she might as well go for broke. She leaned in and brushed a kiss across his lips.

His arm tightened around her shoulders, drawing her closer as he deepened the kiss. His mouth slanted across hers, and he made this crazy, sexy sound—a cross between a sigh and a growl. She loved it. She loved *him*.

Wait. What?

Pump the brakes there, sister.

She pulled back, blinking and trying to catch her breath as the enormity of the situation suddenly rammed into her like a Mac truck.

"Are you okay?" His eyes looked concerned as he tenderly brushed a tendril of her hair from her cheek. "What's wrong?"

She shook her head. "Nothing's wrong. Everything is right. So perfectly right. *Too* perfect."

He narrowed his eyes. "How can things be *too* perfect?"

"You wouldn't understand." Ugh. Had she really just said that? She hated when people said that to her.

"Try me."

"My life isn't like yours. It's not normal. I wanted it to be. I thought moving out on my own and getting an apartment, going to college, would be things I could control, that I could finally be in charge of my life. That things could finally be good. But apparently, that's not the kind of life that I'm supposed to get."

"What are you talking about? What kind of life do you think you're *supposed* to get?"

"Not a good one. Not one like this. With someone like you."

He shook his head. "Why not?"

"Because things like this, like you, don't get too happen for me. Wait, that's not true. They do happen. They just don't last. I've had perfect. I had a perfect family with this great mom and dad, and we were so happy, then my dad was ripped from our lives by a stupid drunk driver and a motorcycle crash. That crash killed my dad, but it took my mom away from me too. Then, after she dumped me at Cassie's, I didn't think I could ever be happy again, but I was. Matt and Cass made me part of their family, and I met this cute guy and graduated and had plans to go to college, then that all got snatched away too when I didn't get into the school I wanted and that cute guy broke my heart. But I moved out anyway and thought getting my own apartment and making my own decisions would make me happy. Then my roommate got murdered, and my new roommate turned out to be my crazy mother."

"Piper, that's just how life works."

"Is it? Is that how your life works? Are both of your parents still alive?"

"Well, yes. But I've had hard things happen too."

She arched an eyebrow at him.

"Okay, maybe not to the same extreme, but still, my life isn't perfect. Nobody's life is perfect, at least not all the time."

"I get glimpses of it—can almost touch it. I can see how things *could* be perfect. And despite the fact that someone is trying to kill me, I can feel those glimmers of hope happening inside of my heart now. I had this great talk with my mom the other night, and I think we have a chance at figuring our mess out and having a real relationship. And I met this amazing guy, he's cute and funny and smart, brilliant even, and I really, really like him."

Fitz's grin came back, and he picked up her hand and linked her fingers with his. "That guy really, really likes you too."

She pulled her hand away and wrapped her arms around her stomach, holding herself together and digging her fingers into her skin. "That's the perfect part," she whispered. "You. You're perfect. Being here with you, kissing you, getting to touch you, that's all perfect."

"It isn't that perfect. We're still in my car in the

deserted parking lot of a city park," he teased.

But she wasn't joking around. "I'm serious. I like you, Fitz. So, so much. And the fact that you like me blows my mind. But I think we're a good fit, and I can actually see us together. See us being happy."

"That sounds like a good thing."

"No, it's not, because that's when things go wrong. As soon as I start to feel happy, that's when my life falls apart, when my heart gets broken, or when someone gets hurt." A hard lump of emotion burned her throat. "I don't know if I can take it if anything happens to you."

He pulled her across the console and into his lap. Cupping her cheek in his hand, he stared into her eyes. "Nothing is going to happen to me. You're not *cursed*. You've gone through some rough stuff—I get that. And I'm so sorry those things happened to you. Losing a parent isn't something any kid should go through. But it doesn't mean you're doomed to a life of grief and that every time something good happens, it will be taken away. Some of that stuff is just life. We all get our hearts broken, all have disappointments and things happen we didn't expect. Sometimes that just means something better is going to happen instead."

She wanted to believe him. Wanted to believe him with all her heart.

But the fear of history repeating itself, of the pattern of her life tearing this remarkable guy away, was too much to bear. "I don't know. The stuff that happens to me isn't normal—isn't everyday kind of bad stuff. People die. Someone is trying to kill me, has already tried once. And now I've got you mixed up in this bizarre mess. And what if something does happen to you?"

"Nothing is going to happen to me. The police are going to find this guy and it's going to be over, and I'll still be here. I'm not going anywhere. I *like* you, Piper.

You didn't get me mixed up in anything. I want to be here. I want to be with you."

"I want to be with you, too," she said, her voice low as she pressed her forehead against his. "It's just hard for me to trust people. Trust that I won't get hurt."

"You've got to trust someone. Can't you start with me?"

"Yes. I want to," she whispered. "I'm just scared."

"I know. It's okay to be scared. But don't let it paralyze you. Don't let the fear of what *could* happen to you keep you from letting *anything* happen to you. Fear is something you meet and then walk through. You have to face it to get to the other side. And fear is temporary, but regret lasts forever. We're way too young to start filling our lives with regret. Fear is just a word. So is strength. And courage. And guts. And you're one of the gutsiest chicks I know. So, stand up, kick fear in the throat, and fight for what you want. Grab it and don't let go. Don't let anyone else take your happiness from you."

Wow. She let out a shuddering breath and swiped at the lone tear trickling down her cheek. "Kick fear in the throat, huh?"

He grinned and nodded. "Right in the freaking throat."

She laughed. A soft laugh, but a laugh just the same. "You must think I'm crazy. All this talk of hanging on to you and us being together. We haven't even been out on a real date."

"So what? We've known each other and worked together for months. And just because I finally kissed you for the first time last night doesn't mean that I haven't liked you, and haven't been thinking about kissing you, for a long time." He stared at her mouth as he ran his thumb softly along her bottom lip.

A quiver of heat tingled down her spine, and she melted into him. "I'm thinking about kissing you right now," she whispered.

"Stop thinking about it and do it," he whispered back, his voice husky.

She leaned in, brushed a kiss tenderly against his lips. "No regrets."

"No regrets," he murmured against her lips, but it wasn't her ears that heard him—it was her heart.

He kissed her again, fully on the mouth, stealing her breath and sending warmth swirling through her chest—warmth and a feeling of finally being right where she was supposed to be. Like she had been waiting for this man her entire life, and here he was. Finally.

And here she was. Finally, right where she belonged.

Wrapping her arms around his neck, she tilted her head and gave in to the delicious torture of want and ache and need. She squirmed in his lap, pressing her chest to his and falling into the blissful oblivion of his kisses.

The rest of the world fell away. All that mattered was this moment, this man whose fingers were caressing her shoulders, her back. His hand slipped under her jacket and inside the back of her shirt, and she shivered as his fingertips skimmed along her spine.

She buried her head in his shoulder, kissing his neck and inhaling the scent of him—the musky tones of his aftershave mixed with a trace of French roast. She would never be able to drink coffee again without thinking about the way his neck smelled, the way his skin tasted.

He laid a hot trail of kisses down her neck then along her collarbone. His touch was like heaven, and she closed her eyes and tipped her head back, a soft moan escaping her lips.

Her moan turned into a scream as she opened her eyes and gazed into the black-hooded face of a man wearing a ski mask and staring into the window of the car as his hand reached for the handle of the door.

"Get away from us," Piper screamed, hammering the window with her hand.

The hooded figure took off, sprinting across the park as Fitz dumped her out of his lap and scrambled to open the door.

She clutched at his jacket, her heart pounding hard against her chest. "What are you doing?"

He pulled his arm back. "I'm going after the guy. What if it was *him*?"

"Then he didn't hurt us. But you can't go after him. Please, Fitz. Just let him go," Piper pleaded.

"This might be my chance to catch the guy," he said, trying to untangle his sleeve from her fingers. "I have to go after him."

"No, please. Don't. Let's just drive away."

He stared into the inky darkness of the trees behind the playground equipment, his breath coming in hard gasps, adrenaline obviously pumping through his veins, as he searched for the hooded figure. He sighed and slumped back into the driver's seat. "He's gone anyway."

Piper leaned over him and pulled his door shut, then pressed the lock button before crumpling back into her seat.

She couldn't seem to catch her breath, and her knuckles were white as she gripped the dashboard. "I think I'm going to puke," she gasped.

"Put your head between your knees," he instructed, turning the key in the ignition and putting the car in gear. "I'll get us out of here."

She did as he said, folding her body over and hugging her knees as she tried to slow her breathing.

He rubbed her back as he drove. "Just take some deep breaths."

"I'm okay." She sat up, trying to convince herself she really was okay as she brushed her hair back from her damp forehead.

Fitz drove them out of the dark park and into the well-lit parking lot of a grocery store. He cut the engine and pulled her into a hug. "Holy shit. That scared the crap out of me. My heart is still racing."

She clenched handfuls of his jacket in her fingers, tightening her hands into fists as she felt tears prick her eyes. A sob escaped her as she pressed her mouth into his shoulder.

"Hey. It's okay. We're okay," he soothed.

She pulled back, anger and despair surging through her veins, as she wiped the tears from her cheeks with the back of her hand. "No. It is *not* okay. You just gave me this whole amazing pep talk about fear and kicking it in the throat, and I bought in to every word. I was ready to lead the charge to face my fears and take them down. But then what do I do at the first sign of trouble? Do I jump out of the car and tear after the creep like you tried to do? No, I cower in terror and plead with you not to go after him either."

"Come on, Piper. You're being too hard on yourself. I was talking about imagined fear and fear of the unknown. I wasn't talking about facing down a strange guy in a mask standing outside your car."

"*You* weren't afraid. You jumped right out of the car. And would have gone after him if I hadn't begged you not to."

"That doesn't make me brave. That just makes me stupid. I was pumped on adrenaline and having a knee-jerk reaction to chase him down, but that was a bone-head move. What if the guy had a gun or a knife? We don't know it was the same guy who is after you. It could have been someone trying to rob us. You made the smart choice by telling me to stay in the car and get us out of there."

"I don't feel very smart. I feel like a coward."

"That's ridiculous. You're not a coward. You got scared. That's how any normal person would react." He gestured to the grocery store. "Want to go inside? We can find some junk food and buy a couple of drinks."

"Sure." Her stomach was still roiling so she wasn't sure about the junk food, but she could use something to drink.

Stretching her legs and walking into the bright store lifted her spirits and the fact Fitz held her hand as they wandered the aisles lightened her mood as well. He joked and teased with her and by the time they'd checked out with some orange juice, a bottle of water, and a giant bag of M&M's, she definitely felt better.

They sat in the car, and he poured a handful of candy into her palm. They shared the treats, passing the bottle of orange juice between them.

Fitz grinned. "You know, the main components of a common date are going someplace together and partaking of food and beverage." He gestured to the last M&M in her hand. "So, I think this constitutes as our first date."

"I've always wanted to go on a date to the grocery store and share a romantic meal of M&M's under the stars," she teased then laughed as she popped the last chocolate into her mouth.

"I don't care if we're eating M&M's, filet mignon, or alligator meat, I'm just happy to be hanging out with you."

"Me too." She offered him a mischievous grin. "But I think you missed the most important part of the first date. The kiss."

"I don't want to miss that." He leaned forward and captured her mouth in a long, lingering kiss.

He tasted like sweet chocolate and cool citrus, and the combination was delicious. He was delicious. His mouth fit perfectly to hers, and she never wanted to stop kissing him.

Heat swirled through her, and she swore she could feel an actual pulse vibrating between them.

Wait. That was an actual pulse.

"Sorry, I'm waiting for a call," he said as he drew back and pulled his phone from his pocket to check the screen. "I've got to take this."

He tapped the screen then held the phone to his ear. "Hello...no, I'm fine...I'm just out of breath because I was running for the phone." He grinned at Piper as he picked up her hand and twined his fingers with hers.

His good-natured smile turned into a frown, and his brow creased as he listened to the caller. "That's so random. But thanks for checking into it for me, bro. It's not what I was expecting, but at least we know something now. Talk to you later." He disconnected the call and tossed his phone on the dashboard.

"At least we know what? Who was that?" Ordinarily, she didn't let her curiosity get the best of her, but these weren't ordinary times, and he had just broken away from kissing her to take a call, so it must have been important. Although, the call could easily be about one of those ridiculously complicated equations Fitz and his classmates were always working on, but somehow she didn't think so. Not with the way he shook his head and was studying her face.

"That was a buddy of mine. He's in Computer Science, and he's a genius at hacking. I told him, hypothetically of course, about a friend of mine who had her online dating profile hacked and asked him to check into it to see if he could figure out who had done it."

"And could he?"

"Sort of. He didn't get the 'who', but he told me the IP address of 'where' it was done."

"So where was it done?"

"That's the part I said was so random. It's weird. He said it was done at the high school. He traced it there, then searched around in some of the documents and is pretty sure it came from one of the student computers in the library."

"What? That is weird. Why would someone hack my dating profile from a computer in my old high school's library?"

Fitz shrugged. "I don't know, but we drive by the school on the way back to your apartment. Do you want to check it out?"

Um...no. Not in the least. The thought of wandering around the high school in the dark sounded creepy and terrifying and like the perfect setting for those terrible slasher movies where the majority of the cast is too dumb to live. Which is why most of them usually ended up dead.

But didn't she just feel like a coward for not being brave enough to face the guy in the park? Checking out a computer couldn't be that hard. Besides, the school would probably be locked, but at least they could say they tried.

"Yeah, sure," she said. "Although I don't know what you think we'll find—besides a computer. And I remember the school's computers being impossibly slow. Do you really think the killer is there right now waiting for the modem to dial up?"

"I don't know what to think. I doubt the guy is there right now, but we're driving right by it, so I just want to look and see. Who knows, maybe the killer somehow inadvertently left a clue."

"I think you've been watching too much television. I

don't think real killers just leave random clues lying around."

"You never know. And it can't hurt to check."

He was right. And they *were* driving right by it.

She took a deep breath. "Let's do it."

It only took a few minutes to get to the school, and Fitz parked in the back next to the gym.

"I figured the school is locked, but there's a window with a busted lock back here," he said, leading her toward the back of the building. "The team used to sneak into the locker room and pull pranks on our coach."

There went her hope they wouldn't be able to get into the school and would be forced to give up and go home. Dang Fitz and his excellent problem-solving skills.

He peered through a window, which opened into a back hallway. "This is it. For once I'm glad our school is old and they used most of their budget on the football program instead of refurbishing the building." He jiggled the window frame, and it popped up. Pushing it open, he boosted himself onto the sill and climbed through then held his hand out to help her.

Here goes the start of a beautiful career in breaking and entering.

Although, technically they hadn't broken anything.

But the window was unlocked, Officer, and I just fell in as I was walking past.

Yeah, that'd work.

She let Fitz pull her over the sill, then did actually fall into the building, so at least that part would be true.

"You okay?" Fitz whispered, helping her to her feet.

"Yep, my pride and my butt are only slightly bruised." She brushed off her backside, and then reached for Fitz's hand as she followed him down the dim hallway.

Between the moon and the glow from the outside security lights shining through the big windows, the hallways were light enough to see where they were going.

Their footsteps echoed in the empty halls, and Piper's mouth had suddenly gone dry as they neared the doors to the library.

"This does seem to prove our theory that the victims are related through something to do with high school," she whispered.

Fitz shrugged. "Maybe. Or it could mean the killer is still in high school. Or maybe he's a teacher. Or what if it's the actual librarian?"

"Considering Mrs. Johnson is like eighty years old *and* a woman, I highly doubt that one."

"Maybe they hired a new guy this year."

"When is the last time they hired anyone new here?"

"Good point." He rested his hand on the doorknob. "You ready?"

No.

"Yes." She gripped his hand, probably crushing his fingers as he turned the knob and pushed through the door.

The library seemed quieter than the rest of the building had been. It could be due to the carpet on the floor or simply the stereotype that it was supposed to be quiet.

The computers were in the back, and they moved quietly through the stacks.

A dim light came from the same area the computers were. She assumed it was the glow of the computer screens.

A hushed whisper of sound broke through the silence, and they froze.

Fitz's eyes went round as he stared at Piper. Her heart was thrashing so hard against her chest, she feared it would explode. That would be awesome—steps away from confronting her killer and her body explodes onto the literary masterpieces of Austen and Tolstoy.

Another sound. The scrape of a chair followed by a turn of a page.

Maybe it's just the janitor. They could be taking a break in the library to read the latest thriller.

The likelihood they would actually come upon the killer sitting at the computer in their old high school was a zillion to one.

Fitz motioned her to follow him as he tiptoed forward. He'd let go of her hand, so she gripped the folds of his jacket, tailing him so closely, she was practically plastered to his back.

He slowly peered around the edge of the bookcase, then yanked his head back, the muscles of his neck tense as his eyes bulged out. He jerked his thumb for her to look.

Icy fingers of dread danced over her skin, causing it to pimple with goosebumps, and she couldn't seem to swallow. She didn't want to look. She just wanted to run away.

But this was what being brave and facing your fear was all about.

Still clutching Fitz's jacket, she edged forward then tilted her head to gaze around the bookcase.

Stifling a gasp, she clapped her hand to her mouth as she lurched back against Fitz.

She'd seen a figure slumped forward, typing at the keys of a computer. The lamp between the computers had been turned on, but his body was tilted away so she couldn't see his face. He was wearing a dark sweatshirt, the hood pulled up over his head, but the jacket was remarkably similar to the one the guy in the park had been wearing.

She stared at Fitz, knowing her eyes had to be as round as Oreos. "What should we do?" she mouthed.

He pointed at her then the door of the library then made the motion of calling someone on the phone.

Okay, she liked the idea of sprinting out of the library and calling the police, but what was he going to do?

She raised her eyebrows, then indicated him.

He pointed to himself then the guy at the computer and made a tackling motion.

What? No!

She shook her head, frustrated at this stupid game of How Do We Face Down a Killer charades.

"Go," he mouthed, then rounded the corner and charged toward the hooded man.

Never having been good at following directions, Piper scrambled after him, letting out a shriek as Fitz tackled the guy, knocking him from his chair and onto the ground.

The hooded guy's face hit the table as he went down, and he let out a howl of pain. He broke free of Fitz's grasp and back-pedaled away from him, grabbing a book from the table and throwing it toward Fitz.

The book glanced off his shoulder as Fitz came at the guy again, staying low and trying to pin him to the ground. He'd told her he'd done some wrestling in high school.

Piper stood frozen, unable to do anything except watch.

The guy frantically tried to crawl away, but Fitz grabbed his ankles and pulled him back.

She hated those scenes in the movies where the heroine stood there indecisively shifting from one foot to the other, not doing anything to help as the hero fights the villain. But that's exactly what *she* was doing.

Fitz seemed to be doing fine on his own, but she still didn't want to remember herself as the one who just stood there while her man engaged in battle.

Spurred into action, she grabbed for the closest thing to her which could be used as a weapon and started heaving books toward the guy. Except she had terrible aim and kept hitting Fitz with the books.

Both men grunted with pain as the books smacked into them.

The guy in the hoodie sent a well-placed kick at Fitz's

shoulder, knocking him back, and giving the guy a chance to scramble backward. He hit the corner of the room and covered his head with his arms, cowering against the wall.

"Don't kill me," he begged.

Piper stopped, her hand in mid-air as she readied another tome to launch.

Fitz paused, his arms outstretched as he prepared to tackle the guy again. He glanced at Piper.

She shrugged.

The guy didn't seem to be fighting back or trying to kill them. In fact, he seemed terrified.

Which wasn't how she would describe her assailant from the night before.

"We're not trying to kill you," Fitz said.

"We thought you were trying to kill us," Piper added.

"Why would I want to kill you?" The guy raised his head and pushed his hood back. A dark red mark smudged his cheek from where he had hit his face on the table. His mouth dropped open as he glanced from his assailant to the book-launcher with the bad aim. "Piper?"

She recognized the guy in the hood and sweat broke out across her back as she gripped the book she was holding tighter. She took a step forward, bumping into the table and knocking another book off. It made a loud thump as it hit the edge of the plastic chair and tumbled to the floor. "Brandon?"

"You know this guy?" Fitz asked.

"He's one of them. One of the guys from the online dating site."

Fitz advanced on him again, but Brandon held up his hands. "I'm sorry. It was a harmless attempt. I know it was wrong, but I didn't mean anything by it."

Huh?

"You didn't mean anything by trying to kill me?"

He dropped his hands as his face went pale. "Trying

to *kill* you? What are you talking about? I never tried to kill you. I didn't even try to hold your hand."

"But you just said you know what you did was wrong. So you know it was wrong to strangle my roommate."

His eyes went even rounder. "Whoa. This is a mistake. I didn't strangle anyone. I'm trying to figure out who *did* strangle Brittany."

She stared at him—she was so confused.

"Look, I'm sorry I asked you out under false pretenses. That's what I'm talking about it—what I did that was wrong. I saw you on the dating site and thought it would be a good way to talk to you, to ask you some questions, to dig for some information about Brittany's murder."

"Why? Why would you do that?"

He sighed. "To get the inside scoop, so I can get a good grade. I'm majoring in Criminal Investigations, and I'm doing my fall project on Brittany's murder."

She shook her head. "You asked me out to grill me about my roommate's death? For an assignment?"

"Yeah, that's what I'm trying to apologize for. After the date, I didn't think you were really that into me anyway, so I figured no harm was done. I didn't mean to hurt your feelings or anything."

"You didn't hurt my feelings, and I'm not into you at all. I thought you were the one who attacked me last night."

"You got attacked last night? Do you think it was the same guy who strangled Brittany?" His eyes lit with interest.

"Yeah, I know it was. But I thought it was you."

"No way. I can barely kill a spider. But I'm totally interested in the way a killer's mind works. That's what I'm doing my paper on. I'm calling it 'A Hometown Homicide.'" He raised an eyebrow at Fitz. "Good title, huh?"

He looked pretty proud of himself, but Piper wanted to vomit. This whole thing seemed to be another dead end. All they'd found was a guy with a morbid curiosity about the murders.

Except something still seemed off.

"Wait. So why are you here? Why did you break into the school at night? And why are you working on this particular computer?"

"I was just following up on a hunch. I had this weird thing happen on the online dating site where I met you. Right after our date, my whole profile was deleted. It was strange and the timing was odd since you were the last person I'd connected with and you were also Brittany's roommate. I wondered if there might be a connection and did a little hacking and traced whoever had been messing with my account to these computers." He gestured to the table. "It seemed like more than a coincidence since the murder victims went to this high school, so I thought I'd come over and check it out."

"And did you find anything?"

"No. But I'm not that sophisticated of a hacker. I checked all six of these and couldn't find anything suspicious or anything to lead to the identity of the person who was messing with my account." His brow creased as he looked from Fitz back to Piper. "What are you guys doing here?"

Piper sighed and set down the book she was still clutching. "Same thing as you—following up on the dating profile stuff. My mom actually set that profile up for me." She held up her hand. "Don't ask. But she only connected to two guys and told them both to show up at the coffee shop wearing a Star Wars shirt and to compliment me on my hair, but *three* showed up instead, and I went out with all three before we realized there were only supposed to be two. I'd never seen the profiles so I didn't know which one was the imposter, and when we went back to check the profiles, they'd been deleted."

"That explains a lot."

"He has a friend who traced the weird activity on my profile to these computers too." She motioned to Fitz. "This is Fitz, by the way. He's my…"

"Boyfriend," he finished for her. "Sorry about the tackle, dude. We thought…you know."

Brandon nodded then tenderly touched his cheek. "Yeah, I know."

"I think you're bleeding a little," Piper told him. "You should probably get some ice on that."

"Agreed. I was pretty much done here anyway. I'm going home." He pushed up from the floor and headed toward the door, then paused and turned back. "Would you consider doing an interview for my paper?"

"I think our coffee date *was* an interview."

He grinned sheepishly. "Could I at least text you if I have any other questions?"

"I don't think that's a good idea."

His shoulders drooped, and he lifted his hand in a half-hearted wave. "Okay. See ya around."

Fitz slumped against the wall. "Well, this whole idea has been a bust."

"Not necessarily. We know now your friend was right and whatever weirdness was going on with the dating profiles thing *did* start here. Which strengthens the connection to the high school, and makes me even more suspicious of those other two guys who asked me out."

"True."

She glanced up as she heard the faint sound of a door closing somewhere in the school. "We forgot to ask Brandon how he got into the school."

"It's an old building. There's probably tons of ways to

get in. And who knows—there could be other kids in here now." He pushed up from the floor and dusted off his jeans.

A shiver ran through her.

Her phone vibrated in her pocket, and she almost wet her pants. "Holy crap. This creepy school is getting to me. My phone just went off and scared the heck out of me." She pulled it from her pocket and checked the screen. "It's a text from my mom." She read it aloud. "Not that I'm worried. I know you're an adult. But Nola was wondering how things were going and if you were okay."

Nice. Leave it to her mom to blame her worrying on the dog. But, surprisingly, Piper wasn't that upset. It was kind of nice to have her mom actually worrying and *noticing* what she was doing. Maybe her mom had changed. A flicker of hope lit in her chest.

She typed back a quick message. "Made a quick stop at old high school. Following a lead."

"High school? Weird. Did you find anything?"

"No. Another dead end." Piper cringed as she typed the word 'dead'. "Heading back. Home in ten."

"I'll let Nola know." Smiley face emoji.

She smiled. "My mom is such a dork. I told her we stopped here but were on our way home." She shook her head then glanced up to see Fitz watching her, a grin on his face. "What?"

"Nothing. It's just nice to see you happy. *And* you have a great smile."

Ugh. People were always telling her she didn't smile enough, and she waited for him to offer the familiar advice that she should do it more often. But he didn't.

He didn't say anything more about it. He just leaned forward and pressed a quick kiss to the corner of her lip. "Let's get out of here."

Wow.

Her lip tingled where he'd kissed it. She *really* liked this guy.

"Good plan. I wasn't a huge fan of this school when I went here, but now it feels downright creepy."

They checked to make sure the computers were shut down then turned off the lamp and left the library.

Fitz held her hand, which was not something that had happened often while she'd actually been in high school, and her thoughts were full of memories of the few months in which she'd attended there.

They passed several display cases on the walls as they made their way toward the gym, and she ran her fingers down the glass of one and peered in at the pictures. "Are you in any of these?"

Fitz pointed to the next one. "I think maybe that one. If they haven't changed it. Remember our soccer team went to state last year? They did have a team picture next to the trophy."

She let go of his hand to cup her palms on the glass of the next case. "I think I can see you." She pulled her phone back out and tapped the flashlight app then shined the light into the case. "Yep, there you are," she said, aiming the light on the team picture. "Nice legs," she teased.

"Thanks." He grinned then held out his hand. "Let me see your phone."

She passed it to him, and he held the light up as he crossed to the next case. "They had a bunch of pictures of the seniors in this one. I think I was in one of those." He peered into the case then pointed into the upper corner. "That one. How about you? Are you in any of these?" He shined the light over the array of pictures as they searched for snapshots of each other.

The display was titled "A day in the life of...", and had obviously been meant to get a cross-section of all walks of the high school's life. There were pictures of kids at dances and in the cafeteria and on the steps of the school. They were cheerleaders, pictures of sports teams, and a shot of the robotics club.

Piper caught her breath as the light panned over a photo of a group of kids all dressed in black. There were six kids, all clothed in Goth attire, and leaning against the stone wall on the side of the school. A spray of lilacs bloomed in the background so it must have been spring, and a hard fist squeezed her heart as she recognized Luna and Dragon.

Who would want to hurt them? Why?

She pointed to the picture. "See that one? With all those kids in black? The two in the middle are Luna and Dragon."

Fitz held the light on the picture. "Are you in the shot?"

"I don't think so." She panned her gaze over the other kids, then another shiver raced down her spine as she recognized one. "Wait. There—that's him! That's the kid in the car. The one I told you about. From the night of the party."

"Are you sure?"

"I'm positive. Look at how his hair covers his one eye. Just like I said." She closed her eyes, concentrating, then popped them open as the name came to her. "Slay. That's it. His name is Slay."

Fitz raised an eyebrow. "Slay?"

She nodded. "I know. Weird. But, I'm sure of it. That must be what freaked me out last night. Remember you said some funny thing about slaying a beast? My subconscious must have been trying to tell me then."

"But surely that's not his real name. It's got to be one of those fake names he picked for himself. Do you know his real name?"

"No. I barely remembered Slay."

He sighed. "I'm glad you remembered, but how does this help or tell us anything? So, what if he went to the party? We still don't know if that party has anything to do with anything."

"But it's our only connection between Kyle and Luna."

"But now that Brittany is taken out of the equation, we don't know if Kyle's connection means anything."

"True." She studied the picture, trying to remember. The boy in the photo stared back at her, his one eye piercing and his mouth curved into the slightest grin, like he knew something the rest of the world didn't.

A tingling jolt prickled across her skin, and a sudden coldness clutched her insides. "I've seen that grin before," she whispered. "That's Clay."

"Clay? That douchey guy who took you to the ice cream place? I thought he was just trying to get you in the sack."

"He was. Or that's what he acted like. But he also seemed familiar to me. Like I knew his brother or something."

"Are you sure? How did you not recognize him?"

"Because he doesn't look anything like this now. Do you remember him from the coffee shop? His hair is light brown instead of deep black, and it's shorter and cut in a totally different style. He was taller too. I'm sure of it. He must have had a growth spurt over the summer. Plus, he acted differently, like with more of a smug superiority or something. I remember the guy I first met seemed angry, but also a little shy. It's like he transformed himself into a totally different person."

"That's what happens when you spend three months in a medical psych ward," a voice said from behind Fitz.

Time seemed to slow as Piper jerked back, her mouth opening as she tried to scream, but no sound came out, her eyes wide with terror as she watched the hooded figure step out from the shadows of the hall, a gun clutched tightly in his hand.

Piper's heart was racing, nearly exploding from her chest, as she stared at the guy who had asked her out to ice cream and put his hand suggestively on her thigh. "Slay."

He winced at the nickname. "Slay is dead. He was a fool. A trusting idiot. He died the night of Senior Sneak—at that great party Luna talked us into going to. You remember that party, don't you, Piper?"

She nodded, unable to tear her gaze from him and the gun in his hand.

Fitz had turned his body protectively in front of hers, his arms held out in a fighter's stance. She was gripping the back of his jacket, the material clenched between her fingers.

"I remember it. In fact, I don't think I'll ever be able to forget it. I was new to the school, too. I'd only been there a few months. My mom and I came to live here to take care of my grandma. I don't know if you ever knew that. I don't know how you would—since you never actually talked to me."

"I'm sorry. It wasn't you. I was just in a bad place and mad at everyone."

"You have no idea what it's like to actually be mad at everyone," he sneered. "But I do. Thanks to you and your friends. I certainly do." His voice took on a sing-song quality which scared Piper almost as much as the gun.

"They weren't really even my friends. I barely knew them," she stammered.

"Apparently, they weren't my friends at all."

"I don't know what you're talking about or why you're doing this. But you don't have to hurt us."

"Oh, but I do," he said, both condescending and disdainful, as if he were speaking down to a servant or disobedient employee. "Because hurting you is the only thing I've thought about for the past four months. It's what puts me to sleep at night and gets me excited when I wake up in the morning."

"Why? I didn't do anything."

He chuckled, but not in a funny way—more like in a homicidal maniac kind of way. "That's what I thought too. Again and again I asked myself *why*. Because I didn't do anything either. I barely talked to anyone at that party, and I just wanted to go home. But when I looked for you guys, I stumbled upon Luna and some boy I didn't know in one of the bedrooms. I know him now, and I can guarantee that Kyle Hammond will soon never forget me." He got a weird look in his eyes and a creepy smirk crossed his face, and the hair lifted on Piper's arms.

"He freaked out and chased me through the house." Clay continued his narrative. "If only I would have run out the front instead of the back, I would have been okay. But I didn't know the house. I got confused. I just wanted out, so I ran through the back door instead. A couple of Kyle's buddies were out there. They were standing by the keg and already piss-drunk, and when they saw Kyle chasing me, they joined in. They didn't know me either. They didn't even know why Kyle was chasing me—it was like mob mentality—or at least that's how my therapist explained it.

"I saw all the trees behind the house, and I thought if I ran into them I could lose them or they would give up. But they didn't. They just kept chasing me. Kyle and his friends were on the soccer team so they were used to running, but I wasn't. I was used to sitting in my room playing video games, which was what I'd wanted to do that night. Except Luna convinced me to go to the party. It was the first time anyone had invited me to do anything." He let out a harsh puff of breath. "I was actually excited to go. I thought I was finally making some friends. Some friends you assholes turned out to be."

Piper didn't know what to do, didn't know how to escape. But she knew if he kept talking, at least he wasn't trying to kill them. "I didn't know about any of that. Not until Kyle told us about it a few days ago. I'm so sorry you were beaten up. That must've been awful. But it doesn't justify *killing* all of us."

"Beaten up?" he scoffed. "Is that what he told you? That they beat me up?"

She nodded.

"I wish they would have only beaten me up. I could have handled that—I'd been bullied and hammered on before—that I could have survived. Make no mistake, they did work me over pretty good. All three of them getting in punches and kicks. Once they caught me and got me on the ground, I knew I was done for, so I just curled in a ball and waited for it to be over. But something came over them. I don't know if it was because they were drunk or just assholes, but Kyle was the worst. It was his idea to strip my clothes off, and it was his belt they used to tie me naked to the tree. By that time, I was half-conscious and bleeding and just praying for them to leave. I was actually praying to be left alone in the woods. And that's what happened. After repeatedly threatening he would kill me if I ever told anyone about what happened that night—about seeing him with Luna and that they were the ones who beat me—they finally left. They left me there, naked and bound to a tree, all alone in the forest."

Piper's heart broke for the boy who had gone through something so awful. But her head reminded her he was somehow blaming her—blaming all of them—for what happened, and he was intent on making them pay.

He glared at her and Fitz, his eyes narrowing to small slits as he raised the gun and pointed it toward them as if for emphasis. "Do you have any idea what it's like to be stranded alone in the woods, naked and strapped to a tree?"

She slowly shook her head, the mere idea of it sending goosebumps over her skin.

"I'll tell you what it's like. First of all, it's cold. Like really freaking cold. And I couldn't curl up and use my own body for warmth because my arms were bound behind me. And when your arms are held that way for too long, they eventually lose their circulation then they'll burn and cramp. And you think if you just yell loud enough or long enough someone will eventually hear you and find you, but pretty soon you've screamed yourself hoarse and no one has come. Then the paranoia sets in, and you're praying someone finds you and also terrified someone will find you naked and bound—maybe an animal who could tear at your flesh, or maybe a deranged madman who will do worse things to you than a few jerky teenage boys.

"But through it all, you hold out hope for rescue. Because you know that you came to the party with three other people—three friends who will eventually come looking for you. Even if one or two of them flake out and figure you found your own way home—one of them—just *one* would have to care enough to try to find you, to spend the time to figure out if you made it home safely or what happened to you.

"So, you hang there, and you blink away the blood that's seeping into your eye from the cut on your head, and you pull and strain and tear your fingernails trying to free yourself from that tree." He stabbed the gun in the air to emphasize each word. "You cry, and you scream, and you beg, and you *believe* someone will come. Until somewhere in that long, cold night, you stop believing and your mind makes a little break—a tiny snap, but enough of a crack that by the time a hunter eventually finds you the next morning, you're barely conscious and have changed into someone else. Someone who has retreated so far into the back of their mind that they refuse to talk about what happened to them or divulge the name of their assailants. The hunter, his name was Floyd, he wanted to call the police but I told him it was just a prank and asked him for a ride home. He gave me his jacket. This jacket." He gestured to the sweatshirt he was wearing, and Piper recognized the faint camouflage pattern she'd seen when he'd attacked her.

"My mother begged me to tell her what had happened, to tell the police, but I refused. She took me to the emergency room, and they hooked me to an IV and treated my wounds, but no amount of fluids would heal my mind. The doctor called it a 'brief psychotic disorder' brought on by a traumatic event, and they put me in the mental hospital. Then my 'brief disorder' turned into what they call a 'psychotic break from reality', which seems like a funny name since it wasn't a break at all. I spent my whole summer in that hospital. That's why I never came back to school. Not that any of you bastards ever noticed I was gone. I finally broke down and told my therapist what'd happened, but I never gave him the names of the boys or told him how much I blamed you all for leaving me there. The hospital was terrible. I despised every minute I was there, despised all of you for putting me there. But those months away gave me plenty of time to plot my revenge and work out the perfect strategy for my final retaliation."

"I'm sorry," she said. "I'm so sorry that happened to you."

"I'm sorry that I accidentally mistook your roommate

for you. It really set back my whole plan. It was that stupid sweater and the way she was wearing her hair. But I won't make that mistake again." Spittle flew from his lips as he spat the words at her. Narrowing his eyes, he pointed the gun at her chest. "I went to that awful party with three people. And all three of you deserted me. Acted like I didn't matter. So, that's how I'm treating you. Like you, and your lives, don't matter."

"But our lives do matter," Fitz said. It was the first time he'd spoken since Clay had stepped out of the darkness. "Don't punish Piper. She told me about that night, and she was just as miserable as you were at the party. She left and walked home before any of those things even happened."

"Shut up," he yelled, shifting the barrel of the gun toward Fitz. "It doesn't matter. It's too late for excuses, too late to try to talk your way out of this. It all ends tonight and tomorrow morning. I have something special planned for Kyle and his friends." He let out another hair-raising laugh. "Something that's going to 'blow' their minds—and their bodies, to smithereens."

Piper caught her breath. Had he really made some kind of bomb? Where was it? And how many people were going to get hurt if he detonated the thing?

They had to get away—had to escape and tell the police.

"This whole thing has been rather easy," he said, almost as if he were bragging. "I thought it would be much harder to actually take a life, but it isn't really difficult at all. And the police are buffoons and don't seem to have even the slightest clue to connect me to any of you. Even finding you all was a piece of cake—none of you had even left town. It was so simple to watch you, to learn your routines, to know when you'd be alone. And you, with putting that dating profile up, it was almost like an engraved invitation to get to you. If only you'd have been a tad sluttier, I would have had you alone and taken you that first day after the ice cream. That date was titillating torture for me. Sitting across from you, talking to you, watching you eat, completely clueless while I was imagining closing my hands around your throat and choking your last breath from your body."

Her stomach pitched, and she swallowed to keep from vomiting.

"That's enough," Fitz said through gritted teeth, the muscles of his neck and jaw tense.

"Yes, it is enough. I'm tired of talking. Sit on the floor," Clay instructed her. "And keep your back to the display case and your hands out in front of you where I can see them."

She lowered slowly to the floor, not wanting to make any sudden moves or do anything to set him off. Her mind was frantically searching for a way to break free or take him down, but until she thought of something, their best bet was to comply with his demands.

He waved the gun between them as he spoke. "You, stay there," he said to her. "You, drop your phone and kick it over here," he said to Fitz.

Fitz did as he said, dropping her phone and kicking it across the floor.

Clay took a step forward and stomped on the phone, cracking the case and smashing it with the heel of his boot. "No one can hear you now," he jeered, then pulled a roll of duct tape from the front pocket of his sweatshirt and tossed it to Fitz. "Tape up her hands and feet. And don't be an idiot. I'm going to check to make sure they're tight."

Fitz gripped the tape as he offered her an apologetic look.

"Do it," she told him.

He ripped a length of tape from the roll, the sound

echoing in the empty hallway. Then he knelt in front of her, gathered her ankles together, and wrapped the tape around them. He tried to tear another piece but fumbled the roll against him.

"Come on, Mr. Brainy Engineer. You're supposed to be so smart, surely you can handle this simple task," Clay chided him.

Fitz kept his chest close to her knees but turned his head to respond to Clay. "I'm doing it. And I *am* smart—smart enough to know you're not going to get away with this."

Shut up, Fitz!

Why was he baiting him?

And how the hell did he know Fitz was studying engineering? Had Clay been following both of them? Her thoughts were interrupted as she felt Fitz push a hard metal object inside the side of her sneaker.

She kept her eyes on Clay, but she knew what it was, what it had to be. Fitz had just slipped her his pocketknife. He wasn't baiting Clay—he was distracting him—diverting his attention away from his hands so he could sneak her the knife. Clay was wrong. Fitz wasn't smart—he was brilliant.

"Make sure it's good and tight, College Boy. I don't want her getting away while I'm dealing with you," Clay said. "I'm not sure what I'm going to do with you yet, but I've always enjoyed eating my dessert first." He licked his lips and eyed her with hunger.

She fought a gag as her stomach went rock hard. Everything in her wanted to escape, and she swallowed at the bile burning the back of her throat.

Fitz wrapped another piece of tape around her wrists. She tried not to cry out as the adhesive tore at her skin and ripped the hair from her wrists. It was okay though—she could take it. Some torn skin was a small price to pay for her life.

"There, it's done," Fitz said. He stayed in a crouch as he gestured to her bound hands. "Check it if you want."

Clay took a tentative step toward them and bent forward to examine her hands.

Fitz took the opportunity of his momentary distraction to lunge forward, driving his shoulder into Clay's stomach and knocking him to the ground.

Clay grunted as his butt hit the floor, but he didn't drop the gun. He kicked his legs out as Fitz tried to tackle him.

But Fitz let out a growl, his face contorted with determination as he dodged his kicks and charged toward him again.

The next few moments seemed to happen in slow motion as Fitz sprang forward, and Clay raised the gun in his hand and pointed it at Fitz's face.

Piper's heart stopped in her chest as the roar of the gunshot exploded, the sound ricocheting through the hallway.

She watched in horror as Fitz's head snapped back, and he fell to the floor, his head hitting the linoleum with a sickening thud.

Swiping at the droplets of moisture that sprayed across her face, she finally let loose the scream that had been building in her as she stared at the smears of Fitz's blood streaked across the back of her hand.

"Shut up!" Clay screamed at Piper as he swung the gun toward her.

She clamped her lips together, biting down on her lower lip to keep from screaming. The coppery taste of blood filled her mouth, and she wasn't sure if it was from where she'd bitten her lip or if it was from Fitz.

Tilting her head to the side, she couldn't hold it back this time, and retched onto the floor. Acid burned her throat and mouth, but it was better than the taste of blood. She coughed and wiped her mouth against the sleeve of her jacket.

Clay had pushed up from the floor and stood ominously over Fitz's prone body. He lay motionless, either unconscious or…

No! He *had* to be unconscious.

She couldn't bear the alternative—couldn't conceive of the idea that Fitz was dead.

His forehead was crimson, his hair and cheek dark and streaked with blood. She searched his face, trying to figure out where he'd been shot and desperately seeking signs he was okay.

A janitor's closet was on the other side of the hall, and Clay tore open the door and peered inside. "This will work," he muttered, more to himself than to her.

Shoving the gun into his jacket pocket, he returned to Fitz, grabbed his arms, and dragged him toward the closet.

A long streak of scarlet blood trailed behind him, and bile rose in Piper's throat again.

Think! Stop freaking out and think!

Her mind screamed at her. This might be her only chance to escape. Fitz had given her a chance, and she couldn't let him down.

While Clay was struggling to get Fitz into the closet, she fumbled inside her shoe, trying to retrieve the small pocketknife. There, she got it. Pinching it between her fingers, she drew it from her shoe and sought to pull the blade open.

Her hands were shaking so bad, she almost dropped it. But she didn't. She finally worked the blade free and attacked the duct tape securing her ankles.

If only she could get her feet free, she could make a run for it. She would have a chance.

Clay disappeared into the closet. She could hear him shoving things aside and his grunts of effort as he must have been maneuvering Fitz's body.

The stupid tape was strong and unwieldy but the little knife was sharp, and she sawed through the tape.

Clay charged back through the door, a folding chair in his hands. He turned his back to her to slam the door and unfold the chair. She guessed his intention was to wedge the chair under the door handle.

This was her chance. And it might be her only chance.

She jerked her legs apart, ripping the last bit of tape and scrambled to her feet.

She didn't know for sure where the gun was. The last she'd seen it, Clay had stuck it in his pocket, but there was no way she could overpower him and try to take it.

Her best bet was to run.

Her legs were achy and tingled from sitting on the floor, but she ignored the pain, and took off, sprinting down the hall.

Heedless of where she was going—except for away from Clay, she heard the clatter of the folding chair and his shriek of frustration.

The gym was at the end of the hall, and she burst through the doors, then froze as she stared at the vast expanse of space. She needed to either get out or hide. The locker rooms were to her right and the windows were across the gym. But she had no idea if the windows were unlocked or how long it would take her to climb out of one.

Her best bet was to hide, then find another way out. She pushed through the door to the locker room as she heard the heavy footfalls of Clay's boots in the hallway.

Rows of lockers ran down the center of the room. The showers were to the left and the coach's office was at the back of the room. If she could get to the office, she could lock herself in and use the phone to call for help. But what if the door was already locked? Or if the phone didn't work? Then she'd be trapped in the office—a sitting duck.

She slipped into the shower area, trying to run softly so he wouldn't hear the slap of her sneakers on the tile. The room smelled like mildew and sweat, and a steady drop of water leaked from one of the showerheads, the sound shattering the otherwise quiet of the room.

Crouching down in one of the shower stalls, she tried to slow her breathing, terrified the loud rasping would give away her hiding place.

The pocketknife was still clutched in one of her bound hands, and she tried to maneuver it around to tear at the tape. But the angle was awkward, and she couldn't get enough traction. She bit at the tape, using her teeth to rip through the strips holding her hands.

Focused on freeing her hands, she still tried to listen for Clay, petrified he would appear in the locker room and discover her.

She gnawed through the last bit of tape, jerking her hands apart at the same time the door burst open, slamming against the wall, the sound echoing against the walls of the shower.

"Piper, where are you?" His voice had the same sing-song quality he'd used before—like they were playing a children's game of hide-and-seek. "Come out, come out, wherever you are."

She pressed her fists to her ears, praying he would give up his search and move on to the other locker room.

The sound of metal sliding along the lockers had her skin going clammy as she knew the thing he was running along them had to be the barrel of the gun.

Then the sound stopped, and she heard nothing at all. No footsteps, no metal clanging, no soft whoosh of a door closing—nothing.

And that was more terrifying than the sound of the gun barrel rattling along the lockers. At least then she knew where he was.

She leaned the slightest forward, straining to hear any whisper of sound. She held her breath, knowing he had to be listening for her, as well.

Clutching the pocketknife in her hand, she held the blade out, the torn strips of duct tape dangling from her wrists as she readied for an attack.

Every muscle in her body tensed, alert, waiting for a sound, a stir, anything to alert her to his location. Her knuckles turned white, and her hand shook as she gripped the knife—it was her only weapon, her only defense.

Her heart pounded so hard she was sure it would give her hiding place away.

She waited, wanting to poke her head into the room to look for him, but also terrified she would see him. Or he would see her.

Finally, she couldn't take another second. Her knees were cramped from crouching, and her back ached from tensing her muscles. She *had* to check, to take one quick glimpse into the room.

Slowly, so very slowly, she peered around the edge of the shower stall toward the lockers where she'd last heard him. The room seemed empty, but she hadn't heard him leave.

She started to turn to check the other side of the room when she felt his presence.

The hair on her neck stood on end.

Her muscles went rigid, her neck so stiff she was surprised it didn't creak as she turned her head another inch and saw him standing on her other side, not a foot away.

His face broke into a macabre grin. "Boo," he whispered.

Piper froze, terror sending chills through her body, her head spinning with dizziness as she struggled to keep her legs from collapsing beneath her.

He must have known where she was hiding and been standing there, like a hunter stalking his prey, just waiting for her to come out. His hands were empty so the gun had to be back in his pocket.

Fight!

The knife was still in her hand, but her body wouldn't move, wouldn't listen to her command.

Fight or die!

His sweatshirt was too thick for the small pocketknife to do much damage. She had to go for some place she could hurt him. She thrust her arm up, stabbing the knife toward his neck.

His eyes widened in surprise, and he lifted his arm in defense, knocking her arm from its intended target. But he wasn't quick enough, and the sharp little blade sliced neatly across his chin and up his cheek.

He howled in pain as he clutched his face, tendrils of blood already trailing down his neck. "You bitch," he roared.

She tried to stab him again, but this time he did block her arm then shoved her backwards with the force of an angry bull.

Her head hit the tiled wall behind her and pain burst through her skull. Blinking her eyes, she fought to stay conscious as tiny bursts of light spun in front of her.

Still clutching his face, he kicked out, sweeping his leg across her shins and trying to knock her legs out from under her.

She went down, her knees cracking painfully on the floor of the shower, the smallest sound of a splash as she landed in a leftover pool of water and cold seeped through the fabric of her pants. Scrambling to get away, she crawled across the shower floor, slipping on the slick tiles.

Just as she thought she'd gained some purchase, his strong hand clamped down on her ankle and yanked her back.

She kicked her leg as hard as she could, her sneakered foot connecting with his chest and sending him back a few inches. The kick must have been enough to startle or hurt him because he let go of her ankle, and she crawled forward, pushing to her feet and running from the shower area.

She heard him behind her, but didn't turn around to look. For all she knew, he could be pulling out the gun and was readying to shoot her in the back. If so, she didn't want to know.

All she could focus on was getting away.

She yanked at the locker room door, half-expecting the feel of his hand on her back or the jerk of her hair as he grabbed for a handful.

But neither of those things happened, and she made it out of the locker room.

A rack of basketballs stood against the wall, and she hurriedly pushed it in front of the door. It wouldn't stop him, but it might slow him down.

Bursting back out of the gym, she sprinted down another hallway, ignoring the throbbing pain in her knee where she'd hit the tile. A set of double doors were at the end of the corridor, and she prayed she could get out and find help, for her and for Fitz.

Was he okay?

She could only pray that he was.

The crash of the basketball cart echoed through the empty hall, and she almost cried with relief as saw the doors leading outside at the end of the hallway. She was almost free.

No. Please no.

A padlocked chain wound its way around the handles of the door. There was no way she was getting out through them.

What the hell? She could *not* catch a break.

She slipped into the closest classroom and flattened herself against the wall. It was decision time. Should she hide or keep running?

The last time she'd hid hadn't worked out very well and hiding wasn't going to help Fitz. She had to keep going—had to find a way out of the school.

She'd had Algebra in this classroom and recognized the set-up. A Jack-and-Jill style bathroom in the back corner connected this room to the biology lab next door. She ran through the maze of desks, careful not to bump into any, terrified she would make a sound that would tell Clay where she was.

Quietly pulling the bathroom door shut behind her, she pushed the lock in, hoping to buy herself a few extra minutes of time if he did follow her into that room.

She pushed through the other door into the biology lab. The room looked exactly the same as when she'd last been there and bile rose in her throat as the memory of trying to dissect a slimy dead frog flashed in her mind.

The smell of formaldehyde, chemicals, and cedar wood chips hung in the air. A row of terrariums lined the back wall, their small bulbs giving off a soft glow in the room as the mice, rats, toads, and whatever other creepy-crawlies were over there slept soundly in their cages.

A cramp bit into her side, and she had to stop, doubling over as she pressed a hand against her stomach. Her palm hit something hard and rectangular in her jacket pocket and for a second she thought it was her phone. But her phone was smashed and broken on the floor in front of the display cases.

Holy crap! She tore at her pocket as she suddenly realized what it was. She'd totally forgotten it was in there. Fumbling with the zipper, her hand still shaking, she finally got her pocket open and pulled out the thing Edna had shoved into her hand earlier that night—her pink stun gun. The Terminator.

Piper turn the gun over in her hands, staring at the plastic case and the metal prongs, as a quiet resolve settled over her. She'd spent the last several months wanting, craving, needing to finally have control over her life, but she'd been waiting for that control to happen, and it suddenly struck her she wasn't going to wait anymore.

She was through with that noise.

The best way to *gain* control of her life and her situation was to reach out and take it. To grab control by the balls and make it her bitch.

Fitz's words came rushing back to her. *Fear is something you meet and walk through. You have to face it to get to the other side. Fear is just a word.*

So is strength. And courage. And guts.

He'd told her to stand up, kick fear in the throat, and fight for what she wanted. To grab it and not let go.

This was her chance. Her chance to face fear—to meet

it, boot it in the face, and walk through to the other side.

Bravery started with *one* step, *one* action.

She gripped the stun gun in her hand. She'd be damned if she'd let this ass-wipe take her down without a fight.

She took a step forward and looked around the biology lab. She might have got a D+ in this class, but she'd seen *Home Alone* four times, and if a ten-year-old kid could take down a couple of thugs with a bucket of paint and some marbles, she could surely disable one deranged psychopath with a biology lab and a pink stun gun called The Terminator.

Her gaze took in all the tools at her disposal. She only had a few minutes so a complicated pulley system with a hot iron was out, but she did have plenty of other resources at hand.

Working through the plan in her head, she quickly constructed what she hoped was a sufficient trap.

The bathroom was locked, so the only way in was through the door leading to the hallway. She spied an extension cord snaking out from under the teacher's desk and set a make-shift trip-wire by wrapping one end tightly around the leg of the desk and the other around the leg of the heavy lab table across from it. A bottle of dish detergent sat on the edge of the sink, and she squirted a thick layer all over the floor in front of the cord.

The sink also held a bucket of liquid with tools soaking in it. She didn't know what the liquid was. A shimmery film appeared to cover the top of the water so it could be soap or some kind of cleaner or it could be plain water. It didn't matter. Its only purpose was to surprise Clay and catch him off-guard just long enough for her to jab him with the stun gun.

Taking a deep breath, she readied herself, calling up all her inner reserves of courage.

I can do this.

She was *not* a victim of her circumstances, and she wasn't about to let herself be a victim of this lunatic.

Gently pulling the door open a few inches, she listened for any signs of him.

A sound, like a scrape, resonated from down the hall, and her heart jumped into her throat. He was out there. Somewhere. She just needed to lure him in.

She didn't want to slam the door—that would too obvious—but she closed it with enough force to make an audible sound.

Gripping the stun gun in one hand, she turned the device on, then grabbed the bucket of tools with the other.

She held her breath as she stood motionless behind the door and waited.

Edna had told her the charge from the gun wouldn't pass through his body to hers so her best bet was to get on top of him and use her body weight to hold him down.

The older lady also said she had to press the gun against the assailant for at least three to five seconds to disable and disorient him, so she knew she had to be patient and wait for the exact moment to have the best chance of stunning him. She tried to imagine herself holding Clay down with the stun gun pushed to his neck while she yelled, "One Mississippi, two Mississippi…"

No. She just had to hit him where it hurt and pray she could hold on long enough.

It felt like ten minutes ticked by as she stared at the doorknob willing it to turn, but it probably took less than one.

This is it. Time to kick fear AND Clay in the throat.

The knob slowly turned, and the door slid open. Then an outstretched hand appeared, the gun clenched in its fingers.

*S*hit.

Piper was hoping he still had the gun in his pocket.

It didn't matter.

It was too late to turn back now.

She just had to be smarter, and faster, than him.

Clay pushed through the door and took three steps into the room.

She'd purposely tipped over a chair in the back corner to make it look like she'd headed that direction.

Her throat burned and she swallowed, praying he would take one more step toward the make shift trip-wire.

He did.

Thank you, God.

He was positioned perfectly. Now she'd see if her plan really worked.

"Hey, asshole," she said.

He whipped around, and she threw the bucket of tools and liquid straight at his chest.

The gun went off, the sound booming through the room.

She swore she felt the disturbance of air as the bullet sped past her shoulder, but she didn't have a second to waste.

Clay took a step back, his right foot landing in the soap. As he pulled his other foot back, his shoe skidded on the slippery surface.

His arms pin-wheeled, the gun circling through the air as the back of his shin connected with the extension cord, and he went flailing backwards.

He swore as he landed on his tailbone, then his head hit the linoleum floor, and the gun went flying from his hand.

Piper barely heard it skidding across the floor over the ringing in her ears, but from the corner of her eye, she saw it slide under the cabinet against the wall as she sprung forward, The Terminator extended in her hand.

A primal scream came from somewhere inside of her as she leapt on top of Clay's legs.

She pressed the button on the stun gun and jammed it against his groin.

The gun made a horrific sound of crackling electricity, and Clay's eyes went wide with shock.

He tried to fight her, roaring out foul names for her as he swung punches against her side and arms. But the whack to his head must have disoriented him, because his blows had little effect.

Either that, or her adrenaline was pumping so hard she didn't feel them. She was sure her body would be covered in bruises tomorrow, but a bruise was a much better alternative than a bullet.

As the current passed through Clay, his chest and legs jerked in spasms, then his arms thrashed out, and finally his body went limp under her.

She pressed the gun harder against him, holding it for another few seconds, just to be sure.

The room was eerily silent as she let go of the button and pushed away from Clay's prone body. Her hands and feet slid in the soapy film surrounding his body, but she backpedaled away, kicking against his legs for traction then pulling herself up using the side of the lab table. She wanted to collapse on the floor, her knees going weak, but she couldn't.

She had to get out of there. She had to get to Fitz.

Zipping the stun gun back into her jacket pocket, she

was tempted to forage under the cabinet for the gun, but chose to take advantage of Clay being disabled and run instead.

Taking a few tentative steps, she rubbed the soles of her shoes clean on the floor, then ran through the door, slamming it shut behind her.

She sprinted back toward the gym and up the hallway toward the closet Fitz was locked in.

Blue and red lights flashed through the windows, their colors reflecting off the lockers. Her ears still rang from the blast of the gunshot, but she could hear the muffled sounds of sirens as she grabbed the chair blocking the closet door and ripped it away.

She jerked the door open and let out a cry as she saw Fitz lying there, his eyes closed, blood pooling on the floor by his head, and his phone on the floor next to his outstretched hand.

His face and the side of his head was covered in blood. So much blood.

The closet reeked of its coppery scent.

Bile filled her throat, but she swallowed it back.

Dropping to her knees, she yanked off her jacket and pressed it to the wound on his scalp, praying he was only unconscious and not dead.

His eyes fluttered open, and she sobbed in relief.

Loud bangs echoed in the hall as the school doors were forced open followed by footsteps in the hall and Mac's voice calling her name. "Piper!"

"We're in here! We need help!" She cradled Fitz's head in her lap as she screamed for Mac.

He appeared in the doorway then knelt next to her as he yelled out orders. "Get the EMTs over here! Now!"

Mac wrapped an arm around her, pulling her away as the small closet was suddenly filled with paramedics and equipment as they went to work on Fitz.

Piper clung to Mac's chest. "It was Clay. He shot him. He's in the biology lab. In the next hall over."

Mac spoke into his mic. "Assailant is armed and dangerous. Last seen in the biology lab on the southeast side of the school."

She shook her head. "He's on the floor, by the desk. I zapped him with Edna's stun gun. Tell them to watch out—the floor is slippery with soap."

The officer's eyes widened, but he relayed the information to his team.

The EMTs loaded Fitz onto a stretcher. Piper and Mac hurried after them as they rushed him out of the school and into a waiting ambulance.

"We got him," a voice crackled through the mic. "Suspect in custody."

Piper wanted to collapse with relief, but she couldn't. She clutched at Mac's sleeve. "There's a bomb. At least one. Clay said he set something for Kyle and the two other guys who tortured him in high school. I don't know their names but Kyle can tell you."

"We know. Fitz told us when he called in. We sent a team, and they've already secured Kyle and the other boys and are working to evacuate their houses and apartments."

She sagged against him. *Thank God.*

Of course, Fitz had told them when he called.

It was only a stroke of dumb luck that he had been holding Piper's phone when Clay found them. If Clay hadn't assumed the phone belonged to Fitz, he wouldn't have locked him in the closet with his own phone still in his pocket.

Who knew how many people Fitz had saved by making that call?

Now all she could do was pray that the same call would save him. She had to get to the hospital—had to see if he was all right.

The siren of the ambulance wailed as the vehicle sped out the exit of the school parking lot.

Another car came tearing in through the entrance, its tires squealing as they bounced up onto the sidewalk and skidded to a stop in the grass. The door flung open, and Claire practically fell out. Leaving the car running and the door open, she stumbled forward, crying out Piper's name as she ran toward her.

"Mom," she whispered, a sob stuck in her throat. Then she didn't think, didn't stop to contemplate her decision, she just reacted as she ran toward Claire and threw herself into her mother's arms.

Claire pulled her tightly to her chest, kissing the top of her head, her voice coming out in hard gasps as she tried to control her own crying. "Oh God, Piper. Are you okay?" She pulled back, still holding her daughter with one arm as she cupped her cheek in her hand and inspected her face. "You're covered in blood. Where are you hurt? Why didn't the ambulance take you?"

"I'm okay, Mom," she said, her arms still wrapped around her. She wasn't quite ready to let go. "It's Fitz's blood." At least she thought so. She had no idea if she was bleeding or what injuries she'd sustained as Clay had chased her around the school.

"I knew something was wrong when you didn't come home. I could feel it in my bones," Claire told her, pulling her tightly against her again. "Then when I heard the sirens, I knew they were headed toward you. I got here as fast as I could."

"Thanks for coming," Piper said. "But we've got to go now. Can you drive me to the hospital?"

❈ ❈ ❈

Thirty minutes later, the emergency room sitting area was

full as Piper sat on the edge of her seat, waiting for news of Fitz. In that time, not only had she and Claire made it to the hospital, but Fitz's parents and most of the Page Turners book club had shown up as well.

It wasn't the ideal way for Piper to meet her boyfriend's parents, but no one seemed to care.

Cassie and Matt had met them at the hospital. She'd had to give her clothes, already crusting with dried blood, to the police, and her uncle had given her his sweatshirt to put on over the thin hospital scrubs they'd given her to wear after she'd handed over her clothes. Her small frame swam in the roomy shirt, but it was warm and not covered in blood, and she buried her hands in the sleeves and wrapped her arms around her stomach.

Sunny and Edna had shown up with coffee and hot tea and made sure everyone had a warm cup in their hands.

Maggie had known Fitz since he was a kid, and she leaned against the wall, occasionally pacing the room, too anxious to sit still.

The occupants of the room rose as one as the emergency room doors opened, and the doctor stepped through.

He held up his hands and smiled warmly. "Mr. Fitzgerald is going to be fine. The bullet only grazed the side of his head. He needed a few stitches, and we've given him something for the pain, but he's doing great."

"A few stitches?" Piper asked. "But there was so much blood…"

"There always is when a head wound is involved," the doctor explained. "We're going to admit him and keep him overnight for observation, but he should be able to go home tomorrow."

Thank goodness. She squeezed her mom's hand. Although she couldn't quite remember when she'd taken it.

245

Claire had been by her side the entire time, she realized. Not pushing or needing anything. Just being there for her. It was a new experience—to have her mom be the one there for her instead of the other way around.

Fitz's parents thanked the doctor and asked if they could see him.

They followed him back toward the emergency room just as Mac entered the waiting area from the street.

"Any word on the kid?" he asked, his brow creased in concern.

"He's going to be fine," Piper told him. "Evidently, the bullet only grazed his head."

"That's what the EMTs had told me. But those head wounds bleed like a bitch. I know you were scared."

She nodded, suddenly unable to talk as memories of cradling Fitz's bleeding head in her lap filled her mind.

"He's young and healthy. And the gun we recovered was a small caliber weapon, so it wouldn't have done too much damage if it only grazed the side of his head. He'll pull through fine. I've seen young guys in my department take a bullet and be back to work the next week showing off their scar."

She hoped he was right.

"I thought you'd want to know the other guys are safe. The team went in and recovered two homemade dirty bombs—one in Kyle's apartment and one in the house the other two guys rent. They were set to go off at midnight tonight."

"That little bastard," Edna swore. "Who knows how many people would have been hurt or killed?" She placed a hand on Piper's shoulder. "You and Fitz were both so brave tonight."

She smiled up at Edna. "Thanks to you and that little pink stun gun you gave me."

"Too bad it wasn't a real gun," Edna muttered. "That

guy deserved more than just a jolt to his man-marbles."

A grin pulled at the corner of Piper's lips. Where did Edna get this stuff? "I'm just glad we got him. And he can't hurt anyone else."

Mac offered her an encouraging smile. "You did good, kid."

She had done well. She'd been brave and stood up for herself against the thing she feared. And she'd won. Clay was in custody, and she and her family were safe.

The important thing now was to focus on Fitz.

Two weeks later, Piper closed her textbook and leaned back in her chair with a smile.

She'd spent the last hour at her desk in her room, studying for an English exam, because time does not stop when it came to college courses and homework. Not that studying for an English exam made her happy, but the fact that things in her life seemed to be getting back to normal certainly did.

She'd always wished for a normal life, but she was finally figuring out 'normal' had many definitions and meant different things to different people.

To her, right now, it meant school and studying for midterms. It meant Fitz was home from the hospital and back to brewing coffee and solving ridiculously complicated engineering equations and making out with her on the sofa at night after her mom had gone to bed. It meant taking Nola for walks and creating frothy cappuccinos at work while she flirted shamelessly with her cute shift leader. It meant things were good with her mom, and the Page Turners had picked a new book club book to read, and Edna's hair had faded back to silver with just the slightest blue twinge.

They'd also heard that Dragon's life was getting back to normal too. He'd made a full recovery and had also been released from the hospital. He was home now but was hoping to return to school next semester.

Which reminded her that she needed to take care of her next payment for school. Evidently, being a poor college student was also part of her normal. But that was okay.

Everything right now seemed not just okay, but pretty great. Like her life was finally settling down into what she'd hoped it would be.

Nola was curled at her feet. She let out a contented doggy-groan as Piper rubbed her belly with her foot while she pulled her debit card from her wallet and placed the call to the Bursars office at the college.

Thankfully, an actual person answered, and Piper gave them her name and Social Security number and explained she wanted to make a payment.

"I'm sorry, Miss Denton, it seems you're mistaken. Your tuition bill has already been paid."

"Um, no. I wish that were the case, but I believe *you* are the one who is mistaken. You must be looking at someone else's account."

The clerk repeated her full name and social. "It says right here the whole tuition for this year and next has been paid in full."

"What? Who paid it?"

"I really couldn't say. The notes only show that it was paid in cash."

"Okay. Thanks then, I guess." Dazed, she clicked off the call. What the heck? Who would have paid off her whole tuition bill? And in cash?

Matt and Cassie certainly didn't have that kind of money, and they had their own two kids' college expenses to worry about. There was no way Fitz could have done it. He was turning out to be a great boyfriend, but not that great. And if he had that much extra money, he wouldn't have to work at the coffee shop.

She rubbed the back of her neck as she tried to think. Who did she know who had that kind of cash laying around? There was only one person who had been flashing mysterious amounts of money around.

But there was no way. It couldn't be.

Claire Denton was not known for her selfless acts.

There was only one way to find out.

Nola followed her as she walked into the living room, where Claire was sprawled out on the sofa, an array of lottery tickets spread across the table in front of her. Tonight was lotto night, and the television was turned to the local news station.

"Hey Mom, do you have a minute?"

"Sure," Claire answered, muting the TV. "The numbers don't come on for another few minutes. What's up?"

Piper sat on the sofa next to her. "I just got off the phone with the school, and it seems an anonymous person has paid my tuition for the rest of this year and next."

"Really? That's crazy. Who would have done that?" It was a good thing she hadn't tried for a career in acting, because her 'I'm so shocked' expression left a lot to be desired.

"Cut it out, Mom. I know it was you." She didn't really know that, but she hoped Claire would fall for her bluff.

"How do you know that?"

"Because no one else cares about me enough to do something so kind and thoughtful."

Her mom stared at her, blinking, as her eyes filled with tears. "Well, Pip, I think that might be the nicest thing you've said to me in a long time. It's not true, the part about no one else caring enough about you, but the kind and thoughtful part is an awfully sweet thing for you to say."

"Then it really was you?"

Claire shrugged.

Piper tilted her head and pursed her lips. She didn't know how to deal with this Claire. She was used to the

Claire who was selfish and only thought about herself.

But maybe that was the old Claire. Maybe her mother really had changed.

Which meant maybe she needed to change too—needed to give her mom a chance.

She blew out her breath. "Thank you."

Her mom smiled. "You're welcome."

"I'm still confused though. Where did you get that kind of money?"

"I told you before. When I left Spider, it wasn't under the best circumstances, and I didn't take much, but I took what I deserved for putting up with that snake for all that time."

"I thought he was a spider."

Claudia shrugged again. "Same difference."

"So you're saying you *stole* it?"

"Stole is really an ugly word. Let's just say I didn't think Spider needed all of that money as much as I needed to get away from him and leave it at that." She picked at a loose thread on the sofa. "And after all this time, I wanted to do something for my daughter—something that mattered. Something to make up for the harm I'd inflicted for not being there when she needed me."

Pain twisted in her heart. But something else bloomed there. Something that felt suspiciously like hope. "You're here now."

Claire rested a hand on Piper's leg. "And I'm not going anywhere."

"I'm glad." And she was. Really glad.

A knock sounded on the door, and Piper leaned in and gave her mother a quick hug before she got up to answer it.

Her stomach fluttered in anticipation of seeing Fitz—his shift had ended ten minutes ago, and he was coming over to study.

Nola raced behind her as she crossed the room. She opened the door and stepped into Fitz's arms. He dipped his head and captured her mouth in a quick kiss as he pulled her to him.

He tasted like caramel and coffee and cinnamon gum, and she melted against him.

Nola let out a tiny yip. Fitz let go of Piper to kneel down and rub the little dog behind the ears. "How you doin', girl?"

Her tail wagged happily as she leaned into Fitz's hand.

Piper knew the feeling.

"Hey, Fitz," Claire called. "I hope you're hungry. I'm making spaghetti and meatballs."

"Sounds amazing."

Her mom let out a shriek, and Fitz held out his hands, a bewildered expression on his face. "What? I said it sounds good."

Claire let out a whimper as she turned toward them. Her eyes were round, and her face had lost its color. Her mouth opened then closed then opened again.

"Mom? Are you okay?" Piper rushed forward. "What's wrong?"

Claire shook her head then an impish grin stole across her face. "Nothing is wrong. Not a dang thing." She held up the lotto ticket she was clutching in her hand. "The numbers on the 'birthday card' just hit."

Piper gasped and pressed a hand to her chest. She could almost feel her heart pounding against it. "All of them?" she stammered.

"ALL. SIX. OF. THEM."

Ho-ly Buckets of Cash.

Her mom let out a shrill bark of laughter then she flew toward her and swooped her into a hug.

The two of them jumped up and down, clutching each

other arms as Nola raced around them, and Fitz stood by, his mouth hanging open in dumb-founded shock.

She'd thought she wanted normal, an ordinary life, but it turns out ordinary was really very just…ordinary.

It's not the life itself, but the people and the experiences that made life remarkable.

As she and Claire drew Fitz into their group hug, Piper decided that's what she wanted—not normal, not ordinary, but a life that was wonderful… and extraordinary.

And it seemed like that was what she was about to get.

THE END

Thanks for reading my book. I hope you loved it! If you did enjoy it, please consider leaving a review.

And be sure to check out all the other adventures in the *Page Turners* series:

Another Saturday Night and I Ain't Got No Body: Book 1
Easy Like Sunday Mourning: Book 2
Just Another Maniac Monday: Book 3
Tangled Up In Tuesday: Book 4
What To Do About Wednesday: Book 5
A Halloween Hookup: Book 6 – A Holiday Novella
A Cowboy for Christmas: Book 7 – A Holiday Novella

Be the first to find out when the newest *Page Turners Novel* is releasing and hear all the latest news and updates happening with the *Page Turners* book club by signing up for the Jennie Marts newsletter at: Jenniemarts.com

My biggest thanks goes out to my readers! Thanks for loving my stories and my characters. I would love to invite you to join my street team, *Jennie's Page Turners* where you can become an honorary member of the *Page Turners Book Club!*

If you enjoy small town contemporary romance
with hot cowboys-
Try the *Hearts of Montana* series

In Tucked Away (Book 1), Charlie Ryan is a city girl who inherits a farm in small town Montana and when she gets there, she finds a lonely teenager girl, a goat named Clyde, a hunky cowboy, and a place she finally feels like she can call home.

Hidden Away: Book 2
Stolen Away: Book 3

If you like hockey romance with cute hockey players and
steamy romance-
Try the *Bannister Brothers Books*

Icing On The Date – A hunky hockey player meets a cute
caterer who will change his entire game.
Worth The Shot
Skirting the Ice

More small town romantic comedy can be found in the
Cotton Creek Romance series:
Romancing the Ranger
Hooked On Love
Catching the Cowgirl

Meet three brothers that are hockey-playing cowboys in
the *Cowboys of Creedence*:
Caught Up In A Cowboy
You Had Me At Cowboy – coming December 2018

Thanks for reading and loving my books!

Acknowledgements

As always, my love and thanks goes out to my husband, Todd, for your steadfast love and support in my writing career and in our life together! We make the best team!

Thanks to my sons, Tyler & Nick, for always supporting me, for listening to a zillion plotting ideas and answering all of my technical questions. I love you more than words can say.

Huge thanks goes out to my mom, Lee Cumba, on this one. Thanks Mom for all of the plotting help and for spending the day feeding me and talking through tons of ideas about murder, red herrings, and deception.

Thank you to the team of people behind putting this book together. Kim Killion of The Killion Group did an AMAZING job on this cover—you are a rockstar, Kim! I so appreciate the formatting talents of Cindy Jackson. And a big thanks to Alyssa Palmer for your awesome editing skills.

Big thanks to my writing sisters, Beth Rhodes and Cindy Skaggs, who helped make this work possible through their constant support and lots and lots of writing sprints—whether I wanted to do them or not. Your accountability and support is invaluable!

Special acknowledgement goes out to the women that walk this writing journey with me every day. The ones that make me laugh, who encourage and support, who offer great advice and sometimes just listen. Thank you Michelle Major, Lana Williams, Anne Eliot, Ginger Scott, Kristin Miller, and Selena Laurence. XO

Big thanks goes out to my street team, Jennie's Page Turners, my incredible Review Crew, and for all of my readers: the people that have been with me from the start, my loyal readers, my dedicated fans, the ones who have read my stories, who have laughed and cried with me, who have fallen in love with my heroes and have clamored for more! Whether you have been with me since the first book or just discovered me with this book, know that I write these stories for you, and I can't thank you enough for reading them. Sending love, laughter, and big Colorado hugs to you all!

About the Author

Jennie Marts is the *USA TODAY* Best-selling author of award-winning books filled with love, laughter, and always a happily ever after. Readers call her books "laugh out loud" funny and the "perfect mix of romance, humor, and steam." *Fic Central* claimed one of her books was "the most fun I've had reading in years."

She is living her own happily ever after in the mountains of Colorado with her husband, two dogs, and a parakeet that loves to tweet to the oldies. She's addicted to Diet Coke, adores Cheetos, and believes you can't have too many books, shoes, or friends.

Her books include the contemporary western romances of the *Cowboys of Creedence* and the *Hearts of Montana* series, the cozy mysteries of *The Page Turners* series, the hunky hockey-playing men in the *Bannister Brothers Books*, and the small-town romantic comedies in the *Cotton Creek Romance* series.

Jennie loves to hear from readers. Follow her on Facebook at Jennie Marts Books, or Twitter at @JennieMarts. Visit her at www.jenniemarts.com and sign up for her newsletter to keep up with the latest news and releases.

Made in the USA
Lexington, KY
21 April 2018